Unforgotten

BOOK ONE
THE SISTERS
OF KILBRIDE

JAYNE CASTEL

WINTER MIST
PRESS

A widowed clan-chief, a knife-wielding nun, and a once in a lifetime love. A sweeping, epic tale of second chances and forbidden love in Medieval Scotland.

Gavin MacNichol once broke Annella Fraser's heart.

After he ended their affair, to wed her elder sister, Ella fled her home and took the veil. Eighteen years later she's shocked to find herself face-to-face with the man she's never forgotten, or forgiven.

Recently widowed, Gavin has lived with regret all these years. He wed for duty, not for love. But when he escorts Sister Ella of Kilbride home to visit her ailing mother, he realizes that the passion he once felt for Ella still burns— hotter than ever.

Yet Ella is forbidden. She's sworn her life to the Cluniac order and is determined to resist the emotional response Gavin's nearness provokes in her.

It's only when Ella falls foul of another clan-chief that Gavin and Ella's lives become entwined once more.

But, this time, their fate is one that neither can run from.

Historical Romances by Jayne Castel

DARK AGES BRITAIN

The Kingdom of the East Angles series
Night Shadows (prequel novella)
Dark Under the Cover of Night (Book One)
Nightfall till Daybreak (Book Two)
The Deepening Night (Book Three)
*The Kingdom of the East Angles: The Complete
Series*

The Kingdom of Mercia series
The Breaking Dawn (Book One)
Darkest before Dawn (Book Two)
Dawn of Wolves (Book Three)
The Kingdom of Mercia: The Complete Series

The Kingdom of Northumbria series
The Whispering Wind (Book One)
Wind Song (Book Two)
Lord of the North Wind (Book Three)
The Kingdom of Northumbria: The Complete Series

DARK AGES SCOTLAND

The Warrior Brothers of Skye series
Blood Feud (Book One)
Barbarian Slave (Book Two)
Battle Eagle (Book Three)
The Warrior Brothers of Skye: The Complete Series

The Pict Wars series
Warrior's Heart (Book One)
Warrior's Secret (Book Two)
Warrior's Wrath (Book Three)

Novellas
Winter's Promise

MEDIEVAL SCOTLAND

The Brides of Skye series
The Beast's Bride (Book One)
The Outlaw's Bride (Book Two)
The Rogue's Bride (Book Three)
The Brides of Skye: The Complete Series

The Sisters of Kilbride series
Unforgotten (Book One)
Awoken (Book Two)
Fallen (Book Three)
Claimed (Epilogue bonus novella)

Epic Fantasy Romances by Jayne Castel

Light and Darkness series
Ruled by Shadows (Book One)
The Lost Swallow (Book Two)
Path of the Dark (Book Three)
Light and Darkness: The Complete Series

Unforgotten, by Jayne Castel

ISBN: 978-0-473-54755-4

Published by Winter Mist Press

Edited by Tim Burton

Cover photography courtesy of www.shutterstock.com
Map by Jayne Castel
Celtic cross image courtesy of www.pixabay.com

Excerpt from the traditional Scottish song 'These are my mountains.'
http://www.rampantscotland.com/songs/blsongs_these.htm

Visit Jayne's website: www.jaynecastel.com

***

For my darling Tim.

And for all those who think it's too late for a second chance ... it rarely ever is.

***

Map

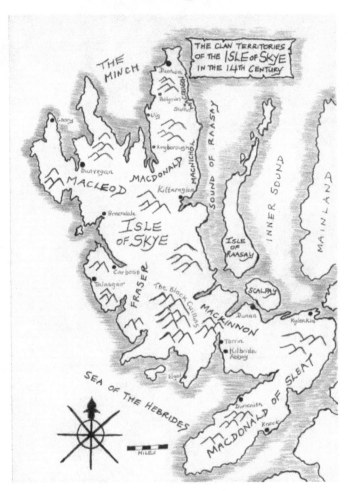

Meminisse sed providere
Remember but look ahead
—MacNichol clan motto

Prologue

I have No Choice

*MacNichol territory,
Isle of Skye, Scotland*

Late summer, 1330 AD

HE WAS LATE.

Annella Fraser should have taken that as a sign, for Gavin MacNichol never kept her waiting. In the three months they had been seeing each other—a long, hot summer that Ella would never forget—Gavin hadn't arrived late once.

Alone in the clearing, Ella started to pace. She couldn't keep still. Butterflies danced in the pit of her belly, and her pulse skittered. She needed to remember to breathe, to calm her excitement.

As she circled the clearing, Ella pulled her linen léine away from her back. She wore only a light woolen kirtle over it, yet the day was humid and she was starting to sweat. The air was heavy, charged. The sky overhead was darkening, and in the distance she heard the unmistakable rumble of thunder.

Ella's mouth curved in anticipation. She wondered what it would be like to make love to Gavin while the storm raged around them. Her chest tightened, and her lower belly turned molten at the thought.

She stopped pacing and peered through the trees— north-east in the direction of Scorrybreac Castle.

Where is he?

Worry crept in, dimming Ella's nervous anticipation. Their time together, illicit and stolen, was so precious that neither of them could afford to be late. She wondered what had delayed him. Matters at Scorrybreac perhaps? His father had poor health these days and relied upon his eldest son increasingly.

Ella's breathing hitched. Maybe he wasn't coming this afternoon.

And then she heard it: the snap of twigs and the rustle of undergrowth accompanied by the 'thud' of approaching hoof beats. A smile flowered across Ella's face, and she loosed the breath she'd been holding, the tension flooding from her. She needn't have worried. Gavin had said he would meet her this afternoon, and he'd always been a man of his word.

An instant later a warrior rode into the clearing.

Even now, months after they had started meeting here, Ella's pulse quickened at the sight of him. Tall, broad shouldered, and strong, the MacNichol chieftain's eldest son had a mane of long dark-blond hair that rippled over his shoulders, and warm blue eyes. His face was ruggedly handsome, and whenever he smiled, a deep dimple appeared upon his left cheek.

However, Gavin wasn't smiling now.

Dressed in plaid braies and a loose white léine that was open at the neck, the young man carried an aura of tension about him. His handsome face was strained, and a groove had furrowed between his eyebrows.

Swinging down from the saddle, he deftly tied his stallion up next to where Ella's courser nipped at grass in the clearing. Around them grew a copse of shady birch trees. A burn trickled through the center of the clearing, its banks mossy. This was a secluded place, known only by hunters who ventured into this densely wooded valley that lay a short ride south-west of the MacNichol stronghold of Scorrybreac.

"I was beginning to worry ye weren't coming." The words rushed out of Ella, before she had the chance to stem them. She didn't want to appear needy, the kind of anxious lass who clawed at her lover. But his tardiness had concerned her nevertheless.

"I'm sorry, mo leannan." Gavin strode to Ella and pulled her into his arms for a bruising kiss.

My sweetheart. The hunger of his embrace surprised Ella. He wasn't usually so forceful. Though young and eager, Gavin MacNichol had proved to be a gentle lover, something Ella adored. She'd always felt so safe with him.

Even so, the hunger of his kiss excited her. She responded eagerly, wrapping her arms around his neck and going up on tiptoe, pressing her body against his.

When they pulled away, the pair of them were both breathless.

Ella tilted her chin, staring up at him, devouring Gavin's strong jaw, kind eyes, and sensual mouth. Lord, how she'd missed their trysts over the past two weeks. Every moment apart from him had been torture. But at Scorrybreac Castle they had to be wary; Gavin's mother always seemed to be watching. Ella sometimes wondered if the woman suspected something.

Now that she was standing this close, there was no denying the change in Gavin's face. Those blue eyes, the color of a summer's sky, were shadowed.

Ella stiffened. "What is it, love?"

Gavin released a long breath before stepping back and dragging a hand through his unbound hair. "Something's happened, Ella ... we need to talk."

Ella went still. He hadn't given any details away, but she instinctively knew that he brought ill news. Even though he had only just entered his twentieth summer, Gavin MacNichol was a steadying influence, a man of even temper and a ready smile. To see him so on edge, and so obviously upset, made a chill slither down her spine.

"My father," Gavin began, his voice husky. "The healer saw him this morning ... he's dying."

The news that clan-chief Iain MacNichol's health had deteriorated didn't come entirely as a shock to Ella. Last time she had seen the clan-chief, he'd been gaunt, his face a sickly-yellow color. Nonetheless, she knew that having the illness confirmed by a healer would have shocked both MacNichol and his kin. "I'm so sorry," she whispered.

Gavin shook his head, his throat bobbing. "My ill news does not stop there," he continued, a rasp to his voice. "There's the matter of my betrothal."

Ella stopped breathing. Over the past three months, the best summer of her life, awareness of his betrothal had cast a constant shadow over her happiness. "What of it?" she finally whispered.

"My parents have insisted that I must honor it," Gavin replied. "They have bidden me to wed Innis before Samhain."

Ella stared at him, her lips parting. "But ye promised ye would talk to yer parents ... tell them ye would not wed my sister?" Her voice started to rise. She hated its shrillness, but she could not help herself. She began to breathe fast, panic rising within her, buzzing like an enraged swarm of hornets. Her ears started to ring.

Gavin shook his head, his gaze clouding. "It's not as easy as that," he replied. "A betrothal isn't a simple thing to break. And with my father's ill-health, there has never been a right time." He broke off there, his expression turning pained. "Neither of my parents had mentioned the betrothal of late ... and I thought it ceased to matter to them." He swallowed hard. "But I was wrong ... it does."

"But ye don't love Innis. Do ye?"

Gavin shook his head. "Ye know I don't," he replied softly. "It's ye I want."

"So go to them, tell them how ye feel."

Gavin took a step back from her, shaking his head. "It's too late, Ella. The agreement was writ and signed upon my thirteenth winter: Gavin MacNichol of

Scorrybreac shall wed Innis Fraser of Talasgair. I thought it could be broken, but it cannot. I tried to tell my father that my heart lay elsewhere, yet he would not listen." Gavin drew in a sharp breath. "He has made it his dying wish."

For the longest moment, Ella merely stared at him.

She'd strayed into a nightmare. It was as if someone else was having this conversation.

Her elder sister Innis was sweet natured and fair of face—much more so than Ella—but she didn't love Gavin and he didn't love her.

Ella and Gavin hadn't meant for all of this to happen. Five years earlier her family had moved from Talasgair—on the western coast of the isle, where the Fraser stronghold lay—to Scorrybreac Castle on the east, so that the eldest daughter could be betrothed to the MacNichol heir.

Ella and Gavin had become friends within the first few days, and then the pair of them had started spending more and more time together as the years passed. Gavin's shrewish mother had always disapproved, but Innis hadn't minded. Ella's elder sister, pious and reserved, preferred to sit at her tapestries or read psalms rather than take walks in the woods or go hunting. These were pastimes that both Gavin and Ella enjoyed—and so they had started going out together.

It hadn't taken long before a bond had forged between them, although they had only become lovers this summer. Ella had felt guilty at first—Gavin was promised to her sister after all—but the guilt soon passed as passion took hold.

"Ye are breaking my heart," Ella whispered, her voice trembling. "Please don't do this."

Gavin stared back at her, his gaze guttering. "I'm so sorry, mo ghràdh," he whispered, his voice broken. "But I have no choice."

1

Facing the Past

Kilbride Abbey
MacKinnon Territory
Isle of Skye, Scotland

Eighteen years later ...

1348 AD

CHANGE ALWAYS APPEARED in Ella's life when she least expected it.

Fortune's wheel didn't turn on the days when she was ready, like after Yuletide when she prepared herself to face the year ahead. Or after a birth or death—significant events that made her pause and take stock of where she was in life.

No, change arrived at happy moments when she was at peace with the world, or on forgettable days when there was nothing but routine to punctuate the moment of its arrival. Fate liked to sneak in and attack from behind. And for that reason, it always caught her unawares.

Sister Ella was hard at work in the gardens of Kilbride Abbey when the second major turning point of her life came.

It was a breathless afternoon in late summer. It wasn't the kind of weather that Ella liked, for it reminded her of another day many years earlier. A black moment. One she had tried her hardest to forget.

There wasn't the slightest breeze to cool the orderly patchwork of vegetable beds inside the abbey's sturdy walls. The air this afternoon smelled of warm earth and grass, and the heat had brought out the noises of surrounding insects and birdlife. Crickets chirped in the nearby herb beds, while somewhere in the hard blue sky above a skylark trilled. Bees buzzed by, traveling from flower to flower, for the nuns had planted roses and lavender around the perimeter of the garden.

A bumblebee droned by Ella's nose then, as she straightened up and wiped her sweating brow with the back of her wrist. She'd been weeding the onion bed for a long while and was pleased with her progress. She had nearly finished. However, her back was starting to ache. The sun was ferocious this afternoon; she could feel its heat burning into her skin, even through the material of her veil and habit.

"Sister Ella!"

A call drew her attention from the neat lines of onions and leeks that stretched before her toward the eastern wall of the abbey. Ella glanced back over her shoulder at where a small figure, garbed in black, hurried toward her. Sister Leanna's habit swamped her. Like Ella, a white wimple framed her face and a voluminous black habit reached her ankles, in the style of the Cluniac order. The young woman's delicately featured face was flushed, her hazel eyes gleaming with excitement.

Ella rose to her feet, grimacing as her joints protested. She had been crouched over weeding for far too long this afternoon. She wasn't old, not like Sister Magda or Sister Fiona, but at thirty-six winters she found that her body sometimes protested at the demands of life in the order. And after hours of gardening on her knees, now was one such time.

"What is it?" Ella asked. "Did I miss the bell to Vespers again?"

It did happen. Sometimes Ella got so immersed in gardening, so lost in her own contemplation, that she even failed to notice the bells calling the sisters to prayer at regular intervals throughout the day.

Sister Leanna laughed. "No, it's too early for that." A smile curved the novice's mouth. "Ye have a visitor."

Ella went still.

For eighteen years she had resided within the walls of Kilbride, this Cluniac abbey upon the south-western shores of the Isle of Skye. In all that time, she'd never once had a visitor.

Ella's mouth flattened into a thin line. She didn't welcome the news. A visitor meant someone from her old life, and that life was dead to her now. It had been for nearly two decades.

"Who is it?" Ella forced herself to ask the question.

Suddenly, she didn't feel well. She was sweaty and incredibly thirsty. Not only that, but her forehead now ached dully, the result of spending too many hours out here in the sun.

"A tall man with blond hair. I caught a glimpse of him ... he's handsome." Sister Leanna's smile widened. She'd been at Kilbride just over a year—not long enough for the outside world, and men, to lose their appeal. "I know not his name," Sister Leanna continued, seemingly unaware that Ella had gone rigid. "But Mother Shona bid me to fetch ye. He awaits ye in the chapter house."

A wave of nausea swept over Ella.

Tall and handsome with blond hair.

Don't panic, she counselled herself. *That could describe many a man upon the isle.*

Ella swallowed, struggling to keep her face composed. "How old would ye say he is?"

"Mature," Sister Leanna replied with a wave of her hand. "At least yer age, Sister Ella ... possibly older."

Ella's mouth curved into a brittle smile. *Mature*. Had she once viewed anyone over the age of thirty in the same way? Even so, Sister Leanna's last words made Ella's heart start to hammer.

No, it couldn't be.

"The abbess bids ye to come now," Sister Leanna said, her gaze turning questioning. "Are ye well, Sister Ella?" She asked with a frown. "Yer cheeks are flushed."

Ella drew in a deep, steadying breath. "I fear I've taken too much sun," she muttered. Brushing off her dirt encrusted hands against her skirts, she walked down the path leading between the rows of vegetables, toward the complex of buildings at their back.

Sister Leanna fell in step next to her.

Ella didn't converse. Instead, she fought the tide of panic that rose within her.

He wouldn't come here. He wouldn't dare ... not after all these years.

"It's nearly time for archery practice," Sister Leanna said, breaking the silence. Ella heard the excitement in her voice. "Mother Shona says I am improving swiftly."

It was true. Ella had seen the novice wield a longbow. She had a steady arm and keen eyesight.

"Do ye think she'll let me go out hunting soon?" Sister Leanna asked, impatience tinging her voice. "I want to be able to bring back deer ... to feed the abbey."

"She'll let ye soon enough, I'm sure," Ella murmured, distracted. "When she thinks ye are ready."

Together the two women left the gardens and entered the abbey complex. Like the high walls surrounding them, the buildings of Kilbride were made of a pale grey stone that gleamed in the sunlight.

The tiled roof of the kirk rose above it all, outlined against a cloudless blue sky. Skirting the edge of the kirk, Ella made her way toward the chapter house. On the way she passed a wide yard. Here, a cluster of nuns were setting up targets, while others approached bearing longbows and quivers of arrows.

"There ye are, Sister Leanna," one of the nuns called out. Her name was Sister Coira. She was tall and broad-shouldered with violet eyes framed by dark brows—and she was one of Ella's closest friends here. "Sister Ella ... will ye practice with us?"

"Maybe later," Ella called back, forcing a smile. She wondered if Sister Coira and the others had seen her visitor. If so, Sister Coira gave no sign. She merely smiled back and nodded before turning to the young postulant trotting up behind her with an armload of quivers. "Hand those out please, Sister Mina."

Leaving them to it, Ella walked on.

Gavin MacNichol favored Mother Shona with a smile that he hoped didn't betray his nervousness. "I trust Sister Annella is keeping well?"

It was an inane question, but the silence inside the chapter house—a small building that was used for meetings—was getting to him. The space, which had arched stained-glass windows lining the walls and a vaulted ceiling, had grown uncomfortably silent during the wait.

"The Lord has blessed us with Sister Ella. She is a valued member of our community," the abbess replied, her tone reserved. "Ye will be able to ask after her health face-to-face, for she will be here soon."

Sister Ella.

Even after all these years, he couldn't imagine her living here as a nun, crow-like in austere black robes.

Gavin nodded and resisted the urge to wipe his palms on his braies. He felt as nervous as a lad before his first dance. As civil as the abbess was, he wished she would leave him alone so that he could pace around and rid himself of the nervous energy that pulsed through him.

He could feel his heart hammering against his breastbone, and his breathing had quickened, sounding overly loud in the silence. It felt airless and stuffy inside the chapter house.

The abbess had brought him here so that he could speak to Sister Annella in private.

"May I ask why ye have come here alone?" The abbess asked after a long pause. "It can't be safe to travel without an escort."

Gavin's gaze settled upon Mother Shona. She was barely a handful of years older than him. She had a pleasant face, warm brown eyes, and good skin—but her habit and veil completely covered her hair and robbed her of any femininity. Perhaps, in other circumstances, the woman may have been attractive, but dressed in such a way it was impossible to tell. That was most likely the point. Brides of Christ had no wish to make themselves attractive to men.

"I wished to travel swiftly ... due to the urgency of this matter," Gavin replied. His mouth quirked then. "However, I did narrowly avoid some trouble on the way here ... two men tried to pull me off my horse yesterday, just after I entered MacKinnon territory, but I managed to outrun them."

Holding his gaze, the abbess's expression turned grave. "It never used to be so dangerous to travel the roads of Skye. Ever since the war with the English, the mood has turned here." She paused, her brown eyes shuttering. "Not only that, but I'm afraid the folk of these lands suffer under Duncan MacKinnon's rule."

Gavin raised an eyebrow at her comment. "Lawlessness is a growing problem upon the isle," he replied. "And I did notice that when I crossed into MacKinnon lands, the villages I passed seemed particularly impoverished."

The abbess's lips compressed. "I do not like my nuns to travel unescorted," she said. Her voice was soft although Gavin caught the edge to it. Mother Shona of Kilbride was highly protective of those within these walls. "I allow this only because ye are a clan-chief and because of the nature of the situation."

Gavin nodded. "I understand, Mother Shona ... and I am grateful."

They both fell silent then, and Gavin shifted his gaze to the arched windows to his left. The afternoon sun streamed through the stained glass, creating squares of red, blue, and gold on the paved floor of the chapter house.

Maybe I shouldn't have come here.

The message he bore could have been brought by another. Why then had he made the effort? It was a two-day journey from Scorrybreac Castle. Just like Mother Shona, his kin and clansmen had found it odd that he'd insisted on riding out on his own like this. But it was something he'd felt compelled to do.

There were some meetings that could not be put off. Some, like this one, were many years overdue.

He'd told himself that the entire journey here. Only, when he'd spied the peaked roof of the abbey's kirk in the distance, standing out against the deep blue of the sea beyond, misgiving had plagued him.

He should have sent a party in his stead, but it was too late now. He was here.

Hearing the soft footfalls of someone approaching outside, Gavin tensed.

He turned his gaze to the door, drawing in a sharp breath as he readied himself to come face-to-face with his past.

The door swung open with a creak, and a nun entered: a small woman cloaked in black.

"Sister Ella," Mother Shona greeted the newcomer, waving her forward. The nun drew close to the abbess and dropped to one knee in front of her. Mother Shona quickly made the sign of the cross and waited till the newcomer had risen to her feet, before she spoke once more. "MacNichol has a message for ye." The abbess's gaze flicked between the two of them. "Are ye happy to speak with him alone, or would ye like me to remain?"

"Thank ye, Mother Shona. Ye may leave us," the nun murmured. Gavin caught his breath. That voice, low and gentle, was exactly as he remembered it.

"Very well ... peace be upon ye both." With a probing glance, first at Gavin, and then at Sister Ella, Mother Shona left the chapter house.

Gavin stared at the figure before him and tried to find a trace of the lass he had once known.

The habit completely obliterated her character. A black veil covered her head, and a snow-white wimple framed a winsome face, while a black habit fell to dusty sandals. A narrow leather belt girded the habit at the waist, where a wooden crucifix hung.

Gavin continued to stare at her. After so many years apart, he drank her in.

It frustrated him that he couldn't see her hair, which he remembered as a soft coppery color. He studied her delicate features. The years had left very little of a mark upon her. The woman's face was perhaps a trifle leaner than he remembered, but she still had the same Cupid's bow mouth, with that sensual upper lip that had once driven him mad with longing. He remembered too her loch-blue eyes, which held a penetrating, intelligent look. Finely drawn eyebrows framed them.

Aye, it was her—and yet it was not.

Once again, Gavin regretted the impulse that had driven him here. He looked into the face of the woman he'd once loved—the woman he had forsaken in order to wed her sister and do his duty.

He realized then that there was a reason why the past was often better left alone.

2

Unchanged

ELLA WAS UNPREPARED for the actual shock of seeing him.

It seemed a lifetime ago—someone else's life—since she'd last set eyes on Gavin MacNichol. She'd told herself that he would look vastly different to how she remembered him. She'd assured herself that he'd have grown old and fat, as his father had as he'd aged.

But he hadn't.

The man who awaited her in the chapter house wasn't so different to the one she'd left behind at Scorrybreac. The years had tempered his boyish good looks, but he still wore his hair long, tied back this afternoon at the nape of his neck. And it was the face of a mature man who looked back at her. Even so, those warm blue eyes were unchanged.

Had he always been this tall and broad? The warrior loomed before her, making Ella painfully aware of her own short stature.

The MacNichol clan-chief was dressed in travel stained braies and a léine, although to enter the abbey he'd donned a sash of his clan plaid: red lined with green. Dust coated his long leather hunting boots, revealing that despite the humidity in the air this afternoon, it hadn't rained in days.

As if sensing her scrutiny, the man's mouth curved into a smile.

Ella went still. His smile hadn't changed one bit. Gavin's face had roughened with the years, but she'd never forgotten the lazy way his mouth curved when he was amused or the deep dimple that appeared upon his left cheek when he smiled.

"I hope I haven't altered too much," he greeted her, his voice soft and slightly hesitant. "Ye haven't changed at all, Ella."

Her spine stiffened. "Sister Ella," she replied. "Why are ye here, MacNichol?"

Gavin's eyes clouded. Her cool welcome displeased him, but she didn't care about his hurt feelings. She'd ridden from Scorrybreac Castle many years earlier and never looked back. Seeing him again here in the flesh brought up memories that she'd long since buried.

She wanted them kept buried.

"Yer mother is dying," he replied after a pause, all business now. His expression had shuttered. He'd been pleased to see her; she'd seen it in his eyes. But that had been before she'd been offhand with him. Now he wore an aloof mask. "She wishes ye to come to see her at Scorrybreac," he continued. "Before it's too late."

Ella stared back at him. She'd had no contact with either of her parents all these years, although her sister, Innis, had written to her. The last correspondence she'd received had been before her sister's death nearly two years earlier. That letter had been a plea for Ella to visit her. She'd been gravely ill and knew she was dying.

But Ella hadn't gone—she had deliberately stayed away from Scorrybreac. Returning there would have brought back too many memories. She'd grieved for her sister, but she hadn't wanted to face her. Guilt still needled her over cutting contact with Innis, although she didn't want Gavin to see it.

"Ye didn't need to deliver the message in person," Ella replied, folding her arms across her breasts in a protective gesture. "A letter would have sufficed."

His brow furrowed, showing that he'd indeed changed over the years. Once, frowns hadn't come readily to Gavin MacNichol. But she could see the fine lines of care upon his brow now.

"I sent word to ye of yer sister's death," he said after a pause. "Yer parents wished ye to attend her burial, but ye never responded." He then folded his own arms across his broad chest, mirroring her action. "I thought that this time, I would come in person." The challenge in his voice was unmistakable.

That was another difference to the amiable young man she had left behind. There was a hardness to Gavin that had been absent nearly two decades earlier. Ella wasn't surprised. The years had a way of shaping folk, wearing at them like waves upon a cliff. One couldn't go through life without being changed by it—even in a place like Kilbride Abbey, where contact with the outside world was minimal.

"I appreciate ye informing me, but I cannot leave here," Ella said after a pause, dropping her gaze to the flagstone floor. "Ye will have to return home and deliver my apologies. May the merciful Lord watch over my mother."

"As God-fearing as yer mother is, I think she'd prefer *ye* did," Gavin replied. "Why can't ye leave the abbey?"

Ella glanced up, her brow furrowing. She didn't have to explain herself to this man. "The Sisters of Kilbride don't travel," she replied, her tone developing a frosty edge.

"But ye are not cloistered?"

"It doesn't matter. We do God's work best here. The farthest I've traveled in years is Torrin. I can't go to Scorrybreac with ye."

"But the abbess has given her blessing."

Alarm fluttered through Ella. What was Mother Shona doing meddling in her affairs? "She should have asked me first."

Gavin raised his dark-blond eyebrows. "So it was just an excuse," he replied softly. "Ye can come with me, but ye don't want to."

They stared at each other for a few long moments. Tension crackled in the air between them with the weight of so many things unsaid.

After that fateful day of their last meeting in the clearing, events had moved quickly at Scorrybreac Castle. Plans had gotten underway for Gavin and Innis's wedding, while Ella had sent word to Kilbride Abbey, requesting admission as a postulant. As soon as she'd heard back from the abbess, who welcomed her to the abbey, Ella had announced the news to her family. She'd left without saying a word of her plans to Gavin.

"If I don't wish to return to Scorrybreac, ye can hardly blame me." Ella didn't like how sharp her voice now sounded. It wasn't her at all. All the nuns here at Kilbride knew her for her gentleness, soft-spoken ways, and ready laugh. But being in the presence of this man gave Ella a sharpness she didn't usually possess. Every nerve in her body stretched taut.

Those warm blue eyes shadowed. "I understand why ye don't wish to return," Gavin admitted finally. "And that's why I came here in person ... to advise ye that no matter what happened in the past, there are times when ye need to see beyond it. Yer mother is seriously ill, Sister Ella. She was in tears when I left. Would ye deny a dying woman the chance to see her only surviving daughter one last time?"

Ella's hand went to the crucifix that hung at her belt, her fingers clasping around it and squeezing hard. *Lord give me strength.*

He was making her feel like some heartless shrew.

He knew the truth of things when it came to her family. She'd confided in him once, telling him of how Innis had always been the favorite daughter. Her father was a kind but weak man, who easily let himself be ruled by his dominant, blade-tongued wife. Ella's mother had always found fault with her youngest daughter. In fact, ironically, the only thing that Ella had ever done right was to take the veil. Ella had saved her parents having to pay a dowry. A relief indeed. Their eldest daughter had found the match they desired; Ella didn't matter.

"Ye know how things are between my mother and me," Ella finally managed. "Please don't paint her out to be saintly."

His mouth curved, although there was no humor in his eyes. "I'm not," he replied, his tone clipped. "I'm well aware that ye were always the best of them. If ye return home, don't do it for yer mother. Do it for yerself."

Sister Ella and MacNichol emerged from the chapter house into the soft late afternoon sun.

Clack. Clack. Clack.

"What's that?" Gavin asked.

Shifting her gaze right to the training yard, Ella's body went taut. Archery practice had ended, but a group of nuns were now sparring with quarter-staffs. Sister Coira, who was the best of them save the abbess at wielding the quarter-staff, was taking a group of younger nuns through some drills.

Ella couldn't believe they were being so indiscreet. She'd thought they would have finished their training by now. They rarely had visitors here at the abbey, and as such, the nuns had gone about their daily routines without worrying that an outsider might see their strange ways.

Hadn't the abbess warned them all not to let strangers see them at practice?

Folk fear what they don't understand, the abbess had told Ella once. *It's better that we appear harmless nuns ... that way no one will ever be threatened by us.*

"Nothing," Ella replied lightly, hoping he wouldn't pursue the subject. "There are harvest games in Torrin every year ... perhaps some of the sisters wish to take part."

It was a weak excuse, but the best she could make at short notice.

A small figure swathed in black and white approached them then, preventing Gavin from questioning her further; Mother Shona had mercifully come looking for them. Relief filtered through Ella. She'd begun to think that the abbess had deliberately abandoned her with this man. She still hadn't forgiven the abbess for telling him that she had permission to travel to Scorrybreac. It had made it impossible ultimately to refuse him.

"Is it agreed then?" Mother Shona greeted them briskly. She had a no-nonsense approach to human relations. Often Ella appreciated her directness, but this afternoon it grated on her nerves. The abbess knew about her past, although Ella had never told her the name of the man who'd broken her heart.

Perhaps if she had, Mother Shona would have sent him away.

"Aye," Gavin rumbled. "Thank ye, Mother Shona. Sister Ella has agreed to travel north with me. We will not keep her long. I will return her to ye within two weeks at the latest."

Mother Shona favored him with a smile, although her gaze was guarded. "I appreciate that." The abbess's gaze shifted to Ella then, and her smile faded. "I'm sorry to hear about yer mother. She will be in our prayers while ye are away."

"Thank ye, Mother Shona," Ella replied, lowering her gaze so the abbess wouldn't see the irritation in her eyes. "Ye are most kind to allow me to go to her."

The abbess nodded before shifting her attention back to Gavin. "It's too late in the day for ye to start yer return journey," she said, her tone turning brisk once more. "Ye are welcome to stay within the walls of the abbey tonight. I will have the guest house prepared for ye, and we would be delighted if ye would join us for supper this eve."

Gavin MacNichol smiled back at the abbess, his eyes crinkling at the corners. It was the first unfiltered smile Ella had seen him give since being reunited with him, and despite that she fought the sensation, warmth suffused her. "It would be my pleasure, Mother Shona," he replied.

3

Revelations at Supper

ELLA STEPPED INTO her cell, closing the door firmly behind her.

"Lord have mercy," she muttered, covering her face with her hands. "Why couldn't he stay away?"

But there wasn't any point in agonizing over *why* Gavin MacNichol had ridden two days on his own to reach the abbey, to deliver a message that could easily have been sent by courier. The fact was, he was here—a guest at the abbey. Two of the sisters were preparing the guest house right at this very moment. And later she would have to suffer through a meal in his presence.

Head still in her hands, Ella sank down onto her sleeping pallet. It was narrow, the mattress stuffed with straw, and covered by a linen sheet and rough woolen blankets. As one of the senior nuns here, she had her own cell. The postulants, novices, and younger nuns shared the dormitory across the courtyard, as she once had. This tiny, sparsely-furnished stone chamber was Ella's refuge.

And at a moment like this, she was relieved to be able to shut herself away.

Mother Mary preserve her, it had been a shock to see him again.

She was still reeling from it. Gavin was even more handsome than she remembered. He'd lost the gaucheness of youth and even suited the harder edge he wore these days.

But the last thing Ella wanted was to travel with this man. He hadn't even brought an escort. It was improper for them to travel together, yet the abbess seemed willing to permit it. There had been many times over the years when Mother Shona's open-minded attitude and views had relieved Ella. The abbess made life at Kilbride a joy for the nuns who resided here. Her approach to religion, and to how a woman should behave, was a refreshing change from the ideas that Ella had grown up with.

But the abbess was being too permissive now. Of course, she didn't realize the history that lay between Ella and Gavin.

Maybe I should tell her?

Ella swallowed hard. No—she couldn't do that.

A bell started clanging then, the sound echoing through the abbey.

Vespers.

Ella wasn't in the mood, but she had no choice other than to heave herself off her pallet, straighten her habit and veil, and leave the sanctuary of her cell. Crossing the courtyard outside the nuns' lodgings, she joined the flood of black-robed figures as they all made their way to the kirk.

Around them the early evening sun had turned the hills gold. As it was late summer, night drew in slowly. After Vespers and supper, there would be time for more chores before Compline. The Sisters of Kilbride were rarely ever idle.

Ella entered the kirk.

As always, the dim interior cast a calming cloak over her. Even on the hottest day, the air in here was cool. Golden-hued light filtered in from high windows, pooling like melted butter on the flagstone floor. Rows of pillars lined the church, leading up to a raised altar, where Mother Shona had already taken her position.

Ella took her place among the orderly rows of nuns that now filled the kirk. Inhaling the heavy scent of incense, Ella sank to her knees, closing her eyes. Although she hadn't been in the mood before, she was now grateful for Vespers. Perhaps the prayers would take her mind off the events of the past hour.

The chanting began. Solemn female voices echoed high into the vaulted ceiling of the kirk, led by Mother Shona in soothing tones. And as Ella joined in the chorus, she felt the afternoon's tension ebb from her. Slowly her shoulders, which had gone rigid, started to relax.

Peace wrapped around her in a soft veil. The ritual always had a calming effect upon her, no matter how upset she was. She loved losing herself in it.

At first Ella concentrated on the prayers, even though she knew them so well she could have recited the words in her sleep. But as Vespers drew out, her thoughts treacherously returned to Gavin MacNichol.

She didn't want to, but she thought back to their last meeting that day in the woods south-west of Scorrybreac Castle.

What a spoiled, foolish chit she'd once been. How she'd paced so impatiently that afternoon. Gavin had treated her like his queen during their time together. He'd never once made her wait for him, and that day his tardiness had irritated her. But it paled into nothing when he arrived and delivered his devastating news.

Ella swallowed hard as the memories assailed her. She hadn't accepted his decision at first. It seemed impossible he could tell her that he loved her with one breath, and then announce that he was going to honor his betrothal with the next. Her sister was a kind and sweet woman, but Gavin belonged to Ella.

Her feelings on the subject didn't matter though. The longer she'd argued it with him, the more stubborn Gavin became. The discussion he'd had with his father, who'd been gravely ill at the time, had set a resolve in him. Even so, she'd seen the tears glittering in his eyes as he faced her.

No matter how she pleaded, he would not be moved. As the eldest son and heir to the MacNichol lands, he had to think about more than just his own needs. Ella had railed against these words. She hated how self-sacrificing he was being. He believed he was noble, but she thought he was acting like a coward. Their future life, their future happiness, hung in the balance, and he was casting it away as if it meant nothing.

Ella wasn't proud of how she'd behaved that day.

In the end she'd flown into hysterics. Wracked with sobs, Ella had stumbled over to her horse and gathered the reins before scrambling up onto the saddle.

Her last words to Gavin still rang in her ears and made her cheeks warm with shame. "Ye shall rue the day ye turned yer back on us." She'd choked out the words. "Ye are casting aside something that will never come yer way again."

Ella squeezed her eyes shut. She'd been so fiery, so impassioned. At eighteen she'd believed that if you wanted something enough, it would be yours. At that age she believed that love conquered all and that somehow she and Gavin would find a way to overcome the obstacles before them.

But now she knew differently. She'd hoped that after a day or two Gavin might have changed his mind. But he didn't. He'd made his decision, and in that stubborn way of his, he was determined to see it through. Ella was stubborn too.

But in the days that followed, she learned a bitter truth. It didn't matter how much your heart yearned for it—some things were not destined to be yours.

Gavin took a mouthful of venison stew and let out a contented sigh. "This is very good." He looked down at the bowl before him. "Do hunters swap ye meat for vegetables?"

Glancing up, Gavin noted that Ella, who was seated directly across from him, tensed at the question. They sat in the refectory, a rectangular building with a hearth at each end. The abbess and a cluster of senior nuns—some of whom were aged indeed—sat upon a raised platform at one end of the hall, while the others sat at long tables down the center.

"Sometimes hunters barter with us," Mother Shona replied. "But the nuns of this order are highly resourceful, MacNichol. In order to do God's work, we must be strong and healthy. Most of the meat we consume here we have either raised or hunted ourselves."

Gavin observed the abbess with interest. Her tone was pleasant, although with a distant note Gavin had come to expect from her. Ever since stepping inside the walls of Kilbride, he'd felt as if he was intruding on a serene world that had no time for the likes of him. Although the abbess was happy to converse with him, he had the sense that she was distracted, as if his questions were taking her from more important matters.

"I saw some of the nuns at practice with quarter-staffs earlier," he said casually. "They looked to possess some skill."

Catching a glimpse of the black-garbed women swinging staffs at each other had indeed piqued Gavin's interest. Ella had tried to throw him off with a weak excuse, yet he wanted to know more.

"As I said ... they were merely practicing for the harvest games in Torrin." Ella interrupted. Her tone was soft, yet there was a pleading undertone, as if she wished he would leave the matter alone. Looking her way, Gavin saw that her face had paled.

"An odd skill for a nun to learn though," he continued, shifting his attention back to the abbess. "Don't ye think, Mother Shona?"

The abbess held his gaze, her own steady. "Aye, I suppose, but as I have said … nuns who are strong and healthy do the Lord's work better."

An awkward silence settled at the table. Gavin ripped off a piece of bread and dipped it into his stew, his attention sweeping around him. The nuns all wore composed expressions, their gazes downcast as they focused on their supper. He finished his inspection, focusing upon Ella. She ate slowly, taking small mouthfuls of stew. Only the lines bracketing her mouth belied her tension.

She didn't want him here.

Eventually, it was the abbess who broke the hush. Putting down her spoon, she met Gavin's eye. "Word reached me a few days ago, of the pestilence that has raged through Europe and England," she said fixing him with a level look. "Our sisters on the mainland tell me that it has now moved to Scotland. Have ye heard such news?"

Gavin frowned. He wasn't a fool; Mother Shona had deliberately changed the subject, away from the abbey. "Aye … my clansmen in Lothian have sent word that the plague has now reached Dùn Èideann," he replied before pausing. He was reluctant to go into more detail, but sensed the abbess would prefer him to speak frankly. "Whole families have been wiped out … some in less than the space of a day. The illness takes a vile form … a terrible fever, chills, and purple boils appearing over the body."

The abbess's brown eyes shadowed, while around her some of the nuns who'd overheard him dropped their spoons and crossed themselves. "How awful," Mother Shona murmured. "We shall pray for those afflicted … and that this isle may be spared such devastation." Her face took on a determined look. "Of course, the Sisters of Kilbride will do our best to take care of those struck down if it does arrive upon Skye … we will never turn our back on the sick."

"They have no cure for it then?" One of the nuns at the table spoke up. It was the tall one that Gavin had spied leading the quarter-staff training in the yard earlier. She had violet eyes, and she wore a guarded expression.

"Not from what I hear," Gavin replied with a shake of his head. "Word is that ye can catch it by simply breathing the air of those who have the disease."

"Indeed ... herbs and medicines seem unable to slow its spread, Sister Coira," the abbess agreed, before her attention flicked back to Gavin. "Sister Coira is our resident healer."

Gavin nodded, looking at the nun in question with fresh eyes. Kilbride Abbey was an interesting place indeed. None of the women residing here were what he'd expected. This was a world where men entered only as guests, and then very rarely. He was in a privileged position indeed to be allowed to visit. In this world, women ruled.

Gavin resumed eating and reached for another piece of bread. The abbess had attempted to distract him from his inquisition about their ways, with her own question about the pestilence, but his general curiosity wasn't yet sated. Eventually, he glanced up and caught the abbess's eye once more. "Mother Shona ... earlier today, ye told me that that the folk of these lands suffer under MacKinnon's rule ... how so?"

Around him the table went still. He noted then that Ella was watching him closely. Her face was impossible to read, although her blue eyes were narrowed and her mouth compressed into a thin, slightly disapproving line.

She didn't like him asking such a question, but Gavin was curious to know about the goings-on in these lands.

"Duncan MacKinnon makes a poor clan-chief," the abbess admitted, her tone turning guarded.

Next to her, Sister Coira was frowning. The nun stared down at her half-finished bowl of stew, a nerve flickering in her cheek. Gavin was intrigued. MacKinnon was clearly not well liked here and, having met the man numerous times, Gavin knew why. Duncan was even more unpopular than his brutal father before him had been.

Taking a sip of beer, Gavin shifted his attention back to the abbess. Her expression was shuttered. He realized then that she'd grown wary of him. He was a clan-chief after all, and for all she knew, MacKinnon might have sent him to spy on the abbey. This was the only abbey upon the isle, and it held more power than some of the chieftains here liked.

"I imagine that ye are a very different leader to MacKinnon," Mother Shona continued after a pause. Her tone was still wary, yet, unlike some of the nuns here, who could barely look his way, the abbess met his eye squarely. Men did not intimidate or embarrass her.

Gavin's mouth lifted at the corners. "I do my best," he murmured. "My father always said it wasn't an easy thing to rule, but it was only when I took over as clan-chief that I realized what he truly meant. Everyone with a problem or a grievance comes to yer door. The weight of responsibility can sometimes be a heavy one, although I try to do right by my people."

Ella felt herself growing increasingly more agitated the longer the meal went on.

Gavin MacNichol was in a conversational mood this evening. He didn't seem to care that he was the one doing most of the speaking, or that his questions were unsettling not only Mother Shona but the other nuns as well. Mealtimes were usually passed in silence, with speaking kept to a minimum, but the abbess had relaxed that rule for this evening. However, MacNichol seemed determined to discuss a number of unpleasant subjects.

Ella didn't live in denial; she knew the problems he and Mother Shona discussed were real indeed. When Ella had first come to live here, the nearby villages had been prosperous. But in the last few years, as MacKinnon demanded higher and higher taxes from his people, folk had grown poorer and increasingly desperate. Just two days earlier, when she'd brought vegetables to the local village, she'd seen too many hungry faces and desperate eyes. The Sisters of Kilbride did what they could to help the villagers, but MacKinnon demanded a tithe from them as well, and last winter had ended up being a lean one.

The conversation drifted on, while Ella found her gaze returning to Gavin. She cursed herself for constantly looking his way, but she couldn't help it.

Gavin appeared at ease as he helped himself to another serving of stew and praised its deliciousness once more.

One of the nuns, Old Magda, smiled at his compliment.

Curse ye, Gavin. He'd always related easily to women. That was how it had started between them. They'd become friends first. She'd found him so easy to talk to. He wasn't like other lads. They all seemed boorish compared to him. Gavin engaged a lass's mind, wanting to know her opinions, her thoughts, and her feelings. He hadn't changed.

Eventually, Ella wasn't able to bear it any longer. It was bad enough that this man had reappeared in her life after so many years, and that she would be forced to travel with him tomorrow.

But to listen to the low timbre of his voice was like a knife twisting in her chest.

Ella pushed away her half-eaten bowl of stew and rose to her feet. "Please, excuse me," she murmured, gaze lowered. "But if I am to travel tomorrow, I will need to ready myself."

"Very well, Sister Ella," Mother Shona replied. "We shall see ye later ... at Compline."

Feeling Gavin MacNichol's gaze upon her, but deliberately avoiding his eye, Ella turned and hurried from the refectory.

4

Ready to Depart

ELLA PACKED THE wooden satchel with some clean tunics, a block of lye soap, and a small leather-bound book of psalms.

"Is that all ye are taking with ye?"

Ella glanced over her shoulder to see Sister Leanna watching her, eyes narrowed.

Despite her bleak mood this morning, Ella's mouth curved. She remembered Lady Leanna MacDonald of Sleat arriving upon a palfrey laden with saddlebags, over a year ago now. A mule carrying the rest of her belongings had followed.

That day, the nuns had watched in thinly veiled amusement as a beautiful lass with pale blonde hair, dressed in flowing blue, had dismounted from her palfrey and looked about her with interest. Leanna hadn't any idea of the life that awaited her. She'd believed she would have her own lodgings and space to hang up her colorful array of kirtles and over-gowns. Ella remembered the shock on Leanna's face when she'd set eyes on the dormitory, and her narrow sleeping pallet, for the first time.

"A nun doesn't need to carry much," Ella reminded the younger woman. She patted the coarse material of her habit, her smile turning rueful. "We never have to agonize over what to wear."

Sister Leanna sighed. "I miss the finery of my old life sometimes, ye know," she admitted. "Don't tell anyone though. I'm sure the other sisters would think me frivolous."

"No, they wouldn't," Ella replied. "I felt the same way during my first year here. But after a while I got used to it. And ye will too."

"Are ye nervous?"

The question made Ella tense. She imagined her displeasure was written all over her face. Sister Leanna hadn't taken supper with them the night before, as being a novice, she dined at the other end of the refectory—but she would have seen Ella depart early.

"It will feel strange to leave Kilbride," Ella replied softly. Of course, that wasn't the real reason for her discomfort, although Sister Leanna wouldn't know any different. "I've had no contact with my parents since I came to live here."

Sister Leanna didn't answer, and slinging the satchel across her chest, Ella turned to her. She saw that the young woman's face was shadowed, unnaturally somber. "I can't imagine having no contact with my kin for that long," she murmured. "I miss my parents so much, sometimes it hurts to breathe."

Ella saw then that Sister Leanna's gaze shone with unshed tears. Something deep inside Ella's chest twisted. How heartless she must seem to the lass. She knew that Sister Leanna was very close to her family. She had confided in her one evening that the real reason for her joining the order was not out of religious fervor. Instead, it had been her father's idea.

MacKinnon had wanted to wed Chieftain MacDonald of Sleat's comely daughter. It had been a drastic move to send her to Kilbride, yet it was the only way they had managed to put MacKinnon off.

Sister Leanna had understood her father's choice, although Ella had seen sadness shadow her hazel eyes at unguarded times—like now.

Stepping close to Sister Leanna, Ella put comforting arms around her. "It does get easier with time," she whispered. As soon as the words left her lips, she realized how little solace they truly gave.

The two women left the cell and walked into the yard beyond. A balmy dawn greeted them. The sun had just risen over the tawny hills to the east, and the air had a sweet smell that promised another hot day ahead.

Ella huffed out a breath. There was so much to do here at the abbey; so much weeding, planting, and harvesting to carry out and oversee. She didn't have time for this trip.

Even so, to change her mind would only cast her in a poor light. All the nuns now knew that her mother was gravely ill. They expected Ella to go to her.

But none of them had ever met Cait Fraser.

Sturdy leather sandals scuffling the dirt, Ella led the way from the nuns' lodgings to the stables. The abbey kept goats, sheep, fowl, and even a couple of pigs. Despite that the nuns didn't travel much, they also had shaggy ponies, beasts that were native to the Isle, and an old sway-backed donkey.

One of the ponies, a bay gelding named Monadh, awaited her. The beast's name was a beautiful one, meaning 'moorland covered mountain'. However, the pony seemed wide as a barrel and hairy as a Highland cow beside the leggy grey courser that waited next to it. MacNichol had saddled both the mounts and was now ready to depart.

He stood, quietly conversing with Mother Shona. At hearing approaching footfalls, the clan-chief glanced up. His gaze tracked Ella's path across the yard. Just like the day before, the sight of him unnerved her.

Ella inhaled sharply, her hand straying to the crucifix looped through her belt. *Dear Lord, please give me the strength to keep company with this man.*

Approaching the abbess, Ella dropped to one knee before her. "Good morning, Sister Ella," Mother Shona greeted her with a smile, making the sign of the cross. "I'm glad to see ye plan to travel light."

Ella forced a smile. "Aye … I've taken yer advice to heart." She then glanced over her shoulder to see that a crowd of nuns had gathered behind her, including Sister Leanna.

Ella couldn't fail to note either that some of the sisters weren't looking at her. One or two of the younger ones were in fact openly gazing at Gavin MacNichol.

Ella frowned. There was a reason why very few men were admitted to the abbey. MacNichol's presence here was a disruptive one. It was just as well he was leaving.

Oblivious to the stir his presence was creating, Gavin met Ella's eye once more. "A sunny day lies before us," he said pleasantly. "The perfect weather for traveling."

"The perfect weather for sun-stroke too," old Magda called out. "Make sure ye keep out of the noon sun, Sister Ella."

"Worry not … I shall look after her," Gavin replied to the elderly nun.

Ella tensed, her throat closing as nervousness got the better of her. Despite his self-confidence, she hated the idea of leaving the abbey. These solid stone walls had been her home for so long, she sometimes forgot that there was a world outside it. Panic fluttered up as she considered the two-day journey to Scorrybreac and what awaited her there.

Masking her rising anxiety with a stern look, Ella crossed to her pony. Then, placing her right foot in the stirrup and facing Monadh's head, she mounted side-saddle. It wasn't easy. She hadn't been on horseback for many years. Once she'd been able to spring up into the saddle with ease, but today it was an effort. She hopped up and down, her habit flapping, as she attempted to launch herself upward. All the while, Monadh patiently waited.

Ella felt gazes boring into her as she scrambled in an ungainly fashion onto the pony's back. Breathing hard, she adjusted her skirts and gathered up the reins.

Had Gavin watched that display?

When she chanced a glance his way, she saw that he too had mounted and was mercifully not looking in her direction. Instead, Gavin met Mother Shona's eye, his cheek dimpling as he smiled. "As I said, Mother Shona, we should return no longer than two weeks hence."

The abbess nodded, stepping back from them. "May the Lord's blessings go with ye," she replied her attention shifting to Ella. Their gazes fused, and the abbess's full lips curved. "Make the most of this time with yer kin," she advised softly. "For many of us never get the chance to say goodbye."

Gavin and Ella rode out of Kilbride in silence.

Gavin's mount, a spirited grey mare, didn't like the quiet pace her rider had set this morning. Yet the pony the abbess had loaned Ella had a short stride. It was also grossly fat and would slow their progress north. Gavin didn't mind. He was to have but a short time alone with Ella. It was stolen time, but he wanted to make the most of it.

Nonetheless, he sensed that his companion wished to keep her own counsel this morning. He cast a glance Ella's way to see that she was deliberately staring at the road before her, steadfastly ignoring him.

Watching her, Gavin stifled the urge to fill the silence between them. Ella was probably just nervous, he told himself. Perhaps she would thaw once they got properly underway.

Rolling hills spread out around Kilbride Abbey. As they crested one, Gavin twisted in the saddle and glanced back at the way they'd come. The spire of the kirk pierced the pale sky, a swathe of blue sea behind it. Woodland nestled in the shallow valleys around Kilbride, and to the north-west Gavin spied delicate wreaths of smoke drifting up into the heavens. He hadn't realized that the village of Torrin lay so close to the abbey.

He had to admit that Kilbride's location—perched just a few furlongs back from a rocky shore, and surrounded by hills and woodland—made it an idyllic spot.

Turning away from the abbey, Gavin focused his attention now on the rutted road before them. They had many furlongs to travel, through the mountainous heart of the isle. In the distance, the shadows of great peaks rose before them—a brutal and sculpted beauty. His lands lay far to the north-eastern side of those mountains.

Finally, he shifted his gaze back to the silent figure riding beside him. It was no good—he couldn't ride all the way to Scorrybreac without speaking to this woman.

"It must feel strange," he said, feigning casualness, "to be leaving the abbey after so many years."

Ella did glance his way, briefly. She studied him coldly for an instant, before she deliberately shifted her gaze back to her pony's ears. "It does," she replied, her tone as frosty as her expression. "A nun should remain in quiet contemplation. I will not be at ease again until I return to Kilbride."

5

Blades

ELLA WELCOMED THE silence.

After a few attempts at engaging her in conversation, none of which had been welcomed, Gavin had duly given up. The morning stretched before them, and as they traveled north-east, the day gradually grew warmer.

In her heavy habit and undergarments, Ella started to sweat.

The sun beat down on her head, and for the first time in many years, she longed to rip off her stifling wimple and veil for a few moments, and let the gentle breeze cool her sweat-soaked scalp. And if she'd been alone, she might have. But with Gavin present, it was the last thing she would do. She'd just have to sweat and bear the heat in stoic silence.

They stopped briefly at noon, on the banks of a glittering burn that flowed over mossy rocks. Ella was glad to take a break. Unused to riding, her backside was already starting to ache.

They were at the feet of the great mountains now. One of them reared directly overhead, tawny red-gold grass rippling in the breeze. This was Beinn na Caillich, the Red Hill, or the Hill of Hag as many local folk knew it.

"Did ye know that a Norwegian Princess was supposed to have been buried at the summit of this mountain?" Gavin said, breaking the silence between them. They sat on two lichen-covered rocks on the edge of the burn, the horse and pony grazing nearby. "Folk say she died of longing for her homeland."

"Aye, I've heard the story," Ella murmured as she helped herself to a slice of cheese. She knew Gavin was only trying to make conversation, but she still felt uncomfortable in his presence. She wished he would leave her to her thoughts.

"There's a cairn of stones up there," Gavin continued. He unstoppered a bladder of water and took a gulp before passing it to her. "I saw it years ago, when I went deer hunting in this area with my brother." He twisted, motioning due north, to where the jagged edges of mountains reared into the sky. They were black and red, as if fire had scorched them. "I remember the herds of red deer roaming in the narrow vales between these mountains." Gavin's expression turned wistful. "That was a good hunting trip."

Listening to him, Ella felt an odd pang.

How she'd once loved hunting. It wasn't a suitable pastime for a lady, her mother had told her that often enough. *Why can't ye be more like yer sister? Innis behaves as a lady should.* It had been true enough. Ella's elder sister had never spent much time outdoors, except for warm afternoons when she would prune the roses in her mother's garden or collect herbs to dry.

When they were younger, Innis's fair skin had remained milky and unblemished, while every summer Ella's face, neck, and forearms burned dark gold.

Very unladylike, her mother had once scolded.

Thinking back on her sister and mother, Ella stopped chewing. She swallowed her mouthful and took a delicate sip of water, attempting to push back memories of the past into the recesses of her mind where they belonged.

Memories of her mother's shrewish words, and of her gentle sister, made her belly clench. She wondered if Cait Fraser's character had softened with the years.

Stoppering the bladder of water, Ella glanced Gavin's way. "What exactly ails my mother?" she asked.

"She has complained of belly pains for a while now," he replied. "The healer initially thought she had digestion troubles, but over the last year, the pains have grown. They eventually got so bad that yer mother became bedridden. She is very frail and spends her days in agony. The healer has done what he can for her, but I'm afraid she has little time left."

Ella listened quietly. Although she didn't like to hear that her mother suffered, she wasn't afraid of illness or death. Life at the abbey had cured her of such fears. For the last few years, she'd worked alongside Sister Coira. The nun was the healer, not just of the abbey but for all the neighboring villages. Ella had assisted Sister Coira with many patients. The nun dealt with everything, from broken limbs, festering cuts, and fevers, to childbirth and wasting sicknesses that no herb or tincture could heal.

"She will be pleased to see ye," Gavin said when a silence stretched between them. Perhaps seeing Ella's features tighten, he shook his head. "I know that relations between ye were never good in the past." He paused there. "Neither of us have had easy mothers to deal with."

"And how is Lady Maggie?"

Gavin pulled a face. "As outspoken and irascible as always, I'm afraid."

Ella's mouth compressed. Cait Fraser was snobbish and narrow-minded, but Maggie MacNichol was a different type of woman altogether. Strong, proud, with a blade-like intelligence, she was the sort of woman who should have been born a man. She would have made a formidable clan-chief, if women had been allowed to gain such positions. Instead, Maggie had always sat in her husband's shadow. However, that had never stopped her from meddling in his affairs, and the affairs of everyone living in Scorrybreac Castle.

"Ye never had much time for her, did ye?" Gavin asked.

Ella lifted her chin, and their gazes fused for an instant. "No," she admitted softly, "but many years had passed since then ... and I'm not the lass I once was."

A hot, gusting wind sprang up as the two travelers resumed their journey once more. Clouds now raced across a pale-blue sky, and all the while, the heat pressed down upon them like a heavy hand.

Gavin's mare walked sedately along, just a few yards before the fat bay pony. She'd finally accepted that this journey would be at a slower pace. Her name was Saorsa—which meant 'freedom' in their tongue—and although she was nearing her tenth year, the horse was as lively as ever.

Gaze shifting around him as he rode, Gavin tried to think of ways to draw Ella into conversation. Despite their brief exchange at noon, Ella had not thawed toward him. Gavin had tried to get her to warm to him numerous times during the afternoon. But when she continued to answer him in short, terse sentences, he got the message and ceased speaking.

The past hung over them both like a heavy storm cloud; the air was charged, crackling with tension. And yet neither of them would address their history directly. Eventually, Gavin intended to bring up the subject with Ella. But so many years had gone by since their last meeting, he wanted to wait a few days first. When they reached Scorrybreac Castle, he would find a way to broach the subject.

Gavin didn't imagine it would change anything. Yet, ever since Innis's death, Ella had been on his mind.

She was lost to him now, but that didn't mean he couldn't try and make amends for the past. He felt that he wouldn't be able to rest, or seek future happiness for himself in any way, unless he mended things between them.

The afternoon stretched on. The days seemed endless this time of year, but gradually, the shadows lengthened, and the afternoon light grew soft and golden.

They were traveling through a vale, its sides studded with rocky boulders, when Saorsa snorted, tossing her head.

The mare sidestepped, and Gavin frowned. Leaning forward, he stroked the horse's neck. "What is it, lass?"

He had barely uttered the words, when dark shapes suddenly burst out from behind the boulders and rushed toward them.

Saorsa squealed, rearing up and nearly unseating Gavin in the process. Only years of experience on horseback prevented him from toppling onto the rocky ground.

Behind him, he heard Ella gasp. "Outlaws!"

There were a few of them—twelve that Gavin could see. His gaze swept over the ragged band advancing upon them. They were dirty, barefoot, and wild-eyed.

One man, a lanky fellow with long dark hair and blue eyes, took a step toward Gavin. He carried a hand-axe at his side. "What's this?" he sneered. "A nun and her ... escort?"

Gavin inhaled slowly, considering his next words. "I'm Clan-chief MacNichol," he introduced himself casually, as if they weren't surrounded by a group of men brandishing axes, dirks, and sickles. "And I'm escorting Sister Annella here back to Scorrybreac Castle to visit her ailing mother. We're in a hurry, so I'd advise ye to let us pass."

A grin stretched across the outlaw leader's face. It made the leanness of his features even more noticeable. "Did ye hear that, lads? We've netted ourselves a clan-chief. He's bound to carry bags of silver pennies with him."

The man took a threatening step toward Gavin. Saorsa tossed her head and sidestepped once more, but Gavin held her steady. "I'm carrying little coin upon me," Gavin replied, his tone low. "But even if I was, I wouldn't be handing them over to ye." He frowned then. "Stand aside and let us pass."

The man's grin faded, his face twisting. He then spat on the ground. "We'll kill ye and take whatever ye are carrying," he growled. "And then we'll strip yer corpse of those fine clothes ye are wearing."

"That's a decent horse ye are riding too," another man called out. "I could sell her at Dunan market and earn enough silver to feed my family for a full year."

Gavin doubted that, but he wasn't going to argue the detail.

Instead, he drew the claidheamh-mor that hung at his side. He never traveled without his sword. The sun glinted off the folded steel blade.

"I don't want any trouble," Gavin said after a moment, when he was sure they'd all had a good look at his sword. "But if ye don't let us pass unmolested, blood is going to be spilled here."

"Aye," the ringleader growled. "Yers ... and the nun's."

And with that, the rabble attacked.

They ran at Gavin and Ella like a pack of howling wolves. Gavin dug his knees in, driving Saorsa forward, blocking their path to Ella. He intercepted the first of them. His blade flashed, whistling through the humid air before it thudded into flesh.

In an instant, the howling turned to screams of fury and pain. And suddenly, Gavin was slashing his way through the fray, fighting for his life.

Panic surged through him—not for his own safety, but for Ella's. Focused on fending off the outlaws, he couldn't make sure none of them had reached his companion.

A man ran at him swinging a vicious-looking scythe. Urging Saorsa forward, Gavin ran his attacker through. He yanked his blade free and glanced over his shoulder then. Ella had been riding a few yards behind him. Apart from her initial gasp of shock, she hadn't made a sound.

And as his gaze fixed upon her, she swung down from her pony's broad back.

Panic surged through Gavin once more.

The Devil's cods ... what's she doing?

She was safer mounted. At least she could attempt to gallop away from the outlaws if Gavin failed to hold them back. Instead, her finely featured face was scrunched up in determination, as if she was preparing herself to face them.

The first of the outlaws were past Gavin now, giving the Claidheamh-mor wielding clan-chief a wide berth while they stalked easier prey.

And then Ella moved.

Gavin's breathing caught as she hiked up the skirts of her habit and underskirts, and reached for the knife strapped to her left calf. He caught a glimpse of creamy flesh and a long, pale, shapely leg.

Ella drew the blade and flung it at the nearest man.

It flew through the air, spinning as it went, and embedded in his neck. The outlaw fell with a strangled cry, fingers clawing at the hilt.

Ella reached for a second knife, drawing it from where it was strapped snuggly to her right leg.

Thud.

Then she whipped out another knife from the satchel she wore across her front.

Thud.

Three men lay groaning and whimpering on the ground before her. Three blades embedded into their flesh.

6

Water Under the Bridge

GAVIN STARED, TRANSFIXED. He'd momentarily forgotten his surroundings. Face creased in a ferocious expression, Ella strode up to the nearest man and yanked her knife free from where it had embedded in his shoulder.

"Please, the outlaw whimpered. "Don't kill me."

Ella ignored him.

Meanwhile, Gavin swiveled around to face the remaining outlaws. Fortunately, they had been as surprised as him by the sight of the small knife-throwing nun.

Gavin swung his blade, causing the leader of the rabble to shrink back, his gaze burning.

"I'd abandon this now," Gavin advised him. "Before it's ye who tastes steel."

Gavin glanced right, to see that the other outlaws, who had formerly been advancing toward Ella, had all drawn back. Some of them were now racing away, scrambling over the rocks in their haste to depart.

Snarling a curse, the leader of the band flung himself toward Gavin, his axe hurtling toward Saorsa's neck.

Thud.

A blade hit his upper chest, just below the collarbone. The man gasped and went down like a sack of barley. His mouth gaped, and he struggled to pull the blade free. His blue eyes were now wide with panic, and Gavin realized that he was young, barely more than twenty winters.

It didn't matter though—this man and his followers had attacked them with murderous intent.

Gavin swung down from his mare, drew a dirk from his waist, and slashed the man across the throat. The outlaw's thin body convulsed, his eyes bulging, and then he lay still.

Breathing hard, Gavin glanced over his shoulder at where Ella stood a few yards back. She had retrieved her other knives and was cleaning them on the léine of one of the fallen men. She looked up, and their gazes fused.

The corners of Ella's mouth lifted then, the closest thing she'd given him to a smile since they'd been reunited. "Getting slow in yer old age, MacNichol?" she chided. "He almost had ye."

A small fire burned, a beacon of red and gold in the smothering darkness.

Night had finally fallen, chasing away the smothering heat. Cool air settled in a blanket over the mountains, valleys, and glens of Skye.

Gavin added a gorse branch to the fire, sitting back as sparks shot up into the air. It was a moonless night, and the flames provided the only light in the lonely vale where they'd made camp.

"Do ye think it's safe to let the fire burn so bright?" Ella spoke up. "What with so many outlaws abroad these days ..."

"We'll be fine here," Gavin replied with a shake of his head. "This valley is too remote for outlaws to bother with."

He broke off there, his gaze fixing upon the face of the nun seated opposite him. The firelight played across her creamy skin and darkened her blue eyes. The habit and wimple and veil she wore were hideous, he had to admit. The former shrouded her figure like a sack, while the latter covered her hair and framed her face in a manner that wasn't flattering to any woman.

Even so, Sister Ella of Kilbride made his pulse quicken.

She sat demurely now, her hands folded upon her lap. There was no sign of the blade-wielding assassin who'd taken down three outlaws in quick succession.

Gavin had never seen anything like it.

And yet, as they'd resumed their journey north-east in the aftermath, they'd barely discussed the incident.

Drawing in a slow breath, Gavin decided it was time. "Did ye learn to fight like that at the abbey?" he asked, breaking the long silence that had stretched out between them.

Ella's mouth quirked. That mouth—it didn't belong upon a nun's face. She had full, finely drawn lips. It was an expressive mouth that was made for sin.

Enough.

Gavin pulled himself up with that last thought. He couldn't let his mind drift back to the past. It was another life; they had both been different people then.

"Mother Shona taught me," she admitted.

Gavin raised his eyebrows, inviting her to continue.

"The abbess learned to fight years ago." Ella looked away then, her gaze shifting to the dancing flames. "Our Reverent Mother was once a novice nun at Lismore in Argyle," she continued softly. "But her convent was attacked by brigands. Most of the nuns were raped and murdered, yet she'd been out foraging for herbs and managed to escape."

Ella paused here, her hand straying to the crucifix that hung from her belt. Her fingers closed around it as she continued, "Mother Shona nearly starved, but then she was taken in by a group of men and women who were living wild in the forest ... outlaws too, but not those who'd attacked her convent. They taught her to throw knives, wield a long-bow, swing a sword, and hold her own with a quarter-staff. She brought those skills with her to Kilbride. And when she was elected as abbess, she decided that we would learn how to defend ourselves should the need arise."

"She did a fine job of teaching ye," Gavin replied. "I've rarely seen such skill."

Ella inclined her head, acknowledging the compliment.

"I thought nuns took vows that prevented them from using violence against others?" he asked.

"We take three vows: poverty, chastity, and obedience. Nowhere is it writ that we are forbidden from defending ourselves from those who'd do us harm," Ella replied. With her fingertips, she traced the lines of the crucifix she now held upon her palm. "We could refuse to wield blades, but that wouldn't prevent us from dying upon them. How can we serve God then?"

Gavin smiled. He hadn't forgotten how sharp Ella's mind was, or her strength of character. Even so, the years had developed those traits further. He'd never met a woman like her and knew he would never do so again.

"Ye were magnificent this afternoon," he admitted quietly. "God's bones, woman ... ye are wasted as a nun."

Ella stiffened, her gaze narrowing. In an instant the easy atmosphere at the fireside dissolved and tension settled over their camp.

"Taking the veil and dedicating my life to serving God was the making of me," Ella said after a chill pause. "I do not see it as a waste of a life ... instead, it is the greatest privilege I could have ever received."

Inwardly, Gavin winced. What had possessed him to say those words? Every time he opened his mouth over the last day, he'd managed to offend her. That wasn't hard to do though, for Sister Ella was far pricklier than the lass he'd known nearly two decades earlier.

Guilt lanced through Gavin. *Whose fault is that?*

"Apologies, Ella," he replied, casting her a conciliatory smile. "It was an ill choice of words."

She didn't smile back at him. "*Sister* Ella." Her tone was clipped.

"I handled things badly ... in the past," he said finally, clearing his throat. "If I could have my time again, I'd do things differently."

Gavin remembered that he'd planned to leave this conversation till they arrived at Scorrybreac—but now seemed like the right time.

Ella's face went taut. "I don't want to talk about the past." Her voice turned brittle. "It is dead to me ... I serve the Lord now."

Gavin leaned forward, snaring her gaze with his. "But there are some subjects that should be aired. Our past is like a festering wound; it needs to be lanced or it will only poison yer time at Scorrybreac Castle." When Ella didn't reply, he continued. "I want ye to know that I have lived with regret, every day of my life since that afternoon in the clearing. I hurt ye greatly, and I'm sorry for it."

"It's too late for this, Gavin." The coolness of her voice was a knife to his heart—and yet it was the first time she'd addressed him by his first name since they'd been reunited. "Like I said, the past is dead."

Gavin swallowed. "Ye left Scorrybreac so quickly. I never had the chance to say goodbye."

A nerve flickered in her cheek as she stared back at him. "Ye didn't deserve it."

"I did my duty," he replied, his voice heavy, flat. "I never wanted to hurt ye, but I could see no way out of it. As the first-born son, I felt I had responsibilities ... I couldn't disappoint my family."

"Aye, ye could have," she whispered, looking away from him. "It would have cost ye, but ye could have gone against them."

Gavin drew in a sharp breath. At last there was a crack in her façade; he'd started to wonder if memories of their shared past affected her at all.

"They would have disowned me," he pointed out. "Would ye have wed a pauper?"

"Aye," she replied, her voice barely audible. She still refused to meet his gaze. "It wasn't yer title that interested me."

"Ye say that now, but—"

"Enough." Ella's choked command splintered the night. "Ye made yer choice, MacNichol ... and I made mine. It's water under the bridge now; let us speak no more of it. My life now belongs to Christ."

7

Scorrybreac

THE SIGHT OF Scorrybreac Castle, after so many years, made Ella catch her breath. Drawing up Monadh upon the rise of the last hill before the stronghold, she let her gaze drink the castle in.

So many memories.

And despite the suddenness of her departure, most of them had been pleasant.

When they'd come to live at Scorrybreac, Ella had loved it. The MacNichol clan-chief had been a jolly, red-faced man with a booming laugh, so different from Morgan Fraser, the chieftain of the Frasers of Skye. The inhabitants of Talasgair, the Fraser stronghold, had all minded their chief, for he could be harsh and had a mercurial temper.

She remembered how beautiful she'd thought this castle's setting—perched out on a promontory, cliffs at its back and the Sound of Raasay before it. Scorrybreac's bulk stretched in a long oval, hugging the shore.

It was still as lovely today, with the MacNichol pennant flying from the keep, the sun glittering on the water behind it. Another warm day had followed them north, and the last of the evening sun was setting behind the mountains that thrust up to the west. Soon dusk would settle.

"Is it as ye remember?" MacNichol pulled his grey mare up next to her.

"Aye." Ella replied softly, deliberately not looking his way. She'd avoided eye-contact with Gavin all day, and had been grateful that he'd had the sense to avoid conversing with her.

Last night's exchange had made them both wary.

Ella's gaze slid over the high granite curtain wall that encircled the stronghold, before she took in the thatched roofs of the settlement before it. "The village looks bigger though."

"It has grown in recent years." She caught the edge of pride in his voice. "We've had a number of folk move here from other areas."

They rode into Scorrybreac village, along a wide road that cut through a patchwork of tilled fields. Indeed, the area looked more prosperous than Ella remembered. It didn't surprise her that Gavin ruled well. His father, although a gentle-hearted man, hadn't been cut out for the role of clan-chief. And his shrewish wife had long pressured him to raise the taxes on the folk who farmed their lands.

There were still men and women out, cottars working the land. An elderly man, who'd been reaping barley, leaned on his scythe and raised a hand in greeting.

Gavin waved back.

"They're working late," Ella observed.

"It's the coolest time of day," Gavin replied, "and with the harvest moon almost upon us, the farmers want to reap what they can before the weather turns."

Ella understood that; the weather of their isle could be capricious. This spell of fine weather wouldn't last.

Reaching the guard house, they rode up a pebbly incline and under the portcullis. Twin crenelated towers flanked the arched gateway, where the men of the Scorrybreac garrison resided. Spears bristled against the dusky sky overhead, and the gazes of the men taking their turn at the watch tracked their path up the causeway.

The outer bailey within was a hive of activity this eve. Guards were sparring with blunted swords to the right of the guard house, their grunts filtering through the warm air, while nearby fowl pecked in the dirt. A group of lads were playing knucklebones on the dusty ground in front of the stables, only to be told off by a stable-hand who was pushing out a barrow of stinking manure.

Ella drew up Monadh once more and looked about her. All was exactly as she remembered. A number of stone buildings flanked the wide space: the stables, armory, stores, and byres. The square stone keep rose to the back, protected by a high stone wall and a second, smaller, guard house.

After the quiet of the abbey, Scorrybreac's outer bailey seemed chaotic. At this hour the sisters would have entered the Great Silence, a ritual she'd come to appreciate over the years.

Upon seeing that their chief had returned, the guards sparring with swords ceased their practice and called out to him. Gavin swung down from his mare's back and responded to their greeting with a warmth and familiarity that didn't surprise Ella.

One glance at these men's faces and she could see that Gavin MacNichol was loved by his people.

"Ye took yer time ... I was about to send out a search party."

Ella's gaze shifted to where a tall man with short blond hair strode toward them.

Blair MacNichol, Gavin's younger brother. The family resemblance was startling, although Blair had a heavier stature, a more florid complexion—and his mother's sharp grey eyes.

Gavin snorted, handing his horse's reins to a stable lad while he unfastened the saddlebag he'd brought with him. "I told ye I'd be away a few days."

"Aye, but since ye insisted on traveling alone, I'd assumed ye had been set upon by thieves."

Ella stiffened at these words. She wondered if Gavin would tell his brother what had befallen them on the way here—or would reveal that she carried a number of blades on her person and knew how to throw them.

But moments passed, and Gavin said nothing.

Blair's attention shifted to Ella then, his grey eyes widening. "Lady Annella?"

"Sister Annella now, Blair," Gavin replied.

"Of course." Blair nodded to Ella, his gaze turning wary.

Ella favored him with a subdued smile. She was used to such a response. Her black robed appearance was a daunting one. Most men no longer saw a nun as a woman—Gavin was the only one who looked at her as if she was.

Checking herself at this thought, Ella swallowed. "Greetings, Blair. I hope ye and yer wife are well?"

"Aye," Blair replied with a nod. "Forbia and I have four strapping lads now ... the eldest has just reached his sixteenth summer."

This news took Ella aback. When she'd left Scorrybreac, Blair and Forbia had only just wed. To think that his eldest son was on the threshold of becoming a man made her feel old.

She glanced over at Gavin, whose face was inscrutable. Did he and Innis have any children? Innis had never spoken of them in her letters, and Gavin hadn't mentioned any on the way here. "Is yer sister still at Scorrybreac."

Gavin's mouth lifted at the corners. "Aye ... Gordana will be happy to see ye."

Warmth filtered through Ella then. Although Gordana was a few years her elder, she had been close to Gavin's sister when she had lived at the castle. She looked forward to seeing her again.

Aware that a number of curious stares from around the outer bailey were now fixed upon her, Ella shifted her attention back to where the square, dun-colored keep rose to the east.

"Where will I find my mother?" she asked quietly.

"I will take ye to her now," Gavin replied.

"We shall see ye at supper ... Sister Annella?" Blair asked. His grey eyes were narrowed slightly as he continued to watch her with an unnerving intensity that once again reminded Ella of his mother.

Ella was opening her mouth to say that she'd likely be taking all her meals in private, when Gavin spoke once more. "Aye ... Sister Ella is a guest here. Of course she will join us in the Great Hall this eve."

Ella's belly tightened at this news, and she drew in a slow breath. Already she felt far too conspicuous here. The last thing she needed was to take a place at the MacNichol clan's table in the Great Hall with kin and retainers all ogling her.

However, as she meekly left Monadh with the stable lad and followed Gavin toward the archway leading through to the inner bailey and the keep, she kept her thoughts to herself.

Gavin walked ahead, ascending a row of granite steps and entering the keep through great oaken doors. Two servants were in the midst of mopping the floor to the entrance hall beyond.

At seeing their clan-chief enter, the lasses straightened up, before curtsying.

"Welcome home, MacNichol," the younger of the two called out.

Gavin cast the lass an easy smile. "Thank ye, Fiona. Don't mind me ... carry on with yer tasks."

Both servants nodded, although they didn't resume their mopping immediately. Instead, their gazes shifted to Ella, curiosity lighting their faces.

Seeing their reactions to her, Ella loosed an inward sigh. She'd have to get used to the stares while she was here it seemed.

Gavin went ahead, leading the way up a spiral stairwell. Picking up her skirts, Ella followed. He didn't try to converse with her, which she was grateful for. She hadn't failed to notice that upon arriving back at Scorrybreac, his manner had altered slightly toward her.

A formality had settled, a distant air that she wished he'd adopted during the journey here.

Leaving the stairwell, Gavin strode down a narrow corridor. Despite that it was a bright day out, there were no windows to let in the sunlight in these hallways. Instead, flickering cressets illuminated the damp stone.

Eventually, Gavin drew to a halt outside a large oaken door. He then turned to face Ella, giving her his full attention for the first time since they'd entered the keep. "Yer mother awaits ye within," he said softly. "I will see ye later ... at supper."

8

Blame

CAIT FRASER'S SICKROOM was dark and overly warm. The air smelt musty and slightly sour, as if no one ever opened the shutters to let fresh air in.

Ella fought the urge to do just that as she crossed the flagstone floor and took a seat beside the bed. Sister Coira believed that fresh air chased away the dark humors that perpetuated illness. Even so, it wasn't Ella's place to come barging in here and open the window so her mother could watch the rose-hued sunset.

Cait appeared to be asleep, propped up against a mountain of pillows.

Lowering herself onto the stool, Ella took in her mother's frail form. She had never been a big woman, yet the illness that now wracked her body had melted the flesh from her bones, withered her arms to sticks, and caused her cheeks to sink in.

Ella's throat constricted as she watched her mother's face. She barely recognized the woman who had once caused her so much anguish. Cait Fraser didn't look capable of causing anyone trouble these days.

Drawing in a deep breath, Ella reached out, her hand covering her mother's. The skin was cool and papery. "Ma?"

Cait Fraser's eyes flickered open, and for the first time, Ella fully knew the woman before her. Those eyes were a deep blue, the same shade as Ella's.

"Ella?" Her mother's voice held a rasp, yet Ella recognized it.

Her vision blurred as she gently squeezed the frail hand beneath hers. "Aye ... it's me. MacNichol came to fetch me himself from Kilbride."

"Ye look so different in that habit," her mother whispered. Ella could hear the weakness in her voice, the whistle in her lungs with each exhale. Gavin was right, Cait Fraser didn't have much time left. "I barely know ye."

"It's still me," Ella murmured, attempting to raise a smile and failing.

"Aye," her mother croaked. "I see that ... and I am so proud that ye are a Bride of Christ."

Ella didn't reply. Her mother had always been pious. Even now, she wore a small iron crucifix around her neck. The cross lay against the snowy white linen of her night-rail. And as Ella watched, her mother's frail hand reached up to clasp the crucifix. It seemed her faith hadn't lessened with the years. Still, her gaze never left her daughter. Cait's blue eyes gleamed.

"I am glad ye came," her mother said finally, breaking the silence.

The genuine emotion in Cait's voice made Ella's chest start to hurt. Her mother had never before used such a tone with her.

Ella leaned forward, cupping her mother's free hand with both of her own now. "So am I."

"I didn't think ye would ... and I wouldn't have blamed ye for it." Cait drew in a whispery breath. "I never treated ye right, Ella ... and I'm sorry for it."

Ella swallowed hard. The pain in the center of her chest had now spread up to her throat. Her eyes stung as she blinked back tears.

Mother Mary, please give me strength. She wasn't sure what she'd expected upon her return—perhaps to encounter a mother as haughty and critical as ever—but this soft, broken individual wasn't it.

It ripped a hole in her chest to see her mother so diminished. She almost wished for a tongue-lashing. It would be easier to bear.

"It's all in the past now, Ma," Ella whispered. "Ye should know that I've been very happy at Kilbride. A nun's life suits me well."

"I would have liked to have done God's work," her mother admitted.

"But ye chose to become a wife and mother instead ... that too is a good choice."

Cait Fraser huffed, some of her old fire returning for an instant. "I thought so once, but with the years, I found myself wishing I'd made a different choice." She broke off there, recovering her breath. It worried Ella to see that even speaking taxed her mother. "Don't mistake me, I don't regret having ye and yer sister," Cait continued weakly. "It's just that I've always yearned for a simple life that I could dedicate entirely to our Lord."

"Kilbride Abbey would have certainly given ye that," Ella replied softly. "I find myself missing its serenity already."

Cait's mouth curved. "Ye were so spirited once ... I was sure ye wouldn't take to such a life." She paused then, her sunken chest rising and falling sharply under her high-necked night-rail. "I was so hard on ye, lass. I favored Innis ... and always compared ye to her."

"I know," Ella replied, her voice still soft. "But all of that is forgotten now."

That wasn't entirely true, yet her mother didn't need to hear it. Best to let a dying woman make peace with her past.

"But I was wrong to do so." Some of the fire of old lit in Cait's blue eyes. Her thin fingers wrapped around Ella's, squeezing with surprising strength. "Innis was quiet and biddable, but ye had a spine. I tried to beat it out of ye, to scold it out of ye ... but for a long while now, I have regretted my actions. Will ye ever forgive me, lass?"

"Aye, Ma." Tears ran down Ella's cheeks, but she didn't reach up to brush them away.

Their gazes locked and held for a long instant, before Cait Fraser's grip tightened around the crucifix she still grasped with her free hand.

"Will ye pray with me, Ella?" she asked, her voice husky.

Ella nodded, smiling through her tears. "Of course I will."

Ella's father was waiting for her when she left her mother's sick room.

Stewart Fraser had gotten broader and greyer in the nearly two decades since they'd last seen each other. His face was even more careworn than Ella remembered, although his hazel eyes were just as kind.

Wordlessly, he enfolded Ella in a bear-hug, and when they drew apart, his eyes were gleaming.

"It is good to see ye, lass," he rumbled. "The years have made ye even bonnier than I remember."

Ella favored her father with a watery smile. "I have missed ye, Da," Ella replied. It was the truth. She'd often railed at her father for allowing his wife to be such a shrew, yet for every harsh word that Cait had rained down upon Ella, Stewart had gifted her three gentle ones.

"Are ye happy, Ella?" he asked softly. "I've often wondered about ye over the years."

"I am content, Da," Ella replied.

A weight appeared to lift from him at her words, and Stewart loosed a sigh. "That is a relief to hear."

Ella's gaze roamed his rugged face. As a younger man, he'd been handsome in that rangy way of the Fraser men: tall and flame-haired. Although he lacked the arrogant bearing of his cousin, Morgan Fraser—the chieftain of the Frasers of Skye. These days his once bright hair had faded to a rusty grey.

"Ma is so frail," Ella murmured, threading her arm through her father's and letting him lead her away down the narrow corridor. Night had just fallen, and cressets now burned upon the pitted stone walls. "I barely recognized her."

"Aye ... she is a changed woman," Stewart replied. "More than just physically ... as I am sure ye noted."

Ella nodded, her throat thickening. "I've never known her so ... soft."

Her father grunted. "Aye ... it's just a pity that it took a fatal illness for her to see clearly."

Ella cast her father a surprised glance. Her mother wasn't the only one to have changed it seemed." She couldn't believe it—her father's tone seemed almost ... critical.

Stewart Fraser let out a heavy sigh, his mouth curving into a tired smile. "I must carry part of the blame too, lass ... for not speaking up when she used to harangue ye. All the same, we are both glad ye have visited her."

Silence fell between them, and when Ella broke it, her voice was heavy with regret. "I should have come earlier, Da. I'm sorry I did not."

"Innis wrote to ye," he replied, his tone guarded now. "We all thought that ye would return when ye heard how ill she was ... but ye never did."

Ella swallowed, guilt thrumming through her. She wished she could tell her father why she'd stayed away. But neither of her parents knew the reason for her taking the veil—and it was too late now to reveal the truth.

It wouldn't change anything even if she was to tell him. It wouldn't erase his disappointment that she hadn't visited her dying sister.

"I regret that, Da," she said softly, a rasp to her voice betraying her churning emotions.

Stewart Fraser halted then and turned to her. Their gazes fused.

"Why didn't ye come?" he asked.

The directness of his question made Ella's breathing hitch. It felt as if someone had grasped her around the throat and was slowly squeezing. Now was her chance to be honest with him. Her father wanted her to speak frankly—and yet she couldn't. She just couldn't.

"We were busy with the harvest at Kilbride," Ella replied, forcing herself not to drop her gaze. "I couldn't get away ... I hadn't realized that Innis was so ill." Her voice trailed off, and when she saw her father's eyes shadow, her chest constricted and a sickly heat washed over her.

He knew she was lying.

9

Lady MacNichol

ELLA HAD HOPED her father would join her for supper
in the Great Hall. However, he begged off with the
excuse that he took all his meals at his wife's side these
days. Ella couldn't criticize him for such devotion; she
only wished she could use the same excuse.

She didn't want to dine with the MacNichols.

Entering Scorrybreac's Great Hall, Ella was taken
aback by its vast size. Had it always been this big, or was
she just used to Kilbride's modest refectory? The hall
was long and rectangular-shaped, with a high dais at one
end. A stag's head had been mounted over a large stone
hearth, and before it sat an oaken table where the
MacNichol family took their meals. Pennants made of
the clan's plaid—red crossed with lines of blue and
green—and a banner of the clan's seal hung above the
hearth. The MacNichol seal was a hawk's head, with the
clan's motto written in Latin beneath.

Meminisse sed providere: remember but look ahead.

Despite her nervousness, a wry smile tugged at Ella's
lips. That motto had meant little to her when she'd lived
here as a maid. But at thirty-six winters, those words
now struck her.

Indeed, one had to keep focused on the future rather than dwelling on the past—yet the wise never forgot. The events almost two decades earlier had nearly broken her, but she would always keep them in her memory. They would inform her decisions and shape the years to come; they would ensure she never walked the same foolish path ever again.

Rows of MacNichol retainers—the clansmen and women who inhabited the keep—sat at the tables beneath the dais. The roar of voices quietened as she passed. Curious gazes followed Ella, tracking her progress down the aisle between the tables.

Spine straight, Ella passed through them and stepped up onto the dais. She'd come here as soon as she could after spending time with her mother, but it seemed she was late. She inhaled the aroma of rich boar stew and saw that servants had already started serving.

Ella reached the table and looked for somewhere to sit. Her belly clenched when she saw that the only free space was to Gavin MacNichol's left—for he sat at the head of the table—next to his mother.

All conversation at the table stopped when Ella took her seat.

Ella's gaze swept over those seated there. Gavin was favoring her with a soft smile, an expression that made her breathing quicken, while Maggie MacNichol was watching their guest with a narrow-eyed stare. Ella knew many others at the table. Gordana was there, sitting to her mother's left; while Blair, his wife Forbia, and their strapping sons sat farther down the table.

"Ye deigned to join us after all." Maggie MacNichol's first words made Ella start to sweat. If her own mother had been remarkable in her change, this woman was the complete opposite. As a younger woman, the clan-chief's lady had been a striking beauty with straw-gold hair, piercing grey eyes, and a regal presence. Time had not withered her, even though her hair had faded and the years had traced fine lines upon her skin. Maggie still sat as straight as ever, the force of her personality radiating out across the table.

"Apologies, Lady MacNichol," Ella replied, holding her eye. "I spent more time with my mother than expected."

Maggie sniffed at this. "And how is she faring today?"

"She is weak ... I imagine her time draws near."

Lady MacNichol's mouth pursed. "Ye should have come sooner." The woman didn't bother to dilute the accusatory tone to her voice. When Ella didn't reply, Maggie frowned. "Instead, my son had to take time away from the running of Scorrybreac to fetch ye."

"Mother." The warning tone in Gavin's voice caused those seated at the table to go still. Even the circling servants, who were ladling out stew, dishing up dumplings, and pouring goblets of sloe wine, paused in their work. "Sister Ella is our guest. Ye are not to interrogate her."

His mother stiffened, drawing herself up like an enraged cat. At the head of the table, Gavin didn't move. He sat, his posture relaxed, in a high-backed chair. Made out of polished oak, the chair had eagle heads carved into the armrests. Ella remembered the chair well, and how his father's corpulent form had spilled into it. There was nothing corpulent about Gavin though. His long body was hard and muscled, even in repose. He held a bronze goblet in one hand, his gaze hooded as he met his mother's eye.

Ella drew in a breath, waiting for Lady MacNichol to explode. And yet she didn't tear into her son as Ella had expected.

There had been many changes at Scorrybreac over the years it seemed.

Nonetheless, Maggie's mutinous expression warned that the woman had not yet finished saying her piece. She would merely bide her time.

The servants continued to serve supper, many of them not bothering to hide their curiosity at Ella's presence. One or two openly stared. It wasn't every day that a nun sat in Scorrybreac's Great Hall.

Behind the chieftain's table, a young woman, seated upon a stool by the hearth, began playing a harp. The lilting music drifted over the hall, filling Ella with memories.

She had not heard music like this since leaving Scorrybreac. The nuns didn't play musical instruments in the evenings. Innis had played the instrument well. Ella remembered her sister's soft smile then, the look of joy upon her face as her slender fingers danced over the harp strings.

Guilt lanced through Ella at another memory of her sister, causing a warm, sickly sensation to creep over her. Ella's conversation earlier that evening with her father needled at her. Innis had never deliberately done Ella wrong—she'd been hurt and confused by Ella's silence over the years.

If there was one thing she would change, it would be her treatment of her sister.

"It's good to see ye." Gordana leaned forward, catching Ella's eye. "Although I hardly recognize ye in that habit."

Ella smiled back. "Ye look no different to the last time we met."

It was true. Gordana MacNichol was around ten years Ella's senior, but age had not dimmed the pretty lines of her face. Gavin's elder sister wore her white-blonde hair braided down her back, and this eve she had donned a dark-blue kirtle that matched her eyes.

Gordana gave a soft laugh. "If only that were true."

Ella held her gaze for a long moment. In her letters from Innis, Ella had learned that Gordana had lost her husband, Rory, ten winters earlier. He'd fallen in the ice just after Yuletide and cracked his skull. It seemed that his widow had never remarried. Their son had been around four winter's old when Ella had left Scorrybreac. "How is Darron faring these days?" she asked.

Gordana smiled. "As tall as Gavin, if ye can believe it." Pride shone in her eyes as she spoke. "He serves the MacDonalds of Duntulm now ... and is captain of the guard." Gordana paused here, her mouth curving. "And he has just wed ... a lass named Sorcha MacQueen."

Next to her Lady MacNichol made a choking sound. "The MacQueen chieftain's bastard ... hardly a match to brag about, Gordana."

In an instant Gordana's face hardened. Her attention snapped to her mother. "My son's happiness means more to me than the parentage of the woman he loves," she said coldly.

Respect filtered through Ella as she glanced from Maggie's haughty face to Gordana's proud one. In the past, neither Gavin nor Gordana had dared to question their mother. Their mother had become even harsher with the years—but it appeared that her offspring had become less tolerant of her sharp tongue.

A servant dished up Ella's supper, and she inhaled the aroma. Mouth filling with saliva, Ella dug her wooden spoon into the stew. She had just taken her first spoonful, when Lady MacNichol spoke once more.

However, this time her words were not directed at her daughter.

"I must say ... that habit does nothing for ye, Ella."

"It's *Sister* Ella, mother," Gavin corrected her wearily. "And please, leave our guest be. Her mother is gravely ill, and she has just crossed the isle to see her."

Maggie shrugged, as if her son had said something of very little consequence, those grey eyes never leaving Ella.

"As I said ... that attire is very unflattering," she continued. "The wimple makes yer face look like a moon. Ye could grow as fat as a sow under all that fabric and no one would be any the wiser."

The urge to laugh bubbled up within Ella. Smothering it, she grabbed her goblet of wine, raised it to her lips, and took a large gulp. "It is lucky then," she replied, her tone deliberately bland, "that the Lord does not judge us on our appearances."

Lady MacNichol's mouth pursed. "Aye ... but the rest of us do. Ye resemble a crow in that garb."

Ella didn't reply. Maggie hadn't changed at all. Always a woman to fixate on the appearance and weight of other ladies, she'd never been without a vicious comment for both Ella and Innis in the past. But even Ella's status as a nun didn't stop her.

"Mother." Gavin's voice was rough with anger now. "Enough."

"What?" His mother favored him with a look of mock-innocence. "I was merely making an observation."

"Ye were being rude," he growled back. Gavin leaned forward then, his face hard. "And ye will apologize."

"The Lord is my light and my salvation—whom shall I fear? The Lord is the stronghold of my life—of whom shall I be afraid?"

Ella paused, raising her eyes from the psalm she was reading, to find her mother watching her with an intent expression.

"What is it, Ma ... I thought this was one of yer favorites?"

"It is," Cait Fraser replied, her voice whispery. "Ye read it so beautifully to me earlier, but yer heart isn't in it, tonight. Is something amiss, daughter?"

Ella stiffened. She hadn't been aware that her mood had shown so clearly upon her face. "I'm just a little on edge," she admitted, lowering the book of psalms to her lap. "Lady MacNichol was particularly sharp-tongued at supper."

Her mother loosed a sigh, sinking back into the mountain of pillows that propped her up. "That's the only good thing about being laid up here," she murmured. "Avoiding that shrew."

"She appears to have gotten nastier with age," Ella observed, before guilt flickered up within her. It wasn't seemly for a nun to gossip about others; nonetheless, she dreaded her next mealtime with Gavin's mother.

"It's bitterness," Cait replied. "Gavin isn't as easy to manipulate as his father was ... she feels powerless."

"I will pray for her soul then," Ella replied, flicking through the psalm book. "Perhaps I can find something to combat her ill humor." She paused then, glancing up at her mother. "What about this: Deliver me from mine enemies, Lord. Defend me from them that rise up against me."

Cait gave a weak laugh. "A little harsh I think, Sister Ella."

Ella continued to leaf through the book. "Ah," she said finally, her mouth quirking. "I have just the thing ... from Psalm Ninety-One."

"Go on, read it then." Cait Fraser's eyes flickered shut. Even short conversations appeared to weary her terribly. "I am listening."

"He will cover ye with his wings," Ella began softly, her voice carrying through the silent chamber. "A thousand may fall dead beside you, ten thousand all around you, but ye will not be harmed. Ye will look and see how the wicked are punished."

10

Regrets

CLIMBING THE WORN stone steps, Ella pushed open the heavy oaken door and stepped into a cool, dimly-lit space. Scorrybreac Chapel huddled against the northern wall of the keep, with the curtain wall rearing above it.

The chapel was much smaller than Kilbride kirk, yet she had fond memories of this place. Indeed, it was her refuge now. She'd left her mother sleeping but made the mistake of going to the women's solar afterward. Gavin's mother had been there, surrounded by her ladies, and Ella had soon felt like a fly trapped in a spider's web. She'd had to get away from the pointed looks and whispered comments.

Inhaling the odor of tallow from the banks of guttering candles lining the walls, and the scent of burning incense, Ella made her way across the polished stone floor. She didn't head toward the altar, but to the small shrine located against the left wall. This chapel was a special place, for it had an alcove dedicated to the Virgin Mary.

Kneeling before it, Ella gazed up at the serene face of the statue before her. A woman cloaked in blue gazed down at the swaddled infant in her arms: Mother Mary. The sight of the statue made peace settle over Ella in a comforting blanket. Even before she'd fled to Kilbride, this chapel had been her safe place. Here, it felt as if nothing could touch her.

Innis had loved this chapel too, and Ella's breathing quickened at the memory of her sister kneeling beside her in front of this shrine. Being at Scorrybreac brought back too many memories.

The ones that included her sister were the most painful.

How she'd wanted to hate Innis for wedding the man she'd loved.

She'd barely spoken to her sister after Gavin broke the news to her. In the days while she'd awaited news from Kilbride, Ella had avoided all of her kin for fear that the disappointment and grief that boiled within her would explode if any of them provoked her.

Innis had written to her often at Kilbride, yet she'd never responded to her letters—not once. But her sister hadn't seemed to mind. The messages had continued to arrive, one each month, until the letter that had revealed she was gravely ill. In that missive her sister had asked something of Ella for the first time since their parting.

She'd requested a visit, so that they might see each other one last time before the end.

Ella hadn't replied—and nor had she visited her dying sister.

At the time she'd buried those feelings deep, busied herself in her life at Kilbride. But now, surrounded by so many memories, they resurfaced once more.

Regret twisted in Ella's breast.

"I'm so sorry, Innis," she whispered. "Ye deserved better."

Her vision misted as the pain just under her breastbone built. "I should have come home to say farewell."

Brushing away the tears that now trickled down her face, Ella heaved in a deep breath. She had visited the chapel for solace, yet she should have known that memories would resurface. Innis had been gone for nearly two years—but her presence was still strong in this place.

Removing the crucifix from her belt, Ella entwined her fingers through the beaded wooden necklace and clasped her hands before her. Then, she closed her eyes and began to pray.

Almost immediately a sense of peace settled over her, calming the churning grief and gnawing guilt. All Ella's cares and worries slid away.

Time lost all meaning in the chapel. It was only when Ella's knees started to hurt that she realized she'd been kneeling for a long while. Around her the tallow candles continued to burn. There was no sign of the priest who oversaw this chapel. He'd likely retired for the night, for it was now growing very late.

It was time for Ella to find her own bed. Servants had taken her satchel up earlier, but she would have to ask one of them to lead her to her lodgings. She'd been too occupied since her arrival at Scorrybreac Castle to seek out her bed-chamber herself.

Wincing, Ella rose to her feet. She rubbed her sore knees and looped her crucifix through her belt.

Despite the grief that had surfaced over her sister, she was glad she'd come to the chapel. Being around so many folk, after years of the peace at Kilbride, had put her on edge. She'd felt overwhelmed, yet her time at prayer and the Virgin's soothing company made her feel stronger—and she knew she'd need strength in the days to come.

She left the chapel, stepping out into the cool night air. Descending the steps, Ella slowed her pace, alarm flickering through her.

She wasn't alone.

Up ahead she spied a man's shadow looming across the cobbles in the light of a flaming torch that was chained to the side of the keep.

Her breathing hitched as Gavin MacNichol stepped into the torchlight.

Ella raised a hand, placing it over her pounding heart. "Heavens," she gasped. "Ye gave me a fright."

"Sorry, I didn't mean to scare ye." The clan-chief stopped and raised his chin to look up at her. "I've been waiting to escort ye to yer lodgings."

Ella stared back at him, the alarm that had just settled rising once more. "Ye don't need to do that ... I can ask a servant."

He inclined his head. "I don't need to, but I'd like to ... if I may?"

Ella tensed. There was no suggestion or flirtatious tone to his words, yet she didn't like them nonetheless. "After our conversation on the journey here, I don't think we have much to say to each other," she said when the silence between them became uncomfortable.

His mouth curved. "I'd like to apologize for my mother's rudeness earlier ... it was inexcusable."

Ella huffed. "Everyone else in this keep has changed somewhat with the years but not Lady MacNichol."

"Ye are mistaken ... my mother has changed. The years have whetted her tongue like a blade. She's even more of a viper than she was when ye lived with us."

Ella raised her eyebrows but didn't respond. Instead, she continued her path down the steps and started across the inner bailey. Gavin walked beside her.

"We shouldn't be alone," she said quietly. "It isn't proper."

"We were alone on the journey here," he pointed out.

"Aye ... but I had no choice about that. Here at Scorrybreac there are sharp eyes and flapping ears and tongues."

Gavin snorted. "I wouldn't worry about that ... I don't give the gossips in this keep a second thought."

Ella cast Gavin a swift glance. "When we met at Kilbride, I thought ye hadn't altered much with the years ... but I now see ye have."

His eyes gleamed as his gaze met hers. "How so?"

"Ye have a harder edge to ye ... and ye certainly wouldn't have told yer mother off like ye did at supper."

Gavin gave a soft laugh. It was a low, pleasant sound that caused an unexpected warmth to seep across Ella's breast. She'd forgotten his laugh, and how much she'd loved it.

"My mother overstepped … something she does frequently these days," he replied. "Gordana thinks I should pack her off to live with kin upon the Isle of Raasay. That way, we'd all be rid of her."

"And why don't ye?"

A heavy sigh gusted out of Gavin. "I don't rightly know … guilt … a sense of filial duty."

Ella looked away, biting at her bottom lip. *Duty*. He hadn't changed that much after all. An overwhelming sense of responsibility still ruled this man's decisions— his life.

"I take it that ye and Innis never had children?" Ella asked after a long pause. They had skirted around the eastern edge of the inner bailey and were now walking past the high wall that circuited the herb garden, a long rectangular space that hugged the southern flank of the curtain wall.

Glancing Gavin's way, Ella saw tension settle over his face. It was a bold, impertinent question, and had she mulled over it first, Ella probably would never have asked it. As it was, she'd been wondering all day about Gavin's union with Innis. Had they truly been happy together? The question had slipped from her lips, before she'd had the chance to stop herself.

"No," he replied, a slightly rough edge to his voice. "We tried for the first few years." He cleared his throat then. "But when Innis's womb didn't quicken, she asked if we could sleep in separate chambers. Once that happened, we never lay together again."

Ella glanced away once more, taking in the news. Years earlier it might have made her feel vindicated. As it was, she just felt hollow—and a little sad. The guarded edge to his voice warned her from asking anything else. Yet his candor made it hard not to.

"Innis wrote to me often, ye know?" she said finally.

"Aye … once a moon."

"I read all her letters."

"But ye never responded to any."

There it was, a faint note of accusation in his tone. Ella wasn't surprised or offended. He had every right to think her cruel.

"Innis told me that she was content with ye," she replied, deliberately not responding to his comment. "Was that not the truth?"

A beat of silence followed. "We were happy enough," Gavin replied. There was a heaviness to his voice now, as if this conversation was starting to weary him. "Innis and I made good companions, and our friendship deepened over the years. But it was not an ideal match ... we both knew that. Perhaps if we'd had bairns, things might have been different." His voice trailed off there, and Gavin drew to a halt.

Ella stopped next to him, surprised. Turning, she faced him, wilting under the intensity of his gaze. The torchlight that flickered across the inner bailey highlighted the handsome planes of his face, but also the regret in his eyes.

Regret for what? That his union with Innis had been lacking? That he'd wed her in the first place?

"I have no heir," Gavin said, his voice low now, "so my brother or one of my nephews will take my place once I'm gone."

Ella inclined her head, wondering at why he was being so frank with her this eve. For the first time since they'd been reunited, she was starting to feel comfortable in his presence. "Does that bother ye?"

"Years ago I thought it might ... but these days I hardly care." His gaze shadowed then, as it held hers. "Maybe it's my punishment for hurting ye, Ella. Perhaps I deserve no better."

11

Saying Too Much

ELLA FOUND GORDANA MacNichol hard at work in the walled garden. Stepping inside the secluded space, Ella inhaled the scents of the last of the summer roses mingled with the strong perfume of lavender.

A few feet away, Gordana stood before a trellis of gillyflowers. She was tying up the stems of the clove-scented, pink and white flowers that grew in large earthen pots, to prevent them from flopping over. Around Gordana spread long beds of rosemary, sage, thyme, chamomile, and myrtle. A large spreading quince tree had been espaliered against the far wall of the garden.

A smile curved Ella's mouth as she took in the scene. How could one *not* smile when standing in such a beautiful spot?

Giving a delicate cough, she moved toward Gordana.

Gavin's sister glanced over her shoulder. Her face had tensed, for she clearly didn't like anyone intruding upon her garden sanctuary.

"Don't mind me," Ella replied, stopping abruptly. "I can leave if ye wish."

Gordana's expression softened. "Stay, Sister Ella ... I thought for a moment that Ma had come to harangue me."

Ella raised an eyebrow, before she drew closer. "She does that often?"

"Ye saw her last night. I deliberately break my fast in my chamber to avoid seeing her first thing in the morning. She tends to sour one's mood."

Ella smiled but didn't reply. Indeed, she had been only too happy to enjoy her bannock, smeared with butter and rich thyme honey, in the seclusion of her bedchamber this morning. She was dreading the noon meal, for Lady MacNichol was likely to be present.

"I'm so sorry about how she spoke to ye yesterday," Gordana continued as the pause lengthened between them. "It was unacceptable."

"It was ... but as ye can see, she hasn't broken me. I didn't come to Scorrybreac for Lady MacNichol."

"How is yer mother this morning?" Gordana asked. Her gaze softened as she spoke.

"Weak ... but glad to have my company," Ella admitted. "I read her psalms earlier. She's sleeping now ... Da says she sleeps often these days."

"Aye." Gordana tied up the last stem of gillyflower and turned to face Ella properly. "She tires easily ... I have visited her often over the past months, but she grows steadily weaker." Gordana hesitated. "I'm glad ye have come."

Ella dropped her gaze, moving over to a seat made from slender willow branches. Arranging the long skirts of her habit, she settled down upon it. "I wouldn't have done," she admitted. "If it hadn't been for yer brother."

Gordana didn't reply. Instead, she too sat down upon the willow seat, her blue eyes settling upon Ella's face in a frank look that Ella recognized. Gavin had the same look.

"Ye should know," Gordana began gently, her face so grave that nervousness suddenly fluttered up within Ella, "that my brother has never forgotten ye."

Ella swallowed and forced herself to hold Gordana's gaze. Of course, Gordana had always been observant; although Ella had never spoken to her of the relationship that she and Gavin had once shared, it appeared that Gordana had guessed at their closeness, unless Gavin had confided in her.

"He has already said as much," Ella replied, her voice tight. "I wish he would keep his feelings to himself. It's too late to voice such sentiments."

Gordana nodded, her gaze clouding. "I feared he'd say something ... when he rode south alone to fetch ye, I suspected he would."

Ella drew in a deep breath, her fingers curling into fists. "I wish ye had managed to dissuade him. All Gavin has done is bring up things that are best left buried."

Sensing Ella's agitation, Gordana reached out and placed a hand over hers. "Perhaps he just wanted to have an opportunity to reconcile." Gordana then favored her with a sad smile. "The mistakes of the past weigh heavily upon my brother's shoulders."

Silence fell between the two women then. It was peaceful in the walled garden, the hush broken only by the buzzing of insects and the faint cries of gulls circling off the coast. The rest of the noise of the busy keep didn't seem to reach them here.

Eventually, smoothing out the wrinkles in her habit, Ella spoke once more. "What of ye, Gordana ... Rory has been gone many years. Why have ye never wed again?"

Gordana's mouth lifted at one corner. "That's another thing Ma has nagged me about over the years." She sighed then, glancing away, a distant look settling upon her face. "After Rory died, I did try to move on ... yet the men who presented themselves to me were awful." She gave a delicate shudder. "The likes of Aonghus Budge of Islay ... ye remember him?"

"Aye." Ella pulled a face. He was a man of her father's age, and although she hadn't seen him in a long while, she remembered him as an overbearing individual with a lecherous gaze. "I understand why ye wouldn't want the likes of him."

"My other suitors weren't much better," Gordana replied. "I kept sending them away ... and eventually what little interest there had been dried up." She turned, meeting Ella's gaze once more. "Truthfully, I am content alone. I have a freedom many women do not."

"Ye could take the veil and come to live at Kilbride?" Ella suggested. "We could do with yer gardening skills."

Gordana snorted. "My lack of piety would make the life of a nun a poor choice for me ... however ..." Her expression turned thoughtful as she studied Ella. "What's it like ... living in a woman's world?"

Ella's mouth curved. "Peaceful ... and structured. We are never idle at Kilbride. There are always chores to be done. I've rarely felt lonely over the years ... the nuns are good company ... most of them at least."

"Ye don't appear to regret yer choice."

"I don't," Ella replied. "If I couldn't have Gavin, I didn't want any man." She broke off abruptly there, having revealed far more than she'd intended. Feeling her cheeks warm, Ella dropped her gaze. "I am content doing the Lord's work."

Gordana didn't reply, although when Ella glanced her way once more, the gleam in the woman's eyes warned her that she had, indeed, said too much.

"A message has come for ye, brother."

Gavin glanced up from where he was going through his ledger of accounts, to see Blair standing in the doorway to his solar, a roll of parchment clutched in his hand.

"Aye?"

Blair approached him, holding out the missive. "It bears the MacKinnon seal," he warned.

Gavin released a heavy breath, replacing the quill he'd been using to scratch out sums, into its pot. "What does Duncan want this time?"

He took the roll of parchment, glancing down at the wax seal bearing the distinctive boar's head with a shin bone in its mouth and the clan motto: *Audentes Fortuna Juvat: fortune favors the bold.* Indeed, it was a message from the clan-chief himself. His lips thinning, Gavin broke the seal and unfurled the parchment. His gaze narrowed as he read the message within.

"Well?" Blair asked after a lengthy pause. "What pot of shit is he stirring this time?"

Gavin lowered the parchment and cast his brother a quelling look. Few on this isle loved Duncan MacKinnon, and Blair never held back when it came to voicing his opinion about the man. As clan-chief, Gavin had to be more diplomatic.

"He's on the warpath," Gavin admitted, handing the message to his brother. "Here ... read it for yerself."

Blair took the missive and did just that. A few moments later he glanced up, his gaze widening. "He's demanding ye *all* meet with him at Dunan?"

"Aye ... in seven days' time. He wants to tackle the lawlessness upon the isle 'once and for all'."

Blair raised an eyebrow at these words.

"This is a discussion we need to have," Gavin reminded him. "Even on our lands, outlaws have become an issue of late." Gavin thought then of a plucky, knife-throwing nun he had accompanied back to Scorrybraec, and a slight smile curved his lips.

"But MacKinnon as host to a meeting? He doesn't get on with the other clan-chiefs and chieftains. Even ye, who can rub along with most folk, can barely stand him."

Gavin's mouth quirked. "Perhaps this is a chance to improve relations upon the isle."

"They won't all come." Blair raised the parchment once more, squinting slightly as he prepared to continue reading it. "MacLeod and Fraser can't be in the same room together ... they'll kill each other."

Gavin snorted. His brother had a point there. The last time Malcolm MacLeod and Morgan Fraser had met, it had been on the battlefield. And then when Fraser's eldest son, Lachlann, ran off with MacLeod's youngest daughter, Adaira, relations between the two clans sank to a new low. However, as he'd just pointed out, lawlessness was a problem that now affected them all.

"What's this?" Blair had continued reading. "He wants ye to wed his sister?"

Gavin leaned back in his chair and ran a hand over his face. Suddenly, he felt every one of his thirty-eight years, and more besides. "Aye ... it seems so."

Blair lowered the parchment and frowned. "This isn't the first time he's made the offer?"

Gavin shook his head.

"Have ye met Lady Drew MacKinnon?"

"Aye," Gavin replied. "Many years ago ... we were both newly wed to others then though. She lost her husband around the time that Innis died."

"And ... ye aren't keen on the match?"

"No," Gavin replied, his tone turning curt. "Lady Drew and I wouldn't be suited."

"Why ... is she ugly?"

Gavin muttered an oath under his breath. Sometimes Blair had such a simplistic view of the world. He wouldn't have minded if Lady Drew MacKinnon was of humble looks, if her character had been sweet.

"I'm well aware I need to wed again," he said after a heavy pause. "However, I'll not choose a scheming and dominant woman as my bride. Lady Drew reminds me of our mother."

Blair winced, and Gavin saw that his point had been made. Blair wouldn't ask after Lady Drew MacKinnon again. Yet her brother wouldn't be as easy to put off. Duncan MacKinnon didn't like being told 'no'.

"Will ye go to this meeting then?" Blair asked. His brother walked over to the sideboard and poured himself a goblet of wine. He then drained it in two gulps and poured himself another. Like their father before them, Blair MacNichol liked his drink. Even though he'd barely passed his thirty-sixth winter, the color in his cheeks was already high, and he was starting to thicken around the middle.

Watching him, Gavin frowned. If he wasn't careful, he'd suffer the same health problems as their father—the gout and bloated liver that had sent him to an early grave.

"Aye, I'll go," Gavin replied heavily. "The outlaw problem needs addressing. Besides ... although MacKinnon isn't my neighbor, I'd rather not make him my enemy."

Across the room Blair gave a rude snort. "Not yet ... anyway."

12

So Soon

ELLA PUT DOWN the book of psalms, her gaze resting upon Cait Fraser's face. Her mother had fallen asleep halfway through the reading. The healer had visited Cait earlier and given her a dose of something strong. Although the herbs dulled the pain, they also made her sleepy.

Rising to her feet, Ella leaned forward and placed a kiss upon her mother's gaunt cheek. The skin was cool and papery beneath her lips. "Sleep well, Ma," she whispered. "I shall see ye tomorrow."

They'd spoken little during this meeting, for fatigue and pain had dulled Cait's senses and she'd preferred to listen rather than converse. Ella could understand why. Her mother's eyes were hollowed with pain.

It was getting late, late enough that Ella could retire for the day without appearing rude. Supper had taken place already. Like all the meals in the Great Hall, this one had simmered with tension. It wasn't only Ella's presence here that caused it, she realized, but the relations between Maggie MacNichol and her three offspring. She seemed to delight in tormenting them, Gavin and Gordana especially.

Still, Maggie would find time—at least once during the meal—to level an insult at Ella. This eve, she had questioned her on life at the abbey before concluding that nuns had spoiled, privileged lives.

Ella sensed the woman's thinly veiled frustration. Maggie had once held a position of power at Scorrybreac. Her husband had been clan-chief, but he had sought her counsel in all things.

Gavin did not.

Ella left her mother's chamber and made her way down the hallway to her own lodgings. Yawning, she let herself into the small yet comfortable room. Although it was still summer, a servant had been in and lit the hearth. In stone keeps like these, the air stayed cool and damp, even on the hottest days. Ella was grateful for the fire. The servants had also brought up fresh water for washing, and left linen drying cloths and a large cake of soap.

Picking it up, Ella gave the soap a delicate sniff: rose. A pang went through her. Life at Kilbride didn't allow for such frivolities. None of the nuns used scented soaps or dabbed rosewater behind their ears.

It felt like a forbidden luxury now.

Even so, Ella would still use the soap this evening. She was far from Kilbride—no one would know or care.

Stopping before her bed, Ella began to undress. It always took her a while, for there were a number of layers to peel off. First came the black veil that she wore over her wimple, and then the woolen belt she cinched about her waist, before she unlooped her crucifix and placed it upon a low wooden table next to the bed. She then wriggled out of the habit itself and removed her guimpe, a starched cloth that covered her neck and shoulders. The wimple lifted off afterward. Then, she removed the scapular—an apron that hung from front and back—and pushed down her underskirt, so that she finally stood clad only in a long ankle-length léine.

Ella let out a sigh. At times, during the summer, she felt like she was being smothered under all those layers of fabric.

Reaching up, Ella undid the heavy braid that hung between her shoulders, freeing her long hair. With a sigh, she shook it free. Her scalp had been itching all day; her hair badly needed washing.

Upon her arrival at Kilbride, Ella had prepared herself to have her hair shorn close to her scalp. However, the abbess held a lenient view on the subject, preferring to let all the nuns keep their hair at whatever length they preferred. Instead, she conducted a symbolic ceremony when they took their vows, snipping off just a single lock.

Ella stripped off her léine, shivering in the cool air despite the hearth burning nearby. She moved close to the wash bowl and poured water into it, humming to herself as she began to wash. When she had cleaned her body, she bent over and wet her hair before lathering it with soap.

The scent of rose floated over her, and Ella inhaled deeply. It was odd how evocative scents could be. Suddenly, she was sixteen years old again, and full of hope for the life before her. She'd been obsessed by roses at that age. She'd embroidered them on all her mother's cushions, pressed rose petals, taken care of her mother's rose bushes, and made rose-scented water and soap.

Drying herself off, Ella donned her night-rail, a loose robe that she wore for sleeping. With a sigh, she perched on the edge of the bed and gently combed out her long hair. The silence and peace inside her chamber wrapped itself around her. At this hour, all the Sisters of Kilbride would be spending time in contemplative silence. In contrast, Scorrybreac Castle seemed to echo with loud voices and laughter until late in the evening. She'd forgotten just how many folk actually lived here.

She retrieved her crucifix from the side table and knelt at the foot of the bed, hands clasped, as she began her evening prayers.

She usually found it easy to concentrate on the words—but this evening thoughts kept crowding her mind, intruding.

Her conversation with Gordana that morning had haunted her for the rest of the day.

My brother has never forgotten ye.

The solemn look on Gordana's face had made Ella's breathing constrict, as did the sadness that shadowed her eyes with the next words.

Gavin knows all chance with ye is gone.

Now that she was here and had started to mend things with her mother, Ella was relieved she had made the journey to Scorrybreac. Yet there were too many memories in this place. Just walking around the shadowy hallways of the keep brought so much back.

The mistakes of the past weigh heavily upon my brother's shoulders.

Ella heaved a sigh. There had been many times over the years when she'd wondered how Gavin was faring. In the first year, she'd thought of him constantly, especially when—

No. Ella squeezed her eyes shut, her comb snagging on a knot in her hair. She wouldn't think of it. *Not now— not ever again.*

Gavin wasn't the only one who carried a burden, who had been scarred by the past. Ella's wounds went deep, deeper than he realized.

"Ella!" Stewart Fraser's voice boomed through the door, jerking her from a fitful sleep. "Ye need to come quickly."

Heart pounding from being ripped from her slumber, Ella pushed herself up into a sitting position. "What is it, Da?" she called back, her voice croaky with sleep.

"It's yer mother," he replied, "she's in a bad way and is asking for ye."

The edge of panic in his voice roused Ella from her bed. Throwing back the covers, she reached for her habit.

"I'm coming," she called back. "I just need to get dressed first."

"There's no time, lass … she has little time left."

Ella froze and straightened up, her pulse accelerating once more. It was forbidden for others to see a nun in such a state of undress, but what could she do? It took her an age to put on all her layers of clothing.

Dropping her habit back over the chair where she'd draped it before retiring for the night, Ella reached instead for a long robe. She would have preferred something with a hood that covered her unbound hair, yet there wasn't any time to braid it. Instead, she heaved in a deep breath, pulled the robe tightly over her night-rail and padded, barefoot, toward the door.

Out in the corridor, one look at her father's face and she knew things were bad.

Stewart Fraser looked scared. His rugged face was strained. A nerve flickered under one eye, and his gaze guttered as it met his daughter's. Wordlessly, he reached out and took Ella by the hand, leading her up the shadowy hallway toward Cait Fraser's sickroom.

Ella knew the smell of impending death. She'd attended many patients with Sister Coira and watched the life fade from them as the healer did her best to make them comfortable.

Death had a sweet, cloying odor that made Ella's bile rise.

The healer, an elderly man named Farlan, stepped away from the bed when Ella entered. His gaze widened as he took in Ella's state of undress, yet he said nothing. With a nod, Farlan moved around the bed and leaned close to Ella.

"Her time is near … shall I call for the priest, or will ye do the last rites?"

Ella swallowed. "I will do them."

Farlan nodded and stepped back. "I will leave ye alone then."

The healer's footfalls whispered across the flagstone floor, and the door thudded shut behind him. Ella glanced over her shoulder, expecting to find her father present. Yet he too had left them alone.

Approaching the bed, Ella's gaze settled upon her mother.

Cait Fraser watched her. The woman's eyes were sunken with pain, her breathing shallow. Her skin was ashen.

"Daughter," she rasped. "Please say the words ... bless me before the end."

Ella swallowed. "Of course, Ma."

The last rites required anointing the forehead of the dying person with oil, yet Ella had none. Instead, she dipped her thumb into a bowl of water that stood on the bedside table and pressed it lightly to her mother's forehead.

"Through this holy anointing," she began softly, "may the Lord in his love and mercy help ye with the grace of the Holy Spirit. May the Lord who frees ye from sin save ye and raise ye up."

Her voice died away, and a smile graced her mother's lips. "Thank ye, lass ... ye were always good, Ella. I'm just sorry I never told ye that."

Ella swallowed once more, in an attempt to dislodge the lump that was making it hard to breathe.

Not now ... not so soon.

Although she didn't like being away from Kilbride, she had wished for more days with her mother before her time came.

She took hold of Cait's thin hand, entwining her fingers through her mother's. "It matters not now," she whispered. "I'm just sorry I came here too late ... I wanted to spend more time with ye."

Her mother gazed up at her. "And I with ye. I have missed ye over the years." Cait's frail fingers tightened around hers. "Are ye truly happy, lass? We didn't all drive ye to a life of misery, did we?"

Ella shook her head, tears trickling down her face now. "Ye didn't drive me to anything. As I have told ye, I am content with this life."

Her mother nodded, her eyes fluttering closed. "That's a relief," she whispered. "Innis blamed herself for ye going away ... and I was sure I'd played a role in it."

"Kilbride was my choice." The words were an effort, for tears now scalded Ella's cheeks. This conversation was tearing her heart out. "I love ye, Ma."

Cait's grip on her hand tightened once more. "And I ye, lass. I wish ..." Cait Fraser broke off there, gasping for breath. "I wish ..."

She never finished her sentence. A heartbeat passed, and then Ella saw the life fade from her mother's face. She'd witnessed such before, the slackening of the muscles and flesh, as the spirit left its mortal shell.

Cait's hand went limp in her daughter's, and she left her last words unsaid.

For a long moment, Ella merely stared down at the woman who'd given her life, the woman she'd resented for so long. One moment Cait had been there with her, the next she'd departed. The suddenness of death was a shocking thing.

A shuddering sob rose up within Ella, a rising wave of grief that had long been held back, like a spring tide behind a seawall. But now that wall was starting to crumble.

Bowing low over the hand she still clasped, Ella began to weep.

13

Laid Bare

ONCE THE GRIEF broke free, it couldn't be stemmed.

For a while Ella couldn't move. She could only cling to the side of the bed, still clutching her mother's hand as sobs wracked her body.

Years of pain, anger, frustration, and grief broke free with an intensity that felt as if she'd just been physically struck.

It hurt to breathe, to think, to exist.

She wept for all of them. For Innis, who'd never spoken a cross word to her, but whom she'd shunned all those years. For her mother, who had been eaten up with regret for too long. For Gavin, who had done his duty and realized too late what it would cost him—and for herself.

She'd run away to Kilbride, and although she'd found solace and peace there, the fact still remained that she'd used it as a hiding place.

But one couldn't hide forever. Sooner or later the past chased you down. Eighteen years of pain and regret toppled down upon Ella.

Gasping, she released her mother's hand and pushed herself to her feet. Her body trembled from the force of her grief, and the tears that still coursed down her cheeks blinded her.

She needed to be alone, she needed to find a sanctuary where she could let grief consume her.

Ella stumbled to the door, ripped it open, and staggered out into the hallway. Her father was waiting there, his eyes widening in shock at the sight of her.

He took a step forward, reaching for his daughter. "Ella?"

"She's dead," Ella gasped out the words, pain ripping through her chest. "Go to her."

She side-stepped her father's embrace and pushed past him, hurrying down the hallway. Her first instinct was to return to her bed-chamber. Yet that wasn't far enough away. She needed the sanctuary of the chapel. And even if she wasn't dressed, she would go there.

Bare feet slapping on stone, she picked up the skirts of her night-rail and robe, and hurried to the spiral stairwell that led down to the bottom level of the keep. It was a foolish thing to do, for tears blinded her, and the heavy material around her legs risked tripping her. But she was too upset to care.

Ella was halfway down the stairwell when she stumbled on the worn stone steps and plunged headlong into the darkness.

A scream ripped from her throat, panic slicing through the blind grief that had sent her running down these steps. In a sickening moment, she realized she was doomed.

And then strong arms caught her.

Gavin had been climbing the steps, on the way to visit Lady Fraser's sickroom, when he'd heard the whisper of bare feet on stone above him. Someone was descending the stairwell—rapidly.

He'd told his nephews off numerous times for sprinting on the stairs. One of the servants had fallen and broken her neck three years earlier, and that had scared all the lads into being more cautious.

But someone wasn't being careful tonight.

A ragged sob reached him and then a long shadow appeared above.

A heartbeat later a frightened cry filled the stairwell, and a woman, encased in flowing white, light copper hair flying behind her, hurtled toward him.

Gavin leaped forward and caught her. However, the force of her fall propelled them both back. Only the fact that Gavin twisted, so that they crashed back against the wall, saved the pair of them from tumbling down the stairs.

"The Devil's cods," Gavin wheezed. The lass had knocked the wind out of him. "That was close."

And then he realized whom he was holding in his arms.

He hadn't recognized her. It had been so many years since he'd seen Ella like this, dressed in a night-rail and robe, her hair tumbling around her shoulders. Holding her soft body in this way, crushed against his chest, made his breathing quicken.

But the desire that arrowed through his groin pulled up sharply when he saw her face.

Tears streamed down Ella's cheeks, her mouth trembled—and her eyes held so much grief, so much pain, that whatever words Gavin was going to speak next died upon his lips.

"Ella," he whispered. "What is it?"

"They're dead," Ella gasped, staring up at him with such a broken expression that it suddenly hurt Gavin to breathe. "Ma is dead ... Innis is dead ... why do I feel like it's all my fault?"

"It's not."

The idea was ridiculous. Who had put such a notion in her head?

"They're gone." The pain in Ella's voice cut Gavin deep. "And I had the chance to put things right, but I didn't ... and now it's too late."

Ella buried her face in Gavin's chest, her shoulders heaving.

Grim-faced, he gathered her against him, lifting her into his arms. Ella didn't resist, for she was sobbing uncontrollably now.

What did Lady Fraser say to her?

He carried Ella up the stairs, back to the floor where her bed-chamber was located. The hallway was empty, the cressets burning low now, for it was well past the witching hour. Most of the keep was asleep, and so had Gavin been before the healer, Farlan, had knocked on his door with the news that Cait Fraser was close to death.

Shouldering open the door to Ella's chamber, Gavin went inside, closing it with his foot behind him. The fire in the hearth had died to glowing embers, although the chamber was warm enough.

Gavin lowered Ella gently to the ground but instantly regretted doing so. He should have carried her over to the bed instead. Letting her down like this made their bodies brush close.

And he felt every curve and contour of her body as he did so.

The Lord strike him down, she felt good. Her body was small yet lush, her breasts soft. He felt their peaks graze down his chest as he set her upon her feet. One of his hands splayed across the small of her back, steadying her. It was an intimate, possessive gesture. In an instant his groin hardened.

Fighting the lust that pulsed through him, Gavin gently hooked a finger under Ella's chin and raised her face so their gazes met.

"Why do ye blame yerself?" he asked. "No one else does."

Her glittering blue eyes fixed upon him. "It was so hard leaving here," she replied, the words coming out in gasps, for she still fought her grief. "The only way I managed it was to shut myself off from my kin. I was angry at Ma for preferring Innis, and I was furious at Innis for taking ye from me." She let out another soft sob. "I know they're both with God now, but guilt still tears me up inside."

"Enough." He hadn't meant the word to sound so angry, but it did. "No one is to blame for Innis and yer mother's deaths. It's just life, Ella. Cruel, callous life."

She stared up at him, her cheeks wet with tears, and something twisted deep within Gavin's chest. Even when she was a weeping mess, this woman was beautiful. She had a soft, earthy beauty, enhanced by that thick mane of light auburn hair that fell around her shoulders in heavy waves.

When they'd been younger, everyone had said Innis was the prettier of the two—yet for Gavin, Ella had always outshone her sister.

Their gazes fused, and Gavin could suddenly hear the thudding of his own heart.

A heartbeat later he leaned down, cupped her face with both hands, and kissed her.

No previous thought went into the act; if he'd stopped to ponder the decision, he'd never have done it. Yet a need so strong that he felt sick from it rose within him, and before he knew what he was doing, Gavin had reached for her.

And the moment their mouths touched, the last of Gavin's restraint snapped. His lips moved hungrily over hers, his tongue seeking entrance. And when Ella's lips parted for him, he sank into her, lost.

Ella let herself drown in him.

For that instant the past didn't matter, who they were didn't matter. For that frozen moment in time they were just a man and a woman. His kiss pushed everything else aside, including her grief.

Ella leaned into Gavin as his lips brushed across hers, as his tongue explored her mouth. Heat throbbed through her, from a fire deep in her belly. Gavin had drawn near so that they were pressed close. The feel of his long, muscular body, the strength and warmth of him made her want to crawl inside him. The male musk of his skin filling her nostrils was overwhelming, dizzying.

In an instant that one kiss brushed away years of restraint, of denial. And when he gently bit her lower lip before soothing it with his tongue, Ella's body trembled.

Aye, for just a few instants, she gave herself to it. She allowed herself to be greedy, to break her vow of chastity. She let want take over.

But alas, this moment wasn't really frozen in time. Instead, it slid into another and then another, and Ella couldn't deny reality.

She was a nun, he was a clan-chief, and her mother lay dead in her chamber at the end of the hallway. This was wrong on all kinds of levels.

And yet breaking off that kiss and stepping away from him was hard. Even harder than riding away from Scorrybreac all those years earlier. Losing physical contact with Gavin was like tearing off a limb.

Ella's throat ached when she twisted out of his arms and took a few rapid steps back. The space between them now felt like a yawning gulf.

Gavin was watching her; the look of predatory lust upon his face, mixed with tenderness and raw need almost undid her. She didn't want him to look at her that way, and yet at the same time, it was the only thing she'd ever wanted.

She hated herself for needing this man. Even now, all these years later, he had the power to scatter her wits and turn her will into porridge.

She should be outraged at him for taking advantage of her at a weak moment. But she couldn't summon the will. Grief had laid her bare, and she had responded to that kiss as eagerly as he'd given it.

She wouldn't turn her desire for him into a lie. She would just have to live with knowing that this man was her one weakness.

But the incident proved that the two of them couldn't be alone together, ever again.

Ella took another step back and bumped up against the bed. Panic flared. How easy it would be for him to push her back upon the coverlet, tear her flimsy night-rail from her body, and claim her. And to her shame, if he tried, she wasn't sure she'd have the strength of will to stop him.

She wasn't sure she wouldn't welcome it.

Desire crackled between them, their gazes still fused. Gavin's blue eyes had hooded in that look she knew well from the past. He was only just holding himself in check.

Eventually, Ella cleared her throat, breaking the heavy silence. "I think it's best ye go now, Gavin," she whispered.

14

In Ruins

GAVIN CLOSED THE solar door behind him and walked over to the sideboard, where a decanter of wine and a row of goblets sat. His hands shook as he poured himself some wine.

Dolt. Lack-wit. Fool.

He'd made some poor decisions in his life—but kissing Ella when she was in the midst of weeping over the death of her mother was one of his worst. He'd known it was wrong, from the moment he'd cupped Ella's wet cheeks with his hands, and yet he'd been unable to stop himself.

The wine burned down Gavin's throat, warming his belly. But it didn't ease the ache under his breast bone or slow his pounding heart.

Gavin set the goblet down with a thud. Unlike his brother, he couldn't use wine to wash his problems away. It wouldn't matter how much he drank, he'd never stop wanting Ella, never stop aching for her.

Breathing a curse, he stepped forward, leaning his forehead against the cool stone wall next to the sideboard. The chill seeped through his skin, although the pounding in his temples remained.

What a terrible mess he'd made of things.

He'd believed that seeing Ella again would give him the opportunity to put things right—so that he could move on with his life. After Innis's death, his clansmen had been putting pressure on him to wed again. There was still time for him to produce an heir. He hadn't been opposed to the idea, yet he'd had the burning need to face Ella again so that he could look forward rather than backward.

That had been a grave error.

Seeing her again had just confirmed that he'd never be able to give his heart to another. Ever.

Gavin squeezed his eyes shut. He hadn't wept in years, but his eyelids burned now. Disappointment, yearning, loneliness—it all churned within him. The force of the emotions made his belly clench, his chest and head ache.

How he wished he could return in time, go back to that day in the clearing eighteen years earlier. He'd have acted differently. He'd have seen beyond the sense of duty that had blinkered him. He'd have broken the betrothal and wed the woman he really loved.

Instead, he'd done what was expected of him, and his life lay in ruins around him as a result.

The fine weather had come to an end.

Long days of shimmering heat and blue skies gave way to grey skies and a chill wind that blew in from the north, ruffling the water of Raasay Sound to the east.

Leaving the chapel, Ella craned her neck up at the sky. Seabirds wheeled and screeched overhead, a sign that the weather was about to become even more unsettled. This was the first day in months that the air had a real bite to it. The warm days of summer were drawing to a close, and autumn was breathing down their necks.

Ella continued on her path through the inner bailey, returning to the keep. On the way she passed Blair MacNichol, who was overseeing the shoeing of his horse. He waved to Ella as she walked by but didn't attempt to engage her in conversation. Even though she'd been here a few days, Gavin's younger brother's gaze was still wary whenever he looked at her. Likewise, his wife, Forbia, had barely spoken to Ella since her arrival.

They had buried Cait Fraser that morning. The kirk at Scorrybreac had a secluded graveyard behind it. Just a small crowd had come to see Lady Fraser off: Ella, her father, as well as the clan-chief and his closest kin. Ella had remained at her father's side, her hand clasping his in silent support. Father Blayne, the local priest, gave a fine service, and then they had laid Cait to rest.

Ella hadn't wept during the burial. After Gavin's departure from her bed-chamber the night before, she had allowed herself to weep softly for a short while longer. Then she'd dried her tears, telling herself that the events of the past days were a test. It was easy enough to serve God within the confines of Kilbride Abbey. But in the world beyond, she'd met challenges at every turn. Stubbornness had filtered over Ella then. She would not fail the Lord. Instead of going back to bed, she'd knelt on the floor by the window and prayed for the rest of the night.

This afternoon she felt in control again. Her mother was at peace, and now Ella could focus on what lay ahead.

Entering the keep, she asked a passing servant the clan-chief's whereabouts.

"He's in his solar, Sister," the young woman bearing an armload of clean linen informed her.

Spine straight and jaw locked in determination, Ella climbed the stairwell to the second floor and made her way to the double oaken doors that led into the clan-chief's solar. Then she knocked.

"Come in," a male voice reached her through the doors.

Ella drew in a deep breath, steeling herself for the meeting, and pushed the doors open. She stepped into a large chamber with a south-facing window. A great hearth dominated one corner of the room, and deerskins covered the flagstone floor. A large tapestry, showing a group of men at a stag hunt, covered one pitted stone wall.

The clan-chief himself sat at a vast oaken desk, bent over a pile of parchments.

Gavin glanced up as she entered. "Sister Ella," he greeted her, his tone formal although his gaze was shadowed. "Good afternoon ... how are ye faring?"

"Much better, thank ye," she replied. "Ma is at peace now."

Gavin nodded, his expression turning guarded. That was better, how it should have been from the beginning. Ella welcomed this new distance between them.

"I'm sorry to intrude." Ella's gaze dropped to the pile of parchments he appeared to be working his way through. "Ye are busy."

He sighed and leaned back in his chair. "Just accounts that have to be paid ... nothing that cannot wait. How can I be of assistance?"

Ella fought the urge to drop her gaze. Even though his manner was reserved, there was still an intensity to his look that unnerved her. The sooner the pair of them parted ways the better.

"I thank ye for organizing my mother's burial so quickly," she began, her voice low. "But now it is done, I wish to return to Kilbride."

"And ye shall," he replied. "Is tomorrow soon enough for ye?"

His response took Ella aback. She had worried he might try and delay her. Swallowing her surprise, she inclined her head. "No, I will be ready."

"Good." Gavin was watching her steadily now, his expression unreadable. "Ye will be traveling in my company again I'm afraid." He held up a hand to forestall her protest. "But fear not, there will be a company of my men with us. We will be making a detour to Dunan on the way, if ye don't mind."

Ella frowned. She had a feeling that it wouldn't matter if it did bother her. She was hardly going to say 'no' to a clan-chief, and they both knew it.

Silence stretched out between them for a few moments, before Ella spoke. "What business takes ye to Dunan?"

"MacKinnon has called a meeting ... between all the clan-chiefs and chieftains of the isle."

"Really?" Ella's interest was piqued now, and she almost forgot to feel uncomfortable in this man's presence. "Why is that?"

It was an impertinent question and none of her business, yet Ella knew that Gavin wouldn't mind her asking. He'd always spoken frankly to her in the past.

"The unruliness upon the isle gets worse ... as ye and I well know. MacKinnon wants something done about the outlaws and thieves."

Ella pursed her lips, remembering their journey to Scorrybreac. "Is it really that serious ... has Skye turned lawless?"

"Not yet ... things are worse on MacKinnon lands, but throughout the isle folk are restless. A meeting between the clan-chiefs and chieftains is long overdue." Gavin pulled a face. "I just wish MacKinnon wasn't hosting the gathering."

Ella's brow furrowed. Although she'd never met him, she'd heard plenty about Duncan MacKinnon. She also knew that many folk within MacKinnon territory, in which Kilbride sat, loathed him. "Perhaps he'd find it less of a problem controlling those on his land if he didn't rule them with an iron fist," she pointed out. "He increases the taxes every year."

Gavin raised an eyebrow. "I'm sure that'll be pointed out to him during the meeting. Have ye ever been to Dunan before?"

Ella shook her head.

"Well then, ye should find it interesting. The broch sits on the site of an ancient fort. It's a bonny spot ... in a wooded valley."

"How long will we remain there?"

"Not long," he replied, still watching her. "I'm hoping our business should be concluded within a day or two."

Ella left the solar and descended to the ground level of the keep. Despite the grey weather, she knew she'd find Gordana in her garden. She needed to tell her friend that she was leaving.

Frowning, Ella made her way down the spiral stairwell, taking care this time. She wasn't happy about the detour to Dunan. She'd already been away from Kilbride long enough. With the breaking weather, there were fruit and vegetables to be harvested. She needed to be there to oversee the work. Still, part of her was curious to see Dunan, for she'd never visited the MacKinnon stronghold. The other sisters would be full of questions about it when she returned home.

Ella left the keep and stepped outdoors once more. Light drops of rain splattered against her face, brought in by the wind, and in the distance, Ella caught the forbidding rumble of thunder.

Gordana wouldn't be at work in her garden for much longer.

Ella found Gavin's sister on her knees weeding an onion bed when she arrived. Although flowers and herbs filled the garden, Gordana had squeezed a few vegetables into the corners.

"A storm's coming," Ella advised her friend as she settled herself onto the willow seat and watched her work. "Hopefully, it'll spend itself overnight ... I don't fancy traveling in the rain."

Gordana stopped weeding and sat back on her heels, glancing over her shoulder. "Are ye sure ye should leave so soon?" she asked, concern edging her voice. "Ye must still be grieving for yer mother?"

Ella favored her with a brittle smile. She knew that Gordana meant well, yet the last thing she needed was to prolong her visit to Scorrybreac. "God's work calls," she replied. "Gavin and his men are riding to Dunan tomorrow ... and I shall go with them. When they have concluded their meeting there, we will continue on to the abbey." Ella paused, seeing the disappointment filter over Gordana's face. In the days since her arrival, they had struck up their old friendship as if they'd never been apart.

"I will miss ye," Gordana said, her gaze shadowing. "As ye have seen, I spend little time with the other ladies in the keep ... but ye and I have always understood each other well."

Ella smiled once more. "Then ye must visit me at Kilbride, Gordana. I know ye aren't interested in taking the veil, but we have a guest house at the abbey, and ye would be welcome whenever ye care to visit."

Gordana's eyes gleamed at this. She rose to her feet and brushed the dirt off her fingers before crossing to the willow seat. Lowering herself down next to Ella, she took hold of her hands, squeezing tightly. "I would love that," she murmured.

15

Unchaste Thoughts

"I WISH YE would stay a little longer, lass." Stewart Fraser squeezed his daughter tightly against him. "I feel like I've hardly seen ye, and now ye are off again ... ye are all I have now."

Ella blinked back tears before drawing away. Her father appeared to have aged years over the past few days. Deep lines bracketed his mouth, his expression looked care-worn, and his once vibrant hair seemed far more grey than red. However, it was the sadness in his eyes that cut Ella to the quick.

"I have to return to Kilbride, Da," she murmured, her voice suddenly choked. "Ye know I must."

He looked so forlorn then that Ella nearly broke down. Blinking rapidly, she stepped close to her pony and checked its girth. Only when she'd mastered herself, did she glance in her father's direction once more.

Stewart still looked bereft. He was gazing at Ella as if he was about to lose her forever.

"Please, Da," Ella whispered. "Ye know I will be alive and well at Kilbride." She drew in a deep breath. "I have invited Lady Gordana to visit ... why do ye not join her?"

His expression brightened just a little. "Are men allowed to visit the abbey?"

"Aye … if they're kin," Ella lied. The abbess generally dissuaded the sisters from inviting family to stay. She said that it made transitioning into a nun's life much harder. But she'd make an exception in this case, Ella hoped. After all, Ella had resided for nearly two decades in the abbey without seeing anyone.

A determined look settled upon her father's face then. "I will organize a visit in a few weeks' time … as soon as the harvest is done."

A smile curved Ella's lips. She hadn't expected him to make a date now; he really was keen to spend time with her. Warmth spread through her at this realization. Of course, with everything that had happened, she'd overlooked the fact that her father had missed her all these years.

"Ready to go, Sister Ella?"

The clip-clop of hooves intruded, and Ella tore her gaze from her father to see Gavin approach upon his grey mare, Saorsa. Like the day before, his expression was shuttered. It was hard to believe this was the same man who'd pulled her close and kissed her so passionately.

But, once again, his altered manner came as a relief to Ella. If he'd put up those walls to begin with, neither of them would have ended up in such a compromising position.

Ella nodded before turning her attention back to Stewart Fraser. Her father's eyes glistened as he watched her. Although she'd invited him to visit her at Kilbride, they both knew the truth of it. Her life was dedicated to God—they would see very little of each other in the years to come.

Stepping forward, Ella threw her arms around him one last time.

They started their journey under leaden skies. Storms had raged over the isle during the night, leaving cold, damp weather in their wake. Fortunately, although it was a dull day, no rain fell as Gavin's party left Scorrybreac.

The clan-chief led the way out of the castle, flanked by the captain of the Scorrybreac guard—a heavyset man named Ceard. Ella rode directly behind them while the rest of the party, four MacNichol warriors, brought up the rear.

They passed through the village, hailing folk as they went, before pushing their horses into a brisk trot. Monadh had a short, bouncing gait, but Ella settled into his stride easily. It had been years since she'd ridden, yet the journey here had brought it all back.

Leaving Scorrybreac behind, the party headed south, hugging the coastline. Mid-morning they crossed into MacLeod territory and skirted the coastal village of Kiltaraglen. Yet they didn't pause, instead continuing on their path across the rolling hills of the eastern coast of Skye. To the west rose the dark shadows of great peaks, ominous against the iron-grey sky.

"It'll rain again," Ceard announced, motioning west. "Those storm clouds over the mountains are headed our way."

Gavin gave a grunt, acknowledging the comment.

Watching the two men, Ella realized that Gavin had hardly spoken since they'd left Scorrybreac. Luckily for him, Ceard wasn't a garrulous man. But after receiving such a brusque response from his clan-chief, the captain didn't make any other attempts at conversation.

Gavin is sore about all of this.

Ella pursed her lips. Of course he was. She wasn't sure what he'd hoped having her return to Scorrybreac would achieve, but she'd wager he hadn't planned on kissing her.

That had been a poor decision.

As was yer reaction to him.

Her conscience wasn't about to let her place all the blame on him. Aye, Gavin had taken liberties he shouldn't have, yet she had melted into his arms like hot tallow; she had parted her lips so he could deepen that kiss.

The memory of it made heat flush across her body.

Stop it. This wouldn't do at all. A nun couldn't have such unchaste thoughts. She needed to stop them, before they tormented her further.

"Jesus, Lover of chastity ... Mary, Mother most pure," Ella whispered a prayer that Mother Shona had taught her in her early days at Kilbride, "and Joseph, chaste guardian of the Virgin, to ye I come at this hour, begging ye to plead with God for me. I earnestly wish to be pure in thought, word, and deed in imitation of yer own holy purity."

The other riders were far enough away that no one heard her softly murmured words. Moments passed, and still, Ella didn't feel any more at peace. The melting sensation that thoughts of that kiss had provoked, still lay heavily within the cradle of her hips.

Heaving in a deep breath, she began to whisper another, more strident prayer. "Jesus, bless me with Yer infinite graces, That I may remain in a state of purity. Strengthen my body, spirit and soul to continually reflect Yer chastity—"

Up ahead Gavin twisted in the saddle, his gaze settling upon her. "Did ye say something, Sister Ella?"

"No," Ella replied swiftly, her cheeks flaming. She had taken care to keep her voice low. Surely, he hadn't heard her?

And yet there was a knowing light in his blue eyes that made the heat in her cheeks burn brighter still. He didn't smile; his face was a study in inscrutability. Yet somehow he knew where her thoughts had been, and what her whispered words were in aid of.

Ella dropped her gaze to her hands; they gripped the reins tightly. A moment later she sensed him look away from her, leaving Ella and Monadh alone once more.

Inhaling deeply, Ella promised herself that she'd wait till she was alone in future before murmuring any more prayers.

Gavin knelt next to the fire pit, watching as the tender flames caught alight. It had taken a while, for the wood was slightly damp. However, the tinder he'd brought with him had worked.

It had been a long, tiring day of travel. Heavy sheets of rain had swept in from the west in the afternoon, drenching the party. Thankfully, it had been a short squall, and by the time they made camp for the night, on the edge of a hazel thicket, the skies had cleared once more.

Rising to his feet, Gavin glanced around him. There was no sign of Ella. After rubbing down her pony, she'd disappeared into the woods, possibly to pray. He hoped she hadn't gone far.

His men had put up tents and begun gutting and plucking some grouse they'd just caught. The birds would be spit-roasted over the embers of the fire pit.

"I'm going to collect some more wood," Gavin informed Ceard. "Ye had better get those grouse on to roast soon or we'll all be eating at the witching hour."

Ceard snorted as he sat with a half-plucked grouse upon his knee. "Ye just make sure the fire doesn't go out."

Grinning, Gavin walked off. Ceard could be a curmudgeon at times, but there wasn't anyone he trusted more at Scorrybreac. Not even his brother.

The air inside the hazel thicket was damp and rich with the odor of wet earth and vegetation. Picking up branches and sticks as he went, Gavin surveyed his surroundings. The trees were tightly packed in here. Dusk would settle soon, and he wondered where Ella had gotten to.

Thud. Thud.

Gavin straightened up from retrieving a fallen hazel branch and frowned.

What was that?

Thud. Thud.

His frown deepened. Following the noise, Gavin walked deeper into the copse. A few yards on, he pushed aside some undergrowth and halted.

Sister Ella had her back to him and was throwing knives at a large tree.

Thud. Thud. Two more blades embedded, side-by-side, in the trunk.

Swathed in black, her head covered by the veil, Ella looked like a deadly shadow come to life in the gloaming.

She moved then, striding over to the trunk, and yanked her six knives, one by one, from their neat row.

Gavin cleared his throat.

Ella whipped around, her face pale and startled. The white wimple framed her face, an austere look that highlighted the delicacy of her features. Yet her hair was now tucked away out of sight.

Gavin's chest ached at the memory of how her hair had felt—fine and soft—tickling his skin and sliding through his fingers. What a terrible thing, to hide such beauty from the world.

"I thought I'd find ye at prayer," Gavin greeted her.

Recovering from her fright, Ella frowned. "What do ye want?"

Gavin dipped his chin to the pile of branches in his arms. "Nothing ... I was out collecting wood and heard a noise." His gaze went to the slender blades that she was now tucking into the belt around her waist. "Please continue ... don't let me interrupt yer practice."

Ella shook her head. "I'm done."

Irritation flowered within Gavin at her frosty welcome. She probably thought he'd planned to seduce her, that he wanted her to break her vows. He'd heard her whispered prayers earlier, and although he'd only caught snatches of the words, he'd known what she was praying for.

She was seeking strength to ward him off. Like he was the Devil and had been sent to tempt her.

Gavin's mouth twisted into a humorless smile at the thought, and he met Ella's eye. "Good," he replied evenly. "Now that ye have finished, ye can help me collect firewood."

"Ye always had a lovely singing voice, Sister Ella ... I remember it well."

Ella glanced up from where she'd been staring into the glowing embers of the fire. Ceard sat across from her. A smile softened his usually severe-looking face, and his pale blue eyes were warm.

"Ye do?" she asked, surprised. Of course, Ceard had been at Scorrybreac all those years earlier. He'd been a much younger man then, but already gruff in voice and manner.

"Aye," he replied, looking slightly embarrassed then. "There's nothing I like more than listening to a woman sing."

Next to him, Gavin smiled. "Ye rogue, Ceard ... what a charming tongue ye have."

To Ella's increased surprise, Ceard's whiskery cheeks reddened a little as some of the other men around the fire chuckled. However, his gaze remained on Ella. "Will ye not sing for us tonight, Sister Ella?"

Ella stiffened, feeling the weight of many male gazes—Gavin's included—settle upon her. "I only sing hymns these days," she murmured, shifting her attention back to the firepit.

"What of 'These are my mountains?'" Ceard asked. "Do ye remember the words?"

Ella drew in a deep breath. She did. The song—a patriotic ballad—was also one of her father's favorites. At least he didn't want her to sing of love and loss. Finally, she nodded.

Ceard's mouth curved. "Will ye sing it?"

Ella glanced up to see all those gathered around the fire still watching her, their gazes hopeful.

"Go on, Sister Ella," Gavin prompted gently. "Just one song won't hurt."

"Very well," Ella murmured. Drawing herself up, she recalled the tune, wishing that Innis was sitting at her side with her harp to accompany her. Time drew out, and then she began to sing, her voice carrying through the chill night air.

"For fame and for fortune I wandered the earth

And now I've come back to the land of my birth
I've brought back my treasures but only to find
They're less than the pleasures I first left behind

For these are my mountains and this is my glen

The braes of my childhood will know me again
No land's ever claimed me tho' far I did roam
For these are my mountains and I'm going home."

Warmth filtered through Ella as she finished the last verse of the song. All her companions were smiling now, their eyes gleaming with love for their land. The men of Skye were often called away to fight for king and country—but most returned home to this rocky isle where the mountains met the sky.

"That was bonny," Ceard said, his face glowing. "Thank ye, lass."

Across the fire, Ella's gaze fused with Gavin MacNichol's. His clan had inhabited their corner of the isle for a long while, had dug their roots deep into its peaty soil. This land would always be his home—as it would be hers.

16

Duncan MacKinnon

A SMILE SPREAD across Duncan MacKinnon's face as he read the letter.

"Ye look pleased with yerself, brother." His sister's acerbic voice intruded. "Why are ye so smug?"

Duncan glanced up, his gaze meeting Drew's across the table. "That was a letter from Niall MacDonald," he replied. "He will be attending the meeting."

Drew raised finely shaped eyebrows. "That makes all seven of ye?"

"Aye." Duncan's smile grew. "And there was ye telling me not one of them would attend." He favored her with a wolfish grin. "Ye will pleased to see Gavin MacNichol again."

His sister's answering smile was sly. "I will." She observed him, her expression turning thoughtful. "So this is how ye will finally rid yerself of Craeg, is it?"

Duncan held his sister's eye as he put the missive he'd just received from the chieftain of the MacDonalds of Sleat to one side. "Aye ... if all goes to plan."

"How exactly?"

Duncan frowned. He didn't like Drew asking questions, yet his sister had a mind like a whetted blade. "Ours isn't the only territory where brigands attack travelers and outlaws raid villages ... they too will want the lawlessness dealt with."

He shifted his attention to the spread of food before him: a large platter of bannocks and pots of butter and honey. Taking a wedge of the large flat cake made with oatmeal and cooked upon an iron griddle, Duncan spread it with a generous amount of butter. He was reaching for the pot of heather honey when he felt someone's gaze upon him.

It wasn't his sister watching him this time, but his wife.

Duncan cast the dark-haired woman seated opposite an irritated look. "What is it, Siusan?"

"When is this meeting?" she asked, her voice low and soft.

Duncan had always liked the sound of Siusan Campbell's voice. Unfortunately, these days it was the *only* thing he did like about her. Since she'd gotten with child, she'd lost her looks. Her body had bloated, her face was blotchy, and her once dark hair had become limp. As soon as her belly had started to swell, he'd lost all desire for her.

"Two days hence," he replied curtly. "Why?"

Siusan put a hand to her swollen belly, shifting in her seat with a grimace. "The bairn is coming soon, husband ... I can feel it."

Duncan shrugged. "And?"

Siusan gave him a pained look. "What if it comes on the day of the meeting?"

Their gazes locked for a long moment, and Duncan's irritation rose. He often felt vexed in Siusan's company these days. She looked at him with those reproachful midnight-blue eyes, and he just wanted to slap her.

A year they'd been wed.

The longest year of Duncan's life.

"Let it," he said before turning his attention back to his bannock, which he drizzled with honey. "I'm sure ye can manage birthing my son on yer own. The healer will be with ye."

Drew let out a soft snigger at this. Duncan glanced up to see his sister eyeing his wife. "It might not be a son," Drew pointed out. "Siusan might bear ye a bonny wee daughter."

"Nonsense," Duncan growled. "The healer is convinced the bairn will be male." The last thing he wanted was a daughter. This broch felt overrun with women as it was. With no brothers, he'd grown up with a dominant mother and blade-tongued sister. He'd had enough of women.

But ye have a brother, a voice chimed in his head. *And he still lives.*

Aye, a bastard. Duncan's brow furrowed as he dwelt on the unsavory fact. *But if this meeting goes to plan, he'll soon be dealt with.*

Bastard brothers aside, the fact remained that Duncan had few male kin still living, which made it all the more important that his wife provided him with a son. Duncan had taken great pains to find himself a submissive wife. However, Siusan wasn't his first choice; the lass he'd really wanted had been taken from him.

His frown deepened. He didn't like reminding himself of that disappointment; it had galled him at the time, and every time he reflected on it, his ire rose anew. Shoving the thought aside, Duncan took a large bite of bannock and chewed vigorously.

Leaning back in his seat, the MacKinnon clan-chief took in the view from his solar window. It was a grey morning, and a watery sunlight filtered in. Beyond the window, the wooded sides of Dunan Vale were wreathed in mist. The hottest summer he could ever remember had given way to the inclement weather he was used to.

"Is everything ready for yer guests?" Drew spoke up again.

"Aye," Duncan replied, glancing his sister's way once more. "Or it will be when they arrive."

His sister was delicately buttering a sliver of bannock. Everything about Drew was dainty. She was a small woman with hair the color of peat, smoke-grey eyes, and milk-white skin. These days, Duncan often felt disconcerted when he looked at her; for with the passing of the years, Drew MacKinnon was starting to look more and more like her mother. She had the same cunning face, sharp gaze, and queenly bearing.

A shiver ran down Duncan's spine. He didn't want reminding of that hag. He needed to find a husband for his sister so he could be rid of Drew. MacNichol had been evasive thus far; perhaps Drew would manage to convince the clan-chief if she was able to corner him.

Stuffing the rest of the bannock into his mouth, Duncan brushed the crumbs off his léine and rose to his feet.

"Where are ye going?" Drew demanded, eyebrows arching once more. "Ye only just sat down."

"Ye have reminded me that there are things to be done," he grumbled, grabbing another wedge of bannock from the tray. "I can't sit around yapping with ye two."

Leaving his sister and wife in offended silence, Duncan left the solar.

Bran was waiting for him in the hallway beyond. The coal-black wolfhound leaped to his feet, tail wagging.

"Here, lad." Duncan threw the dog the bannock, which Bran swallowed in one gulp. Then the hound bounded forward, falling into step with his master as Duncan strode along the hallway to the stairs that led down to the lower levels of the broch. Reaching down, the clan-chief ruffled the dog's ears.

Bran was a good dog. Duncan had raised him from a pup, and he preferred the hound's company to anyone else's in the broch.

In the Great Hall, which took up most of the ground floor, Duncan found Ross Campbell, his right-hand and captain of the Dunan Guard, and Carr Broderick, another of his most loyal warriors, seated at one of the long tables with the other men.

"Finish yer bannocks," Duncan barked, approaching the table.

Ross lowered the piece of cake he'd only been able to take a bite from. Raven-haired, with the same midnight-blue eyes as Siusan—Campbell blue—Ross was one of the few at Dunan who weren't cowed by the clan-chief. Duncan had always liked that about him. Ross had fostered here under Duncan's father as a youth but then had stayed on afterward. He'd served Duncan loyally over the past few years, although he could sometimes question him when others wisely knew to hold their tongue.

Ross watched him now, his face impassive, while around him many of the other warriors shot each other nervous looks. "What's the hurry this morning, MacKinnon?" he asked, his voice a low drawl.

"I'm in the mood to go hunting."

More surprised looks were exchanged around the table. Carr, a stocky warrior with pale blond hair cut close to his scalp, frowned. Ross's gaze also narrowed.

"My cousin is due to give birth any day," Ross said after a pause. "Don't ye want to stay close to her?"

Duncan snorted. "No. I want to ride out into the woods and stab a great big boar through the heart. Then I want the beast roasted and pride of place upon the banquet table when my guests arrive."

Silence followed this comment, before Ross abandoned the rest of his bannock and rose to his feet. He was a tall man at full height, easily meeting Duncan's eye—and Duncan towered over most. "They will all attend the gathering then?"

"Aye ... even MacLeod."

Ross grinned, showing his teeth. "He'll want to avail himself of yer fine MacKinnon hospitality."

Laughter echoed around the Great Hall at this comment. Carr grinned, although Duncan barely raised a smile. Campbell was being facetious. Ever since his father's death and his mother's departure for a convent on the mainland, Duncan received few visitors. This was the first time he'd ever extended an invitation of this kind to the other leaders upon the isle.

"He will," Duncan growled. "It's time MacLeod learned that Dunan outshines Dunvegan in every way."

He'd visited the MacLeod stronghold once, years earlier. It was an impressive fortress to be sure, a square stone keep perched upon rocky crags overlooking a loch, but Dunan was more beautiful, and the village that surrounded it was twice the size of the hamlet on the outskirts of Dunvegan.

"I thought ye wanted MacLeod's help?" Ross stepped away from the table and moved toward Duncan. "Ye don't want to anger him ... Malcolm MacLeod isn't a man lightly crossed."

Duncan snorted, making it clear that he cared not if he angered MacLeod. He then turned and strode from the Great Hall, Bran trotting at his heels. He didn't look over his shoulder. He didn't need to, for he knew that Ross, Carr, and the other men would be following as faithfully as his hound.

Leading the way out of the broch, Duncan descended a steep row of steps into a wide bailey. "Saddle our horses," he yelled to one of the lads who was carting fresh hay into the stables. "We're going on a hunt."

Duncan then spun on his heel and found himself eye to eye with the captain of his guard. Ross stared back, unflinching. "MacLeod's held too much clout upon this isle for too long." Duncan growled out the words. "It's time for him to step aside, for younger blood to make the decisions that affect us all."

This time Ross Campbell, wisely, didn't respond.

17

Arrival at Dunan

ELLA'S BREATHING CAUGHT when she spied the
broch of Dunan rising out of the mist. Gavin hadn't
exaggerated; the MacKinnon stronghold was indeed a
majestic sight, especially on an afternoon like this, for
mist wreathed the Dunan Vale. It drifted amongst the
dark spruce and pine that carpeted the sides of the valley
and curled like smoke around the base of the broch,
making the fortress look as if it were floating upon a
cloud.

"What do ye think?" Gavin's voice intruded, and Ella
tore her gaze from the broch to see that he had reined in
his mare and now rode alongside her. It was the first
time he'd spoken to her all afternoon. They'd exchanged
a few brief words at midday, when the party had stopped
for a light meal of coarse barley and oaten bread and
cheese, but had traveled apart since then.

"Impressive," Ella admitted. "It reminds me of
Talasgair."

Gavin's mouth lifted at the corners. "Of course ... I
sometimes forget ye are a Fraser."

Indeed, Ella had lived at the Fraser stronghold on the
north-western coast of Skye until she was around

thirteen. Despite that many years had passed since she had last seen it, she still remembered the fortress clearly.

Shifting her gaze back to the stone broch looming before her, Ella studied it. "Ye can see it was built on the site of an ancient fort."

"It is," Gavin replied. "Although the MacKinnon clan-chiefs have built up from the base of the tower and raised it much higher than the original. It's now three stories high, whereas the original broch only had one level. The village below is interesting too ... they call it 'the warren', for it's a network of narrow lanes that are easy to get lost in."

Intrigued, Ella continued to observe the approaching stronghold. As they neared it, she spied a high stone wall that ringed both the broch and the village. They clattered over a bridge that spanned the meandering An River and rode toward the North Gate.

Despite the enshrouding mist and poor light levels, there were plenty of folk working the surrounding fields: cottars bent over rows of kale, cabbages, and turnips. There were also a number of huts scattering the edges of the fields, tiny dwellings of stacked stone with sod roofs. Smoke wreathed up from some of the huts, and as she rode past, Ella inhaled the aroma of baking bread and braised onions.

Her belly rumbled in response. It had been a long while since the noon meal, and her appetite was now sharp. Even so, the thought of being a guest at Dunan, where she knew no one, put her on edge.

Once again she felt a pang of homesickness for Kilbride—a place where she knew every face. The abbey also offered her protection from the outside world, which could be so harsh and cruel. Her mother's death had left her feeling exposed, and the incident with Gavin had unnerved her. She was vulnerable away from Kilbride and looked forward to having routine back in her life again.

Not long now, she promised herself, urging Monadh through the gate and into the village beyond. *And I'll be back where I belong.*

"Welcome to Dunan!"

A tall man dressed in black leather strode out to meet them as they dismounted in the bailey before the broch. A leggy wolfhound, with a brindled black coat and a lolling tongue, loped at his heels. Ella stared at the newcomer, tracking his path across the yard.

Duncan MacKinnon ... this must be him.

Ella didn't know what she was expecting, but this wasn't it. Many of the tales that circulated MacKinnon lands portrayed the clan-chief as a depraved beast. Yet the man who embraced Gavin was fine looking: tall and broad-shouldered with a mane of peat-brown hair, storm-grey eyes, and a ruggedly handsome face. He looked to be around Gavin's age—in his late thirties.

"Good afternoon, MacKinnon," Gavin greeted him. "Am I the first to arrive?"

"Niall MacDonald is here already ... and the rest of them should be here by tomorrow morning." MacKinnon pulled back from Gavin and slapped him across the back. "Leave yer horses with my lads and come up for a cup of mead."

The MacKinnon clan-chief stepped away from Gavin then, his gaze sweeping over the small party that MacNichol had brought with him.

But when he saw Ella, his face froze. "Who's this?" he asked. His bluff tone had completely vanished, and his voice sounded strangely brittle.

Gavin stiffened before taking a step toward Ella. "This is Sister Annella," he replied. "She is a nun at Kilbride and has just been to Scorrybreac to visit her mother. Sadly, the woman has passed away, and I'm now escorting Sister Annella back to the abbey. I hope ye don't mind her staying here?"

MacKinnon continued to stare at Ella, his grey eyes shadowing. When he didn't answer, Gavin cleared his throat. "Can she stay at the broch?"

MacKinnon started slightly, before he dragged his gaze from Ella's face and focused on Gavin once more. "What?" he mumbled. "Aye, of course she may."

MacKinnon then clicked his fingers, and two stable lads came running. "See to their horses," he barked before flashing Gavin another broad smile, Ella seemingly forgotten. "Follow me."

A woman's wails drifted through the broch, greeting Ella when she entered the Great Hall. A stairwell led off it, climbing up to the higher levels, from where the cries of agony were issuing.

Ella's step faltered, and her gaze swiveled to MacKinnon. "What's that?" She blurted the question out before she could stop herself, dropping the reserved demeanor she'd adopted away from Kilbride.

He frowned, irritated. "It's my wife ... she's giving birth. It's been taking her a while ... she's been wailing for hours now."

"Don't mind us then," Gavin cut in. "Leave us with some mead and go to her."

MacKinnon's frown deepened into a scowl. "Birthing is woman's work," he muttered. "I'll not interfere."

An uncomfortable silence followed, before Ella spoke up once more. She knew she should hold her tongue, but the wailing clawed at her. "Do ye want me to go up and see if I can help in any way?" She paused here, aware of the clan-chief's glower. "I have aided births before."

MacKinnon shook his head. "There's no need. My sister and the healer are with her."

Ella's lips parted as she readied herself to argue. A swift warning glance from Gavin stopped her. He was right; she'd only just stepped over the threshold. It wasn't her place.

Even so, the poor woman's piteous cries ripped into Ella, shredding her nerves. She couldn't bear to listen to them and know that she wasn't allowed to help.

They took a seat at the far end of the Great Hall, upon a raised dais. A fire burning in the nearby hearth threw out a blanket of welcome heat. Ella sat down upon a low bench, next to Ceard, while MacKinnon lowered himself into a great oaken chair. Above him a huge boar's head hung upon the wall. Ella stared at it, taken aback by the beast's size and massive tusks.

Seeing the direction of her gaze, Duncan MacKinnon grinned. "Impressive, isn't he? I brought the rogue down three summers ago ... I've never seen the likes of him since."

"It's certainly a prize," Gavin admitted. His gaze flicked between MacKinnon and Ella, and she saw a wary expression settle over his face. He didn't like the interest that MacKinnon was showing in her; he didn't trust the man.

Ella dropped her gaze then, cursing her outburst earlier. She had done a foolish thing in drawing MacKinnon's attention. *A nun should be serene and silent.*

Servants appeared then, bearing jugs of mead. They filled MacKinnon's cup first before moving on to his guests. Ella shifted restlessly upon the hard wooden bench. The woman's wailing was not as loud here, but she could still hear it.

How could MacKinnon sit there drinking mead when his wife was in so much agony?

A chill slithered down Ella's spine when she dared a glance back at the clan-chief—and immediately regretted it. MacKinnon was watching her under hooded lids: a sensual, brooding look. Maybe the stories about this man had some truth to them.

She'd only spent a few moments in MacKinnon's company, and already she had the urge to bathe in a tub of scalding water and scrub her skin with a hog-bristle brush. Lowering her eyes once more, Ella resolutely ignored his stare.

Around her the rumble of men's voices filled the hall. Warriors were filtering in after finishing work for the day, and as they settled at long tables, calling out to the serving wenches to bring them drink, Ella realized that she couldn't hear Lady MacKinnon's cries at all now.

She glanced up, her gaze shifting to the stairwell. Perhaps the woman had finally given birth?

Meanwhile, she could hear Gavin making an attempt at conversation with MacKinnon. Gavin's ability to get on with anyone had always impressed her; he was easy company and although strong-willed, didn't have that competitive streak that many other warriors possessed.

Seated beside the MacKinnon clan-chief, the difference between the two men was striking. Ella chanced a surreptitious look, noting that apart from the fact that they were both tall, muscular, and of a similar age—the similarities ended there.

MacKinnon had a hungry, intense look to him, a restless coiled energy like a trap primed to spring. In contrast, MacNichol was watchful, calm, his blue eyes veiled.

Ella glanced away and raised her cup of mead to her lips.

It was no good denying it—Gavin MacNichol still captivated her.

She'd wanted to hate him all those years ago, she really had, although becoming a nun had made that difficult. Mother Shona had told her that letting hate into her heart was allowing herself to be consumed by darkness. She couldn't serve God while dwelling in the shadows.

The events of the year after their parting had tested her, brought her to breaking point. She had lain upon her pallet at night, weeping herself to sleep. She had railed at him, blamed him for her fate, and missed him with an ache in her breast that felt as if it would make her heart stop.

But it didn't. Time had helped ease her loss, her bitterness, her shame.

Yet despite it all, Ella knew that she could never really hate Gavin. Being back in his company confirmed it. Even when she was sore at him, even when his behavior troubled her, all it took was one look, one smile, and her heart melted.

Mother Mary give me strength. Ella took a gulp of mead, her fingers tightening around the earthen cup. *For just a couple more days.*

18

Reacquainted

A TALL, DARK-HAIRED man walked into the Great
Hall, his expression grim. A brown-haired woman
dressed in a pine-green kirtle followed him. Her face was
pale, her eyes red-rimmed.

Ella didn't know either of the newcomers, yet one
look at both their faces and she grew still.

Around her the Great Hall quietened, men and
women swiveling around to watch the pair who made
their way across the paved floor toward the dais. No one
spoke a word. Silence settled like an indrawn breath.

Slowly, Ella shifted her attention to MacKinnon.
She'd been making a point of ignoring him while the
mead flowed and he'd started regaling Gavin with tales
of his hunting exploits. But she looked at him now.

His face was impassive, his grey eyes hooded. When
the man and woman neared the dais, he broke the heavy
silence. "What news? Has my son entered the world
yet?"

The man halted. He was one of the handsomest men
Ella had ever set eyes on, with chiseled features and
penetrating midnight-blue eyes. He didn't look like the
sort of man given to displays of emotion, for there was
pride upon his face, and arrogance. Yet his eyes glistened

and his throat bobbed before he answered, and when he spoke, there was a rasp to his voice.

"My cousin gave birth to a boy, Duncan," he said softly, "but the bairn was still-born." He broke off there, his gaze fusing with the clan-chief's. "Siusan is dead."

The words fell like an axe-blade in the hall.

Duncan gaped, his fingers clenching around the horn of mead he'd been drinking. "What?"

"The birth was too long." The woman spoke then. She was pretty with sharp grey eyes. Her voice was low and surprisingly strong, despite the haunted look on her face. "She bled out ... there was nothing any of us could do."

Another silence fell. This one crackled with tension, like the air before a summer thunder storm.

Ella's chest constricted, and a wave of dizziness swept over her.

Still-born.

How she wished she'd never come to this place.

She'd never met Lady MacKinnon, yet her heart wept for the woman. Her heart wept for all women who'd died giving birth, for there were far too many of them.

MacKinnon snarled a curse and hurled his horn of mead across the hall. It smacked one of his warriors across the back of the head, drenching him. The man grunted, clutching the back of his skull.

MacKinnon ignored him. "All she had to do was bear me a son—a live one!" The words were savage. The man's voice trembled, not from grief but from rage. "She had but one task, and she failed."

Shock rippled over the Great Hall of Dunan.

In an instant Ella realized exactly why folk hated Duncan MacKinnon so much. The selfishness, the cruelty, of his words ripped into her. The faces of those surrounding her mirrored Ella's own response.

Gavin's lips parted as he stared at MacKinnon, while the man and woman who'd delivered the news both went stone-faced.

But MacKinnon didn't appear to notice or care. Another tide of obscenities spewed from his mouth, and he launched himself to his feet, shouldering the dark-haired man aside as he strode out of the hall.

Many gazes watched him go. But still, not one person uttered a word.

Gavin escorted Ella from the Great Hall. Together, they ascended the stairwell to the upper levels of the broch.

Ella didn't speak as she climbed the stairs. She wished Gavin hadn't insisted on accompanying her. He should really have remained downstairs with the other chieftains. However, he'd been insistent.

Chieftain Alasdair MacDonald of Duntulm had just arrived. While his pregnant wife had retired to their quarters immediately, Alasdair had taken a seat upon the dais to share a mead with Niall MacDonald of Sleat and Gavin.

After his outburst earlier, MacKinnon hadn't reappeared to join them. It was a relief. Ella wondered if, after his rage had subsided, he'd gone to see his wife.

Reaching the landing to the second floor, Ella turned to Gavin. "I can make my way from here," she murmured. "Ye should return to the Great Hall."

Gavin grimaced. "In truth, I've got no stomach for mead this eve." Studying his face, Ella noted the lines of tension that hadn't been there before their arrival at Dunan. "I'm sorry, Ella," he said softly, taking a step toward her. "I'd known MacKinnon can be a brute ... but his behavior today was inexcusable. Ye didn't need to witness that."

Ella swallowed as the ugly scene flashed before her once more. She'd never forget MacKinnon's angry, red face as he railed at his dead wife: "She had but one task and she failed."

Instead of grief, he'd been filled with rage.

What kind of man behaves that way?

"Is the meeting still going ahead?" she asked when a pause drew out between them. "Surely, Lady MacKinnon's death will prevent it."

Gavin shook his head. "MacKinnon should really delay our talks by a day or two ... but seeing as he's been so eager to discuss matters, I doubt he will."

Ella stared at him, aghast. "But Siusan MacKinnon isn't even buried yet."

Gavin gave her a pained look. "If the meeting is postponed, I will accompany ye back to Kilbride first," he assured her. "With MacKinnon's mood so volatile, I'd prefer ye didn't remain here."

Their gazes held for a long moment, and Ella knew he'd noticed how MacKinnon had stared at her earlier. Yet she didn't bring the incident up, for even recalling the man's stare made her skin crawl.

Ella took a step back. "I should retire now."

"Do ye know the way to yer chamber?" Gavin asked, frowning.

"Aye ... it's the last door on the right."

Gavin nodded, his expression shuttering. "Goodnight then ... I shall see ye tomorrow."

Night settled over Dunan, bringing the encircling mist in closer. Gavin stood at the window of his bed-chamber and looked out over the valley. Tall spruce poked up through the milky fog; it was an eerily beautiful sight, and Gavin might have enjoyed it, if his mood had been different.

As it was, he felt on edge.

Ella had suggested that he return to the Great Hall, yet he wasn't in the mood. The scene he'd witnessed earlier had been damning. Even the memory of it made Gavin's ire rise. MacKinnon was a heartless cur. Afterward, Gavin's first instinct was to gather up those of his party and depart from Dunan without a backward glance.

But he'd given his word he'd take part in tomorrow's meeting, and the problems facing their isle needed to be sorted.

Even so, the thought of dealing with MacKinnon the following day, of listening to his demands, made Gavin grind his teeth. Right now, the only thing he wanted to do was smash his fist into the clan-chief's mouth.

The clatter of hooves below drew Gavin's gaze then from the mist-wreathed valley, to the bailey below. A party had arrived, and judging from the booming male voice that echoed against the surrounding stone, it was Malcolm MacLeod.

Gavin relaxed his jaw a little. MacLeod could be bullish, but beneath all his swagger and bluster, the man had a heart. Gavin wasn't sure Duncan MacKinnon did.

He had spoken briefly to Alasdair MacDonald of Duntulm and his wife, Caitrin, after supper. It had been a year since he'd seen them both—but much had changed in their lives since their last meeting.

Caitrin MacDonald.

Despite his bleak mood, Gavin's mouth curved. Just over a year ago now, he'd been one of three suitors all vying for her hand. Ross Campbell, captain of Duntulm Guard, had also been one of them.

Blonde, proud, and recently widowed, Caitrin had been sought after. After losing Innis, Gavin had told himself that it was time to leave the past behind, time to make a fresh start. But when he and the other suitors met with Caitrin at Dunvegan, it had become quickly apparent that the woman's affections lay elsewhere.

She was in love with her dead husband's brother, Alasdair.

They'd both been determined to deny their feelings for each other, but Gavin liked to think he'd played a small role in bringing them together. Once he'd realized that he'd never win Caitrin's heart, he met with Alasdair and forced him to face the truth. The man was deeply in love with Caitrin; Gavin knew the signs and also had to face a few truths himself.

For as lovely as Caitrin was, there was only one woman for him.

Reaching up, Gavin scrubbed his face with the palm of his hand. The Devil take him, he'd miscalculated when he'd thought that seeing Ella again, apologizing to her, would help him move on with his life.

In truth, the opposite had happened.

A soft knock at the door intruded upon his thoughts.

Stiffening, Gavin turned toward it. The hour was late—too much so for visitors.

"Who is it?" he called out.

With a click, the door opened inward, and a slender figure encased in pine-green stepped inside.

Gavin stiffened. "Lady MacKinnon," he addressed her formally, no warmth in his voice. "To what do I owe this visit?"

"With all of today's excitement, we didn't manage to get reacquainted, Gavin." She smiled and shut the door behind her, leaning up against it. "I thought I would rectify that."

Gavin raised an eyebrow. He'd forgotten how bold Drew MacKinnon could be. Of course, she'd been newly wedded the last time they'd seen each other. However, that hadn't stopped her from flirting shamelessly with him—right under her husband's nose.

"This meeting could have waited till tomorrow," Gavin replied, folding his arms across his chest.

Drew's smile became coy. She was comely; Gavin had noticed that years ago. She shared her brother's coloring: pale skin, storm-grey eyes, and peat-brown hair that she had braided and coiled around the crown of her head, revealing a long, slender neck.

However, just like years earlier, her beauty left him cold.

He'd never liked the shrewdness in Drew MacKinnon's eyes, the cunning edge to her smile. She thought she was cleverer than him—than most men—and she could barely conceal her arrogance.

"I know it's late, Gavin," she said, a sultry edge to her voice, "but ye have time to share a cup of wine with me, do ye not?"

Gavin held Drew's gaze, resisting the urge to show her the door. Drew knew he had manners and wouldn't cast her out. At the same time, she was playing a dangerous game. It was not seemly for a widow to be entering a guest's bed-chamber, at any hour.

Silently, Gavin moved to the sideboard, where a jug of bramble wine and a stack of clay cups sat. He then poured some wine and handed Drew a cup, noting that she deliberately brushed her fingers against his as he did so.

Gazing up at his face, Drew took a sip of wine. "Ye grow more handsome with the years, Gavin ... age suits ye."

"Ye look well too," Gavin replied, his tone still cool. Compliments were expected, so he would give them. It was true though; the past decade since he'd seen Drew hadn't aged her at all.

Drew's smile widened, although her gaze remained sharp.

"I'm sorry about yer loss today," Gavin said after a pause. He'd noted that although Duncan hadn't been upset about his wife's death, Drew had been, as had Lady Siusan's cousin, Ross.

Drew's grey eyes guttered. "I can't believe Siusan is gone." She gave a delicate shudder then. "I am glad I've never had to suffer the horror of childbirth." She reached out, placing a hand on Gavin's forearm. "It was horrible."

Gavin went still. The grief in Drew's eyes had been real, although she'd used it to gain closer proximity to him, hoping that he'd comfort her. Exhaling slowly, he took a deliberate step back so that her hand fell away.

"Aye ... it must have been ... especially for Lady MacKinnon. Were ye close?"

Drew held his gaze, her mouth compressing slightly as she realized he hadn't fallen for her ruse. She then nodded. "Siusan was an easy lass to like." She paused there, favoring him with a wry smile. "Unlike some of us."

Finally. For the first time since entering his bed-chamber, Drew MacKinnon had said something that hadn't been carefully thought out beforehand, something that wasn't designed to ensnare him. Something sincere.

Gavin took a gulp of bramble wine; it was delicious—dark and spiced. "Ye are who ye are, Drew," he said finally. The use of her first name made her gaze widen. "As am I." He halted there, letting his words sink in before continuing. "I know ye are looking for a husband, but I'll save ye the effort now by telling ye that I'm not looking for a wife."

Drew stiffened, her eyes narrowing. "That's not what I heard ... ye were keen to wed Lady Caitrin last year, were ye not?"

Gavin smiled, not remotely chastised by her shrewish tone. He was used to women like this, having grown up with a mother that made most men run for cover. "I was," he admitted, "but since then I've changed my mind. I'm not wedding again, Lady Drew ... ye are wasting yer smiles on me."

19

Meeting of the Clans

"I HOPE YE have some solutions for us, MacKinnon." Morgan Fraser's voice echoed across the Great Hall. There was no mistaking the threatening note. "This better not have been a wasted trip."

The chieftain of the Frasers of Skye limped across the floor toward the dais. Watching his approach, Gavin noted that Morgan had aged significantly since he'd seen him last. He'd always been a tall, proud man, although his mane of once flame-red hair was now laced with white, and deep grooves cut into his austere face.

As he approached the dais, Fraser's sharp gaze swept across the table.

Gavin wasn't surprised to see that it froze upon Malcolm MacLeod.

This was the first time that Fraser had met in peace with MacLeod since his wife, Una, had left him for the MacLeod clan-chief a few years earlier. The look on Malcolm MacLeod's face wasn't friendly as he stared his arch-nemesis down.

Gavin shifted uncomfortably in his seat. Fortunately, both men were unarmed; MacKinnon had wisely insisted upon it for the meeting.

He knew all about the bad blood that existed between the Frasers and the MacLeods, and that the last time these two men had seen each other, it had been in battle. Fraser's rounded posture and limp were the result of a serious wound dealt to him by MacLeod's claidheamh-mor.

"Aye ... although this isn't my problem alone." Seated at the head of the table, MacKinnon watched Fraser with a narrow-eyed stare. Gavin had heard that relations between the MacKinnons and the Frasers hadn't been good either of late—not ideal since they were neighbors. "Take a seat, Fraser."

Morgan Fraser grunted before climbing up onto the dais and taking a seat between Alasdair MacDonald of Duntulm and Niall MacDonald of Sleat, directly opposite Gavin. He acknowledged the others seated at the table with a brusque nod.

Malcolm MacLeod and Brodie MacQueen flanked Gavin. Both men wore formidable expressions. None of the leaders here liked that MacKinnon presided at the head of the table, lording over them all as if he were king of the isle.

Gavin certainly wasn't happy about it. It was clear that this meeting wasn't just about the grievances that MacKinnon wished to air, but about the balance of power upon this isle.

The seven chieftains of Skye rarely met under the same roof. Whether or not the coming years brought war or peace, this meeting would decide it.

The realization put Gavin on edge.

A tense silence settled at the table. The seven men were alone in the Great Hall; even the servants had let them be. Two ewers of wine sat at each end, and seven pewter goblets lined the table.

Fraser poured himself a large goblet of wine and took a gulp. "Come on then," he growled. "Let's talk."

All gazes swiveled to MacKinnon, who was leaning back in his chair, fingers lightly drumming on the table before him. "Did ye all travel here without problems," he began, his voice low. "No encounters with outlaws on the road?"

This comment brought a snort from MacLeod. "No one would dare attack a clan-chief."

"That's not entirely true," Gavin spoke up. "I've been attacked twice of late." He paused here, his gaze shifting to MacKinnon. "Both times on yer lands."

This caused a stir at the table. The men seated there exchanged surprised yet wary glances.

"Exactly," MacKinnon growled. "When even a clan-chief cannot travel unmolested, things are grim indeed."

"The roads to the north have become more dangerous of late," Alasdair MacDonald spoke up. The youngest of the men at the table, Alasdair wore an inscrutable expression. *Clever lad*, Gavin thought. *Don't trust any of them.* Alasdair's gaze swept around the table, a challenge in his blue eyes. "Although we didn't encounter any outlaws on the way here."

"Criminals will always exist," Fraser muttered, taking another gulp of wine. "What are ye going to do, MacKinnon, stamp them all out?"

"Outlaws and cutthroats abound on this isle these days," MacKinnon replied, his dark brows knitting together. "Twice over the last six months, supplies that have come in from the mainland have been attacked."

"What did they rob ye of?" MacQueen, a heavyset man with wild dark hair, spoke up then.

MacKinnon screwed his face up. "The usual ... silver, as well as grains and livestock."

"Maybe they were hungry," Niall MacDonald pointed out. He was a tall, lean man of around fifty winters with pale blond hair tied back at his nape. "Ye tax folk too heavily, MacKinnon."

It was a bold statement, and Gavin felt the temperature at the table drop as a result.

MacKinnon met the older man's challenging stare, his own narrowing. Gavin had heard that there was no love lost between these two either. They shared a border and there had been skirmishes between them over the last few years. A rumor also circulated the isle that

MacKinnon had wished to wed MacDonald's eldest daughter but had been thwarted.

However, watching the way MacKinnon looked at MacDonald now, the way the muscles flexed in his jaw, Gavin knew that the slight hadn't been forgotten.

"Theft is theft," MacKinnon eventually bit out the words. He then tore his gaze from Niall MacDonald's and let it travel over the other faces at the table. "Brigands must be dealt with."

"And how do ye suggest we do that?" Fraser replied. He was watching MacKinnon with a gleam in his eye.

"We must make an example of them. Those caught should be given a public hanging and left to rot at crossroads."

"And ye think that will stop desperate men?" Niall MacDonald leaned forward, his large hands clenching upon the table before him.

MacKinnon stared back at him. "Aye."

"Lawlessness has become a problem in my lands," MacLeod admitted, shattering the tension. "Cattle rustling has gotten worse, and travelers between Kiltaraglen and Dunvegan were attacked just last week."

"Those men moved onto the north afterward," Alasdair MacDonald added, "they have been caught and imprisoned."

A tense silence followed these words. Gavin studied the young MacDonald chieftain's face, impressed by his impassive delivery.

"Of course, there's a reason why things are so bad in MacKinnon territory," Niall MacDonald said, helping himself to some wine. "And it's not just because ye raise yer taxes higher every year." He paused there, his mouth curving at the scowl upon MacKinnon's face. Meeting the younger man's eye, MacDonald of Sleat raised his goblet to him in a mocking salute. "Yer brother has a score to settle with ye."

Gavin tensed at this news. *His brother?* To Gavin's knowledge, Duncan MacKinnon didn't have one. His only sibling was a younger sister, Drew. Likewise, the other men at the table looked on in surprised silence, their gazes keen.

Niall MacDonald had revealed something of great interest.

"My *bastard* brother, MacDonald," MacKinnon eventually answered, his voice low and hard, "as ye well know."

MacLeod let out a loud, rumbling laugh. He was a big, corpulent man with thick auburn hair and a ruddy complexion. The laugh suited him. "Why doesn't it surprise me that auld Jock MacKinnon spread his seed away from the marital bed."

The words, crude as they were, made some of the men at the table grin—although Fraser didn't look amused. Nothing MacLeod said would please him. Gavin didn't smile either; he could see that MacKinnon was seething.

"My father plowed a whore," MacKinnon bit out the words, "and Craeg was the result."

"Ah, so the bastard has a name." Fraser rubbed his chin, his sharp gaze narrowed. "And what trouble has Craeg *MacKinnon* been causing?"

Duncan MacKinnon's face flushed then—a deep, ugly red like raw liver. Gavin could see he didn't want the likes of Fraser giving his bastard outlaw brother the MacKinnon name. And yet, to react to it would weaken him in the eyes of all present. MacKinnon knew it, and so he held his tongue—barely.

"He leads a band of fugitives," MacKinnon said eventually, his voice hoarse with suppressed wrath. "They move from place to place, hiding in the forests, the mountains, and the vales of my lands as it suits them." MacKinnon's hand grasped the stem of his goblet so tightly that his fingers turned white. "He steals from me ... no one else ... and gives *my* silver and *my* possessions to the poor."

Gavin went still, casting his mind back to the ragged group who'd attacked him and Ella on their way to Scorrybreac. Surely those men hadn't been part of Craeg MacKinnon's band?

"And the people love him for it," Niall MacDonald added with a smirk. "Many wish it was Craeg ruling Dunan, not ye."

MacKinnon's fist slammed down upon the oaken table with such force that wine sloshed over the brim of some of the goblets. His grey eyes glittered as he stared Niall MacDonald down. "So ye say, MacDonald. But I've not heard such tales. How do I know ye are not in league with the bastard? Ye have obstructed me at every turn of late."

Niall MacDonald's face turned thunderous. "Yer brother doesn't need my help," he replied coldly. He leaned forward then, his expression deliberately goading. "Ye are making a mess of things all on yer own. Yer father wasn't much of a clan-chief … but at least he realized that folk need to eat. He knew that if ye oppress yer own people, eventually they'll rise up against ye … only now we're *all* paying the price."

Ella studied the rose she was embroidering upon the pillow case, a pang of homesickness flowering within her. But it wasn't longing for Kilbride this time. Instead, nostalgia for the years of her childhood returned. There were many things about her youth she'd have preferred not to dwell upon, but her love of roses, and the afternoons she'd spent with her mother and sister tending the garden, would always remain among her fondest memories.

"It's a lot of trouble to go to, Sister Annella." Drew MacKinnon's voice made her glance up from the delicate pink rose she'd been embroidering. "For MacNichol to escort ye to Kilbride in person. Why would he do that?"

Ella glanced up, meeting Lady MacKinnon's eye. The woman, who was of a similar age to her, sat opposite, a wooden spindle in one hand, a basket of wool upon her lap.

"He was wed to my sister," she replied. "God rest her soul."

Drew inclined her head. "Ye are a Fraser?"

"Aye."

"I take it that yer hair is flame red under that veil."

Ella smiled. "Not really ... it's more like tarnished copper."

A low laugh answered her. "I've never heard red hair described that way before." Rhona MacKinnon had glanced up from the child's woolen tunic she was knitting.

Ella and Drew weren't alone in the women's solar—a spacious chamber that looked out over the mountains to the west of the broch—for two other women had joined them: Rhona MacKinnon and Caitrin MacDonald. Ella had learned that the women were sisters, both daughters of Malcolm MacLeod.

Ella dropped her gaze, embarrassed at being made the center of attention. "My hair isn't as fiery as yers, I'm afraid, Lady Rhona."

"Ye should see my son, Cailean's, locks," Rhona replied with a chuckle. "Barely a year old and red curls so bright I'll never have to worry about losing him in a crowd when he starts to walk."

Drew MacKinnon's mouth curved at his, although there was little mirth in her gaze. Ella wasn't sure that MacKinnon's sister liked her two companions much. Every comment she'd issued toward them thus far had carried a barb.

Observing her companions, Ella had never seen three women who contrasted each other more. All of them were beauties, although Drew's sharp grey eyes and knowing expression detracted from her loveliness. Caitrin was the only one of them with child. Under her blue kirtle, her belly was noticeably swollen.

The sight of a pregnant woman unnerved Ella slightly, especially after the events of the past day. Caitrin would know of Lady MacKinnon's death; they had buried Siusan in the kirk yard just outside the walls of Dunan shortly after dawn. But Caitrin didn't seem unnerved by the tragic birth; instead, she wore a serene expression as she embroidered a coverlet.

In contrast, Ella was still on edge after the incident. She'd joined the mourners; she'd done so out of respect for she'd never met MacKinnon's wife. The clan-chief had stood, his face stone-hewn, while the priest murmured prayers for the dead woman and her still-born child.

As soon as the priest was done, MacKinnon had turned on his heel and stalked away, his wolf-hound loping along behind him.

Ella had watched him leave, wondering if he grieved for his wife at all.

"Still," Drew MacKinnon shifted her attention back to Ella. "Gavin must be fond of ye, if he'd accompany ye to Kilbride himself. After all, he could have just asked one of his men to do it. I have to say ... it all appears a bit unseemly ... a nun traveling alone with a band of men."

The woman was fishing. The intelligence in those grey eyes made Ella wary. Not only that, but the familiar way she said Gavin's name made Ella tense. She seemed to be showing a particular interest in him.

Ella favored her with a demure smile. "Haven't ye heard, Lady MacKinnon? Outlaws infest these lands ... MacNichol is merely concerned for my welfare."

20

Mine

SUPPER THAT EVENING was an awkward affair.

Ella would have preferred to have begged off. She'd spent the afternoon in the small kirk outside the walls of Dunan. It was a tranquil spot, where she'd been able to pray in peace. The priest had then given her a tour of the grounds, before she'd retired to her chamber later.

However, a servant had knocked upon her door as the day drew out, advising her that as one of MacKinnon's guests, she was expected to attend supper.

Being seated next to Gavin just made the meal even more awkward. She'd managed to avoid him for most of the day, but sitting between him and Alastair MacDonald, she felt anxiety flutter up under her ribcage.

Gavin was too close. She could feel the heat of his body and smell the spicy scent of his skin. It made her flustered and on edge.

"Are ye enjoying yer stay at Dunan?" Gavin asked lightly. He had just helped himself to a slice of venison pie, after serving Ella first—something which had raised a few eyebrows around the table.

Drew MacKinnon was sitting directly opposite, watching Gavin like a she-wolf stalking her prey.

She's after him. The realization hit Ella then. A strange sensation filtered through her: hot and prickly.

Jealousy.

Mother Mary … please get me through this. Jealousy was an ugly emotion, one that a Sister of Kilbride didn't entertain. The last time Ella had felt like this, she'd been preparing to leave Scorrybreac while Gavin and Innis's wedding loomed.

Ella swallowed hard and focused on answering Gavin. "Aye," she said softly. "I spent some time in Dunan kirk today … and Father Athol showed me the crypt where the MacKinnon clan-chiefs are all buried."

Gavin inclined his head, his gaze meeting hers. Ella's breathing quickened. She wished he wouldn't look at her like that, not with so many eyes upon them. He watched her as if she were the only woman alive.

He watched her as if she weren't sitting there shrouded in yards of black cloth.

A memory resurfaced then, one that she had deliberately put away into the deepest vaults of her mind: the pair of them lying under a spreading birch, the dappled sunlight bathing their naked skin. Gavin was propped up on one elbow, his fingertips gently tracing shapes across Ella's breasts and belly. "Ye are so bonny, Ella," he'd whispered. "I shall never tire of gazing upon ye."

Ella blinked. There were many more memories that she kept under lock and key, ones that heated her blood and made her pulse race.

And when Gavin looked at her as he did then, he risked freeing them all.

"How did the meeting go?" she asked, suddenly breathless.

The moment shattered, and Gavin's gaze clouded. "Badly," he murmured. "I was hoping we'd come to some resolution this afternoon, but MacKinnon has insisted we continue discussions tomorrow."

Disappointment lanced through Ella at this news. She'd been hoping to leave Dunan the following day. The atmosphere within the broch smothered her, made her uneasy. She didn't belong here. She needed to return to Kilbride.

"None of ye could agree on things?" Ella asked. She too deliberately kept her voice low. Around them most folk were deep in conversation. Nonetheless, it was best to avoid being overheard. Especially since they sat near the head of the table, where their host lounged in his oaken chair.

Ella had noticed that MacKinnon appeared in a sour mood this evening. A scowl twisted his handsome face, and he was drinking heavily.

"MacKinnon wants us all to take a harder line with outlaws," Gavin replied, bending closer to her so that he wasn't overheard. That was a mistake, for the heat and scent of him enveloped her, and his breath feathered against the shell of Ella's ear. "He wants them strung up and left to rot at crossroads. But there are also bandits who only target MacKinnon himself, and those men are led by the clan-chief's bastard brother. MacKinnon wants our help to hunt him down."

Ella drew back, eyes widening. "Bastard brother?"

"Aye." Gavin's mouth quirked. "Things are more complex than we all realized—well, most of us anyway."

Ella became aware then of a hard stare boring into her. She glanced across the table to see Drew MacKinnon glaring at her.

"Lady MacKinnon hasn't taken her eyes off us since we sat down," Ella murmured, shifting her attention back to Gavin. "Ye especially."

Gavin's face tightened. "She's a widow ... and looking for a husband."

Ella raised her eyebrows, feigning nonchalance, even as her heart thundered against her breast bone. "And ye are in need of a wife, are ye not?"

Gavin held her gaze. "I was," he said softly. He paused then, silence drawing out between them. "But not anymore."

Heart racing, Ella dragged her attention from Gavin to the slice of venison pie she'd not yet touched. Truthfully, her belly was now in knots. This was a hazardous conversation, although it was her fault for asking him about Lady MacKinnon.

And as she struggled with everything that was forbidden to her, everything she dared not want, she became aware of another gaze upon her.

It wasn't that of Lady Drew, who was now attempting to flirt with her cousin, Taran MacKinnon. The big scarred warrior sat with his wife, Rhona, at the table. The widow wasn't having much luck engaging Taran in conversation, for he answered her in short, curt sentences.

No, the person staring openly at Ella wasn't a woman.

Duncan MacKinnon reclined in his chair, goblet of wine in hand, and stripped her naked with his gaze.

Kneeling by the bed, Ella clasped her hands together and began her evening prayers. It had been a long, exhausting day. She wasn't used to having contact with so many new people, or to making idle conversation. Some of the folk she'd met—like Lady Rhona, Lady Caitrin, and their husbands—had been good company. But others had worn upon her. Lady Drew especially.

Ella squeezed her eyes shut, shoving back the sharp dislike that twisted her gut every time she thought about the comely widow. Not only had she succumbed to the sin of lust while away from Kilbride, but now jealousy plagued her.

Inhaling deeply, she began a prayer. "Dear Lord, please free me from all envy and jealousy," she murmured, her voice fervent. "I will only look to ye for all I need. I pray I will be more and more like ye. Conform my mind and thoughts to yer thoughts, Lord."

Ella broke off there, concentrating as she prepared to repeat the prayer.

However, a knock at the door interrupted her.

Rising to her feet, Ella smoothed her habit. It grew late. She couldn't think who could be knocking upon her door at this hour.

Was it Gavin?

A mixture of dread and excitement churned through her then. She hated herself at that moment, for her weakness where he was concerned.

"Aye," she called out. "Who is it?"

The door swung open, and a tall figure stepped inside. Yet it was not a man with dark-blond hair, warm blue eyes, and a boyish smile, who turned her will to porridge.

The man who invaded her space was dark-haired with storm-grey eyes and a wolfish expression.

"Mac ... MacKinnon," Ella stammered, shocked by his presence. "What do ye want?"

It was a rude, direct question. But then, any man who strode into a nun's bed-chamber didn't deserve a polite greeting.

MacKinnon kicked the door shut behind him, the hungry look in his eyes quickening. A grin stretched his lips.

"That's a fine question, Sister Annella ... one I intend to answer."

He advanced upon her. Suddenly, Ella's bed-chamber seemed a cage. There was nowhere to run, nowhere to hide.

Breathing fast, she backed up and found herself pressed against the wall with MacKinnon looming over her.

This close he was overwhelming. He also reeked of wine, and Ella noted that his gaze was glassy. He'd come here on a drunken impulse, one he was likely to regret come morning. She had to convince him to leave.

"Please go," Ella gasped out the words, hating how nervous she sounded. "Ye shouldn't be in here."

"This is my broch," he drawled before reaching out and stroking her cheek. "I decide where I'm permitted to enter." His grin widened. "Ye are a pretty one ... too bonny to give yerself to God."

Ella froze, her jaw clenching. His touch made her skin crawl, as did the feral look in his eyes.

"I've always been fascinated with nuns," he continued, oblivious to her reaction, or perhaps not caring. "Ye are forbidden, with yer pious faces and secretive ways ... but I know the truth. Behind closed doors, ye are all whores."

Anger started to pulse within Ella's breast, a living thing that wouldn't be quietened. *How dare he?*

MacKinnon stepped closer still, his muscular body pushing her hard against the wall. She felt his arousal pressing against her lower belly and panic surged.

"There's a lass at Kilbride," the clan-chief whispered. "Lady Leanna MacDonald of Sleat ... do ye know her?"

The question caught Ella off guard. Her hand was inching down, gathering the material of her habit so that she could reach the knife she always carried strapped to her left calf. But his words stalled her.

"Aye," she replied cautiously. "Why?"

"She was promised to me," MacKinnon growled. His hand slid down Ella's jaw to her neck, before the fingers splayed across her throat. "Before I wed Siusan."

Ella stilled as she remembered the conversation she'd had with Sister Leanna nearly two years earlier. Like Mother Shona and Sister Coira, she knew the reason behind the young woman's arrival at Kilbride. It was to avoid this man.

"That's right." MacKinnon's mouth twisted. "We were to wed, Lady Leanna and I ... but her father came between us." His hand tightened around Ella's throat then. "I want ye to give the lass a message for me. Will ye?"

Ella swallowed. The pressure on her neck was getting uncomfortable, and the look on his face scared her. She wanted to deny him, but she knew to do so would be foolish. "Aye," she whispered.

"Good," MacKinnon murmured. He leaned forward, trailing his lips down Ella's cheek. "Tell Leanna that I'm free to wed again ... tell her that I'm coming for her, and that the walls of Kilbride will not stop me from taking what is mine."

Horror bubbled up within Ella. His wife and son had only just been laid to rest. In the space of a day, he'd become a widower, and all he could think about was having Sister Leanna.

Beast.

His fingers tightened around Ella's throat. "Will ye tell her that?"

Ella nodded.

"Say the words, swear ye will tell her," he snarled.

"I swear," Ella rasped. His grip was so tight on her neck she could barely breathe. "I will tell her."

A hungry smile spread across Duncan MacKinnon's face. "That's a good lass. Ye are the biddable sort ... I like that." His free hand reached up and grabbed her breast through her habit, squeezing hard. "Ye have a lush body under yer crow's garb too ... I like that even more."

The panic that had been simmering within Ella exploded, and she realized with sickening certainty that he was going to rape her—right here against the wall in her bed-chamber—unless she did something to stop him.

Ella moved.

She dropped her weight, dragging him down with her, while her left hand grasped beneath the layers of her habit and underskirts to the knife hidden beneath them. Whipping the blade free, she stabbed him in the chest.

The look of surprise on Duncan MacKinnon's face would have been comical, if she hadn't been so scared.

He reeled back, mouth gaping. In an instant he released his grip on her neck, and Ella slipped past him, making for the door.

But MacKinnon was a warrior. He'd fought in battles and had no doubt taken wounds before. As such, he recovered with frightening swiftness.

Cursing, he yanked the blade free, flinging it away from him. It clattered to the flagstone floor. MacKinnon staggered and lunged for her, blocking Ella's way out.

She needed to reach for another knife, but unlike when she traveled, she only kept one blade on her indoors. The others sat in her satchel beside the bed.

Flying across the room, Ella grabbed a large clay jug full of water.

MacKinnon gripped her round the waist and hauled her back toward him. Ella twisted and hurled the jug at his head.

It smashed across the clan-chief's skull, bringing him down like a charging boar gored by a pike.

Duncan MacKinnon crashed to the floor.

Trembling, Ella stood there a moment, staring down at him.

Dear Lord, preserve me ... have I killed him?

No—he was breathing.

A mix of panic and relief swept over Ella. She glanced around her, frozen in place for an instant. She couldn't think what to do. Fear turned her witless, and then as she took in one deep breath and then another, she was able to move.

Heart pounding, she grabbed her satchel and made for the door. She didn't stop to check on MacKinnon on the way, or even to retrieve the blade that lay on the floor behind the unconscious clan-chief. It was too risky. She needed to get out of this chamber, and far from MacKinnon, before he awoke.

21

In the Dead of Night

GAVIN WAS JUST drifting off to sleep when someone shook him awake.

In an instant he lashed out, his fingers fastening around a slender arm. The gasp that followed made the last vestiges of sleep fall away.

"Ella?"

"Aye," she said, her voice tight with pain. "Please let go of me ... ye will break my wrist."

In the pale glow of the nearby hearth, Ella's face was pale and taut, her gaze wide with fear.

Gavin abruptly let go of her wrist, and she stepped back, rubbing it gently. "I'm sorry." Gavin ran a hand over his face. "Reflexes, I'm afraid." He observed her once more. She wore her satchel slung across her front, and despite that her habit covered her from head-to-toe, Gavin saw that Ella was trembling. "What's wrong?"

"MacKinnon just attacked me." The words tumbled out of her. "In my bed-chamber. I stabbed him and knocked him out with a jug of water ... but he's bound to wake up soon. We need to go ... now."

For a heartbeat Gavin merely stared at her—and then fury hammered into him like a sledge hammer to the chest.

With a curse, he swung his legs over the bed and stood up.

And then he froze.

Like most folk, Gavin slept naked.

Ella was staring at him. And as the moment drew out, her gaze slid down the length of him. It was not an innocent gaze, but one that had known carnal desire, the look of a woman capable of great passion.

Yet she didn't utter a word. And as Gavin watched her, Ella's throat bobbed. "Ye should get dressed," she said huskily, a pleading note in her voice.

Gavin drew in a deep breath. Anger pulsed within him; all he could think about was finding MacKinnon and beating him to death. Clothes hardly seemed to matter.

Looking around, Ella spied his braies and léine slung over the back of a chair. She grabbed them and handed them to him, her gaze averted now. However, Gavin saw the pink stain that colored her cheeks.

Gavin took the clothing and started to dress. "That piece of dung," he snarled as he laced his braies and grabbed his boots. "I'm going to rip him apart."

"No!" Ella gasped, rushing forward. "Please, Gavin." She placed her hands upon his bare chest, her sea-blue eyes glistening. "We need to go ... gather Ceard and the others and ride. We must get away from here."

"I'm not leaving without getting my reckoning against that bastard."

"Ye will only make the situation worse."

"I'll make him wish he'd never been born."

"Ye will destroy relations between yer clans ... because of me. I can't let ye do that. It's bad enough that I have to involve ye in my escape."

They stared at each other for a long moment, before he growled a response. "I don't care about that." Gavin reached up, placing his hands upon Ella's shoulders. He could feel the tremors that wracked her. She was terrified. "Did he hurt ye?"

She shook her head. "I stabbed him before he had the chance." Her fingertips splayed across his chest, and she pressed into him. Her touch was a brand upon his skin. Did she have any idea what it did to him?

"I beg ye, Gavin," she gasped. "Leave yer need for reckoning. Take me away from Dunan, away from that man, before it's too late."

The desperation in her voice cut him to the quick. He hated to see her like this. What had MacKinnon said and done to make her so afraid?

"This doesn't end here, Ella," he said, his voice hoarse with the anger that still pulsed in time with his heartbeat. "MacKinnon's not going to get away with this."

She nodded. "And he shouldn't ... but right now, we must go."

They stared at each other for long moment, and then, reluctantly, Gavin nodded.

A waxing gibbous moon lit the way as the MacNichol party clattered under Dunan's south gate and into the night.

The guards had let Gavin pass without argument. He was a clan-chief after all and had told them that urgent news had reached him by carrier pigeon, calling him back to Scorrybreac.

Ella rode behind Gavin and Ceard. The cool night air kissed her face, and she drew in great lungfuls of it. Never had she been so grateful to leave a place. As beautiful as Dunan was, the broch was rotten at its heart.

The man who ruled it was poison.

Tell Leanna that I'm free to wed again ... tell her that I'm coming for her, and that the walls of Kilbride will not stop me from taking what is mine.

MacKinnon's rasped words echoed in Ella's mind, tormenting her. She'd said nothing of his whispered threat, or of the ugly things he'd said, to Gavin. MacNichol needed reasons *not* to kill MacKinnon. Telling him what had happened in that chamber would have ensured that he murdered the man.

Part of Ella wanted MacKinnon dead. The clan-chief was dangerous; the air inside her bed-chamber had crackled with menace the moment he'd stepped into it. He was twisted, cruel, and manipulative. Nothing good could come from letting such a man live.

Yet she was a nun. For years now the abbess had shown her the way of forgiveness, of peace.

We only use weapons to defend ourselves, Mother Shona had told the sisters sternly during arm's practice. *We never strike out in rage, or for vengeance, for that makes us no better than those who seek to do us harm.*

Ella knew the abbess had spoken true. But more than that, she didn't want Gavin to get into trouble. Even if he were to cut MacKinnon down in righteous rage, the other chiefs weren't likely to see things his way, and nor were MacKinnon's family and retainers.

She wouldn't have Gavin put his own life at risk for her.

Ella didn't glance over her shoulder as she rode, even though she felt the weight of Dunan at her back. With each furlong that Monadh's feathered hooves ate up, the shroud of anxiety that had been smothering her gradually lifted.

Around her the moon cast its hoary light over a wild, mountainous landscape. They left the dense forest of conifers behind and entered a bare, bleak valley. Great sculpted peaks rose either side, dwarfing the party. Ella was grateful for the moonlight, for without it they would have had difficulty traveling. Even so, Ceard and two other warriors carried flaming torches aloft, illuminating their path further.

None of the MacNichol party spoke as they rode west. Ceard and the two others had been hauled from their beds and told they were leaving. There had been some grumbling in the stables, yet the men had followed his orders anyway.

They understood that if Gavin MacNichol needed to depart urgently in the dead of night, he had good reason.

Ella's attention shifted to Gavin's back, and an image of him standing naked before her in his chamber flashed across her mind.

The Lord strike her down, he'd been magnificent.

His body was long and well-muscled, but it was the body of a mature man, and a number of fine, pale scars traced his torso. The glow from the nearby hearth had kissed his naked, golden skin, and for a long moment, Ella had merely devoured the sight of him.

Shoving the image from her mind, Ella squeezed her eyes shut. She needed to forget she'd ever seen that.

The sight of Kilbride Abbey, silhouetted against the lightening sky, made Ella's vision mist with tears. Relief swamped her, drowning out the fatigue of the past few hours. They had ridden with barely a break all night in order to reach their destination.

The high walls, made of a grey local granite, gleamed when the first rays of sun touched them. A chorus of birdsong accompanied the riders as they slowed their mounts to a walk and approached the gates. Drawing near, Ella reflected how well fortified the abbey was. Mother Shona, having already lived through a brutal attack on her previous abbey, had been determined to keep raiders out; as such, the nuns had hired men from Torrin to dig a deep ditch around the base of the abbey's walls. The walls themselves were around twenty foot high, as were the heavy oak and iron gates that barred their way inside.

Reaching the gates, Ella dismounted and walked to where a heavy iron knocker hung.

She lifted the knocker, letting it fall three times. Touching it was enough for sanctuary, had she been pursued, but Ella would not rest until she was indoors.

None of the party accompanying her spoke as they waited for someone to answer her knocking. Gavin had been worryingly silent on the way here; and whenever Ella glanced his way, she'd seen that he wore an unusually stern expression, his eyes narrowed.

He was angry; she could feel waves of ire emanating from him.

Nerves twisted in her gut as she realized he wasn't going to let this go. Duncan MacKinnon had just made an enemy of clan MacNichol.

And although she knew she wasn't to blame for MacKinnon's behavior, Ella still felt responsible for this turn of events.

If Gavin hadn't brought her with him to Dunan, this would never have happened.

Ella shook her head, irritated by the direction of her thoughts. Life was full of turning points. The Lord's will worked in ways she'd never really understood, despite her many years of prayer and contemplation.

At that moment a sound of iron scraping against iron echoed through the still morning, and a small window opened around five and a half feet from the ground. A middle-aged woman, with a harassed expression, peered out into the dawn.

"Sister Elspeth," Ella greeted the nun, stepping forward. "Good morning."

Sister Elspeth's gaze widened. "Sister Annella?" Her attention then shifted to the party of men still astride their horses behind her. "Did ye ride through the night to reach us?"

Ella nodded, noting the acerbic edge to the nun's voice. She and Sister Elspeth had never gotten along. Elspeth had just taken her vow of perpetuity when Ella arrived at Kilbride. And after the events of the months that followed, in which Ella lived as a postulant, Sister Elspeth had viewed the young woman with disapproval.

That same censure lay in her eyes now.

An awkward silence fell, and then behind Ella, Gavin cleared his throat. "Are ye going to let us in, Sister?" he asked, irritation edging his voice. "My men have been traveling without rest for hours now. We'd like to stable our mounts and have some beer and bread to break our fast."

Sister Elspeth's mouth pursed, and then she drew back, slamming the iron window shut.

Moments later the clunk of the locks releasing broke the morning's stillness.

Ella didn't bother to remount Monadh. Instead, she led him into the abbey, entering a wide yard, flanked by stables on one side and the guest house on the other.

Before them rose Kilbride kirk, tall and proud, its steep roof standing out against the pale sky. The sight of it made Ella smile.

I'm home.

22

It's Not My Secret to Tell

ELLA'S RELIEF DIDN'T last for long.

Mother Shona met Gavin and Ella in the chapter house, while the rest of the MacNichol party stabled their horses and went to the refectory to eat and drink.

Gavin and Ella would have to wait in order to break their fast.

The abbess listened in silence as Ella recounted the tale of what had befallen her the night before. But, like she had with Gavin, Ella left out MacKinnon's message for Sister Leanna.

Ella wasn't sure exactly why, but instinct told her to keep those details private. She needed to see Sister Leanna herself, for MacKinnon's words alarmed her greatly.

When Ella told of how MacKinnon had shoved her up against the wall and started to grope her, the temperature dropped inside the chapter house.

Gavin's gaze burned, a nerve ticking in one cheek. She'd never seen him like this. Gavin had always been so level-headed, never prone to the explosive temper she'd seen in other men over the years.

Likewise, Mother Shona's brown eyes narrowed, her usually soft-featured face turning hard.

And when Ella told her how she'd stabbed MacKinnon before knocking him out with a blow to the head from a heavy clay jug, the abbess's gaze gleamed.

"We have taught ye well, Sister Ella," she murmured after Ella concluded the tale.

"No, it was *ye* who taught me," Ella replied, a lump rising in her throat. Now that the ordeal was over and she was out of danger, the urge to weep rose up within her. With difficulty, she pushed it down, swallowing hard. "MacKinnon would have raped me, if ye hadn't shown me how to wield a blade."

"Sister Ella showed her skill on the journey north too," Gavin said, speaking for the first time since they'd entered the chapter house. His voice held a rough edge to it. "We were set upon by thieves, and she brought a number of them down ... and saved my life."

Mother Shona's eyes widened at this news. However, the woman swiftly recovered. Her gaze, when it settled upon Ella, was grave.

"Ye did what ye had to, Sister Ella," she began softly. "MacKinnon would have raped ye otherwise ... but I'm afraid ye cannot remain at Kilbride now."

The words, even though gently spoken, hit Ella like a backhand across the face. She stepped back from the abbess, her lips parting in shock.

"What?"

The abbess shook her head. Her gaze was shadowed, although she wore a determined expression. With a sinking feeling, Ella realized that the abbess—a woman she had long considered a friend—would no longer protect her.

"But I've taken my vows of perpetuity," Ella continued, her voice rising. "Ye can't cast me out."

"Kilbride sits on MacKinnon lands, Sister Ella," the abbess replied firmly. "We cannot risk turning the clan-chief against us or we will lose his protection. He will seek ye here ... and will demand I hand ye over to him."

"Ye could refuse," Gavin interjected.

The abbess glanced over at the MacNichol clan-chief, her expression hardening. "I could," she replied coolly.

"But how would that go for us, do ye think? I have an obligation to the nuns who reside here. I must think of their safety."

Gavin held her gaze. "Ye could hold the abbey ... my men and I will remain here to help ye."

"No!" The word burst out of Ella. Panic curled up through her belly now, making her breathing come in short gasps. "I won't have ye all put yerselves at risk."

Gavin cast Ella a dark look. "I'm tired of hearing ye say that ... I shall decide whether or not a situation is worth risking me and my men over."

Ella held his gaze, her heart hammering now. She felt sick. Her relief at returning to Kilbride had shattered; nowhere seemed safe anymore. She had been innocent to believe MacKinnon wouldn't come after her, wouldn't demand the abbess hand her over.

Of course he would.

I should have killed him.

Ella clenched her hands at her sides. "No," she growled the word. "I will go."

"Sister Ella." Mother Shona stepped forward and reached out, grasping her hands. "If ye leave Kilbride, I don't mean ye to fend for yerself in the wild. Ye will need protection." The abbess cast a look at Gavin then, her expression imploring. "Will ye take her in?"

Gavin's face went taut. "Excuse me?"

Impatience flared in the abbess's eyes. "Will ye wed her?"

It was Gavin's turn to look as if he'd been struck across the face. In the meantime, Ella was so shocked that she couldn't even speak. She merely stared at Mother Shona as if she'd lost her wits.

"I can't wed a *nun*," Gavin finally rasped. "It's forbidden."

"Ella will no longer be part of this order," the abbess countered. "I shall cast her out this very morning."

"For what?" Ella gasped, horrified by the abbess's brutality. All these years at Kilbride, and she'd thought they'd become close friends. Yet now that her precious abbey was threatened, the abbess wanted Ella gone.

Mother Shona shifted her attention back to Ella. "I will tell the other nuns that ye have broken yer vow of chastity ... that ye have fallen in love with MacNichol and gone to live with him as his wife."

A stunned silence followed these words.

Ella tore her hands from the abbess's and drew back from her.

She knows.

Ella had been careful, all those years ago, never to utter a word about the man who'd broken her heart, the man who'd driven her to choose a life of seclusion.

But as she stared at Mother Shona, she realized that perhaps having seen Ella and Gavin interact, the abbess had guessed the truth.

"It's a lie," Gavin said quietly. "Ella hasn't broken any vows."

The abbess ignored him; instead, her attention remained upon Ella. "He doesn't know, does he?"

Ella's breathing hitched, and hot panic surged. She felt as if she were balancing upon a knife-edge with an abyss yawning below her. "Ye are not to say a word, Mother Shona," she said hoarsely. "Ye promised."

"And I will not," the abbess replied, her gaze shadowing, "but ye should ... it is time, Ella."

Ella. Not Sister Ella. Already she was out of the fold; already cast out of the order she'd devoted her life to for so many years.

"What are ye speaking of?" Gavin asked, his voice was low, wary.

Ella didn't look his way; she didn't dare. Instead, she backed up, never taking her gaze from the abbess. Suddenly, her life was falling to pieces before her eyes. Everything she'd worked so hard to hide was about to be exposed. Her life was about to be shattered to pieces.

She couldn't bear it.

With a sob, Ella turned and fled the chapter house.

Gavin watched Ella leave. But instead of following her, he turned to Mother Shona.

Their conversation had both alarmed and confused him. He felt as if he was lagging behind, grasping at snippets of details that meant nothing to him.

He needed some answers.

"I don't understand." Gavin fixed the abbess with a hard stare. "What should Ella tell me?"

Mother Shona dragged in a deep breath. "This is not how it should be told ... by right ye were never to know."

Dread twisted Gavin's gut, although he masked it with a scowl. "Know what?"

The abbess shook her head. "It's not my secret to tell."

Gavin's heart started to pound against his ribs. *Secret?*

Their gazes fused for a long moment, before Mother Shona exhaled sharply. "Go after Ella and ask her."

Gavin nodded and moved toward the door.

"Wait," the abbess's voice halted him, and he turned to see that she was watching him, sadness etched upon her proud face. "Ye will find her in the graveyard."

Kilbride's graveyard was a small space, encircled by a neatly trimmed hawthorn hedge. Rows of grey headstones thrust out of the grass like small stumpy teeth. At the far end of the yard grew a large shady yew.

And under that tree stood a small robed figure.

Ella's back was to Gavin as he approached. Her shoulders were hunched, revealing her misery.

Gavin slowed his step. He hated to see Ella like this. He'd witnessed her control begin to unravel at Scorrybreac after her mother's death. He couldn't bear to see Ella that upset again.

As he neared her, Gavin saw that Ella stood before a low grassy mound that lay under the spreading branches of the yew.

"Ella?" he said her name softly, hoping that she would not flee.

He wondered if she had even heard him. Ella's head was bowed, her arms folded across her chest in a protective gesture.

Stepping up next to her, Gavin shifted his attention to her profile. Ella's cheeks were wet. She wept silently, her gaze riveted upon the mound at her feet.

"Ella," he whispered. "Please talk to me."

She heard him that time. Ella's eyelids fluttered closed, and she dipped her chin, taking a long, shuddering breath.

"They couldn't give him a gravestone." Her voice was faint, broken. "For he was born out of wedlock."

Gavin went cold. He tore his gaze from Ella's profile to the mound. It was a tiny grave, one that sat apart from the others in the yard. Gavin's throat closed up then, his heart thudding against his breastbone like a battle drum. And when Ella spoke again, he felt as if someone had just driven a blade under his ribs.

"This is our son's resting place, Gavin."

23

Second Chances

IN AN INSTANT, Gavin MacNichol's world tilted.

A son.

It hurt to breathe, hurt to think. For a few long moments, he was lost in a churning sea of pain and regret. And when he finally recovered the power of speech, Gavin's voice didn't sound like his own. It was raw, edged with grief.

"Why did ye never tell me?"

"Ye were wed to my sister by the time I realized I was with bairn," Ella whispered. "My courses have never been that regular ... it was only when I couldn't face my morning bread and beer that I realized something had changed." She paused there. "The healer from Torrin confirmed that my womb had quickened."

Gavin stared at her, his thoughts churning. "And the abbess allowed ye to remain here?"

Ella huffed out a laugh. There was no mirth in it, just sadness. "Aye ... she told me that I could take my vows once the bairn was born, and that if it was a girl she could be brought up as an oblate within the abbey walls."

"And if it was a lad?"

"When the bairn was old enough, we would take him south to the monks upon Iona, where he would be brought up."

Silence fell between them then, broken only by the impatient bleating of goats in the enclosure to the east of the graveyard. They were awaiting milking. Neither Gavin nor Ella paid them any mind.

Gavin didn't speak. Instead, he waited for Ella to tell him the rest of the story. He didn't want to hear it, and yet he knew he had to know every last painful detail.

"It was a hard time for me," Ella said after a long pause. "I carried the bairn uneasily." She dipped her head further, her features growing taut. "I was upset when I arrived at Kilbride ... full of grief, anger ... and fear. The birth was long and painful ... and when the bairn came, he was stillborn." Her voice caught as she said those last words, revealing that although many years had passed, Ella still carried the sorrow within her.

They'd just come from Dunan and the death of both MacKinnon's wife and son. Gavin realized what painful memories it must have brought back for Ella.

Bile rose, stinging the back of Gavin's throat. "I should have been there for ye, Ella," he finally managed. "Ye shouldn't have had to deal with all of that on yer own."

Ella opened her eyes and raised her chin. "Ye made yer choice, Gavin, and I made mine," she replied huskily. "I told myself when I came to Kilbride that I would sever all ties to my old life. I never told anyone here who the father of the bairn was."

"But the abbess—"

"She's a canny woman ... she probably guessed when ye came to collect me."

Gavin heaved in a deep, steadying breath. The anguish her news had roused in him was an open wound. He didn't know what to say, what to do. Hunkering down, he placed a hand over the top of the low mound.

"I don't suppose ye gave him a name?" he asked softly.

"The sisters told me not to," she whispered back. "But I ignored their advice. I named him Finn ... after my grandfather."

Sorrow rose within Gavin, wreathing up inside him like winter mist. He could not stop it, could not prevent the tears that forced their way out and trickled down his cheeks.

Finn.

He and Innis had never been able to have children. And perhaps if he hadn't abandoned Ella, let her flee Scorrybreac, their son might have lived.

"I'm so sorry," he whispered. But the words weren't enough, and the moment they passed his lips, Gavin regretted them. An apology wouldn't erase the stain of the past, wouldn't change what had befallen Ella. "I want to make amends for this," he continued, his voice ragged now. "I want to ensure that ye never suffer again."

"Enough." A small hand caught his. Ella had crouched down next to him, and she squeezed his hand tightly. "Blaming yerself is useless. I chose to lie with ye ... even though I knew ye were promised to my sister ... we must both bear responsibility for the past. And we must both let it lie." She paused then. "It's as yer clan motto says: 'Remember but look ahead.' ... we should both do that."

Gavin tore his gaze from the grave and met Ella's eye. She too wept. Her blue eyes were red rimmed, her lovely face strained. And yet there was strength in her; there had always been strength.

"Ella." Gavin swiveled around, catching her hands in his. "The abbess is right ... ye need to leave here. MacKinnon will follow us ... he will have his men search Kilbride. He will deal with ye harshly if he finds ye. The only way ye will stay safe is under my protection. Let me look after ye, as I should have done years ago." Gavin heaved in a deep breath, holding her gaze firm. "Will ye be my wife?"

Ella stared back at him. After a long moment, her mouth quirked into a watery, melancholy smile. "Years ago I used to imagine what a proposal from ye might be like … but I never envisioned this … ye asking me to become yer wife to save me from the hangman's noose."

"Ye think that's why I ask?" Gavin moved toward her then, dropping onto his knees, his grip on her hands tightening. "That I'm doing this out of a sense of obligation?"

Her throat bobbed. "Aren't ye? Ye were always a good man, Gavin … ye have always sought to do what was right."

Her words cut deep. Yet he deserved them. Indeed, he'd spent his life following the rules his forefathers had set out. He'd lived in fear of disappointing those who'd never had his best interests at heart.

"I'm asking ye to be my wife because I love ye, Ella." The words were soft, barely above a whisper. "I've never stopped loving ye." He broke off there, wishing he was more eloquent, that he could express himself better, but it felt as if an iron band gripped him about the throat and was slowly squeezing. "Fate is giving us a second chance … and this time I will not turn my back upon it."

Silence fell between them. Ella did not answer; she merely stared back at him, her blue eyes glistening with tears.

Gavin inhaled slowly. He felt ripped apart, close to pleading, yet he prevented himself. "Will ye be my wife, Ella?"

Another pause stretched out, and Gavin felt sure that her silence was damning. It was too late. They'd both gone too far upon their chosen paths to change course now. Ella would leave Kilbride, but not to wed him.

But then Ella offered him a watery smile. It was like watching the sun emerge after a dull day of low cloud and biting wind. Her smile bathed him, soothed his aching soul. "Aye," she whispered. "I will."

Ella paced the chapter house, awaiting the arrival of Sister Leanna and Sister Coira. She was to leave Kilbride in secret, but when Ella had begged Mother Shona to allow her to say goodbye to her two closest friends at the abbey, the abbess had finally relented.

It was to be a hurried farewell, but Ella was relieved she would be permitted to have it.

Leaving Kilbride was unthinkable. She felt as if she'd strayed into a dark dream.

The chapter house door creaked open, and two black garbed figures appeared: one small and slight, the other tall and broad-shouldered.

"Sister Ella!" The shock in Leanna's voice nearly made Ella smile. "Why aren't ye dressed in yer habit?"

Ella turned to face her friends. She was sure she presented an odd sight indeed. It had been so many years since she had dressed in common-place garb that she felt as if she stood naked before them. The clothes she had arrived at the abbey in had long been given away to the poor. Ella stood before them in far humbler clothing: a plain ankle-length léine covered with a kirtle made of faded blue plaid, laced across the bodice. Around her shoulders she wore a threadbare woolen shawl. Her head was uncovered, her hair braided down her back.

"It's just Ella now," she replied, before attempting a smile. She was sure the expression was more of a grimace. "I'm leaving the order."

Both women gaped at her. Sister Coira's lips parted, her violet eyes growing huge. "But how is that possible? Ye have taken yer vows of perpetuity ... they cannot be broken."

Ella sighed. "Apparently they can, if a nun has broken her vows and does not intend to repent for them."

The color drained from Sister Leanna's face at this admission. "Mother Mary," she whispered, aghast, "what have ye done?"

"We returned to Kilbride via Dunan," Ella replied. "There was an ... incident there. Duncan MacKinnon burst into my bed-chamber and tried to rape me. I stabbed him, knocked him out with a jug, and then fled."

Both women stared at her, shock filtering across their faces. Guilt knifed Ella. Mother Shona had told her to keep the story of what had befallen her at Dunan to herself, but Sisters Leanna and Coira were her friends; she wanted them at least to know the truth of things.

Their reactions were interesting, especially Sister Coira's. A shadow moved across her gaze, and a nerve flickered under one eye. She looked almost ... guilty. In contrast, Leanna clenched her jaw, fury tightening her face.

"That filthy bastard," Leanna growled. "I wish ye had gutted him like a pig." The words were shocking coming from one as delicate and sweet-tongued as Sister Leanna. Her sunny disposition and ready smile were what the other sisters were used to seeing—not this fierce, sharp-tongued young woman.

"That's not all," Ella continued. "MacKinnon gave me a message for ye, Sister Leanna. He said to tell ye that he's free to wed again ... he said 'tell her that I'm coming for her'." Ella paused there, hating the words she was having to relay to her friend. "He said that the walls of Kilbride will not stop him from taking what is his."

Silence followed her words. Sister Leanna reached out, grasping Sister Coira's arm for support. "He can't touch me here," she gasped out the words. "Da won't permit it."

"Of course he can't," Sister Coira soothed. However, the nun's gaze now looked haunted, her face strained. "It's just bluster."

"He *will* come looking for me here," Ella interjected. "And that is why I must go ... I just wanted to warn ye first, Sister Leanna. I hope Sister Coira is right, and that it is just an empty threat. In the meantime, ye may want to advise yer father that MacKinnon hasn't given up on taking ye as his wife."

Sister Leanna nodded, determination filtering over her face. "I will do that." She released Sister Coira's arm and stepped forward. "So this is it, Ella ... we are to never see ye again?"

Ella nodded, her throat thickening. "I'm afraid not. Gavin MacNichol has agreed to take me away ... I will wed him."

Sister Coira gasped at this news, drawing close. "What's this?" she demanded. "Ye never said anything about wedding anyone!"

Ella managed a smile then. Her admissions were shocking, and yet she had little time to explain them to her friends. Nonetheless, she would try. "Come and sit down for a few moments." She motioned to the wooden bench below the stained glass windows behind them. "I don't have much time, but ye both deserve to know the truth about me."

24

Don't Look Back

HEARING FOOTFALLS BEHIND him, Gavin turned.

A woman approached. A few feet away, Gavin heard Ceard grunt in surprise, while one of his other men murmured an oath.

Aye, it was like traveling back in time. The woman who held the skirt of her kirtle up as she crossed the dirt yard was no longer eighteen, her blue eyes brimming with excitement, but Annella Fraser still moved with unconscious grace, her head held high. The passing of time hadn't diminished her. There was a strength to her delicate face at thirty-six that had been lacking at eighteen, and a steadiness to her gaze.

Life had battered Ella, but it hadn't broken her. Instead, it had molded her.

She dressed in poor cloth, yet to Gavin she had never looked lovelier. The kirtle had once belonged to a taller, thinner woman than Ella. As such, it was slightly too tight across the bodice, straining against her full breasts, while the skirt dragged upon the ground. Around her shoulders she wore a shabby blue woolen shawl.

The yard was deserted. All the nuns, save Mother Shona, who followed behind Ella, were in the refectory consuming their noon meal.

Ella was to leave in secret, without a word to anyone except her closest friends. It was harsh, especially after all the years she'd given to the order. Yet Gavin understood why.

Nuns who had taken their perpetual vows didn't just cast aside their habits and leave the order. To be cast out was to leave under a shadow of shame.

Gavin wished he could have spared Ella this. But they couldn't risk lingering at Kilbride. With each passing hour, it became increasingly dangerous for them to remain here—both for Ella and the Sisters of Kilbride.

Approaching Gavin, Ella lifted her chin slightly and met his gaze. She then stopped and drew her threadbare shawl tightly about her, as if aware that he and his men were taken aback by her altered appearance.

It must have felt strange, to wear a kirtle again and to go about with her hair uncovered after so many years.

He stared back at her, unspeaking. He wanted to tell her how lovely she was, how the years had barely touched her. Instead, he merely held her gaze. This close, he could see that her eyes were shadowed. Leaving Kilbride was not a happy occasion.

Gavin turned to where Mother Shona drew to a halt at Ella's shoulder. The woman's face was unusually grave.

"Ye will accompany us to Torrin kirk then, Mother Shona?" he asked.

She gave a curt nod. "I must witness yer union."

Next to the abbess, Gavin saw Ella drop her gaze to the dirt. His chest constricted at the sight. This wasn't what he wanted for Ella; she was wedding him out of her own volition, yet at the same time, the union was being forced upon her.

It was either become his wife or leave the abbey without protection. If she did that, it would only be a matter of days before MacKinnon tracked her down. Wedding Gavin would give her shelter and ensure she remained safe, at Scorrybreac.

"We should hurry." The abbess moved to a shaggy grey mare that had been saddled for her. "The sooner ye are wed, the sooner ye can distance yerselves from Kilbride. MacKinnon will be on his way here by now."

Her words were a sobering reminder.

Ella's chin snapped up, her mouth thinning. Without a word, she crossed to where Gavin awaited her. They would ride together. Reaching down, Gavin took her hand. Ella then placed a foot atop his and sprang up before him. As she settled against him, her back pressing against his chest, Gavin's breathing hitched. The feel of her was distracting. Trying to ignore the quickening of his pulse, Gavin gathered the reins.

"Are ye ready?" he asked.

Ella's voice held a rueful note when she replied, "Aye … ye heard Mother Shona. MacKinnon will be here soon enough. Let's go."

Cottars working the fields on the way into Torrin glanced up from their work, gazes alight with curiosity as the party cantered up the potholed road into the village. Ella kept her gaze straight ahead, hoping that she and the abbess were hidden from view by the other riders.

Very little went unnoticed here, which wasn't a good thing, for MacKinnon would likely come to Torrin asking questions after discovering that Ella hadn't returned to Kilbride after all.

Each stride of the leggy courser brought Ella hard up against Gavin. The heat of his body enveloped her, creating sensations that were both pleasant and disturbing. She found herself wanting to lean into him but fought the urge.

Torrin kirk was a small building perched on the edge of a high cliff. The village spread out behind it, a ramshackle collection of stacked-stone cottages with thatched and turf roofs.

The priest came out to meet them, a small bald man with a sharp-featured face.

He wasn't happy about being asked to perform a wedding ceremony at such short notice, yet since the abbess herself requested it of him, he eventually acquiesced.

There was no time for preparations, no time to find a pretty gown or to weave flowers through her hair.

All the same, nervousness fluttered through Ella's belly when she walked up to the altar.

The early afternoon sun filtered in through the kirk's high windows, catching dust motes on the way down. Ella inhaled the familiar odor of tallow and incense, and her nervousness increased.

Just hours ago she'd been a nun. A kirk was a place where she served the Lord, where she knelt and prayed, and found solace from the rest of the world.

She was no longer a Sister of Kilbride, and yet in her heart little had changed. It felt wrong to be standing here with her hair uncovered wearing this ill-fitting kirtle, about to wed the man who'd broken her heart so many years earlier.

Panic gripped her chest. Dragging in a deep breath, Ella did her best to quell it.

Turning, she met the abbess's gaze and shot her a pleading look.

Mother Shona merely favored her with a soft smile, her eyes shadowed.

With a jolt, Ella realized that the abbess was putting herself, and her position, at great risk by helping her.

She was going against the rules of the Cluniac order. A nun who had taken her final vows couldn't leave the order without a long and lengthy process—one that required seeking permission from the Holy See. And since the Pope resided in faraway Rome, that could potentially take years.

They didn't have years.

The abbess was also about to go against MacKinnon— in order to protect her.

Ella's vision misted.

She would never forget Mother Shona's kindness.

The priest cleared his throat, drawing her attention back to the present. Father Gawen wore a censorious look as he gazed down upon the couple he was to wed. They had given him no details on why the union was to take place today. Nor did they tell the priest that until a few hours ago, Ella had been a Sister of Kilbride.

Even so, Father Gawen's gaze sharpened when it fastened upon Ella. "I recognize yer face," he murmured. "Have we met before?"

Of course, they had, albeit briefly. Ella had seen the priest at spring and harvest fairs in the village over the years, although they had never spoken.

"I think not, Father," she replied, dropping her gaze to the dusty stone pavers that lined the kirk floor.

"Can we start the ceremony now please, Father?" Gavin's voice held a note of impatience. "We have a long road to travel this afternoon."

Father Gawen's mouth thinned at this, although he minded his tongue. Mother Shona had already introduced them as Clan-chief MacNichol and Lady Annella Fraser. As such, the priest was wary of offending Gavin.

"Very well," he replied, his brow furrowing. "Join hands, and we shall begin."

Ella walked out of the kirk with a new identity. No longer was she Sister Ella of Kilbride, or even Lady Annella Fraser. Now, she held the title of Lady Ella MacNichol of Scorrybreac.

Blinking as the bright sunlight assaulted her eyes, Ella glanced around her. There was a magnificent view from the cliff top. To the north the charcoal peaks of the Black Cuillins stood out against a soft blue sky, whereas a craggy coastline stretched south. The waters of the sea were flat and glassy this afternoon. Out of the sun, the air was cool and the breeze had a nip to it; yet staring out at the view, Ella could have been fooled into thinking that they were still in the midst of summer.

"Ready to go ... Lady MacNichol?"

Ella turned to find Gavin standing behind her. Even tired, anxious, and travel-stained, the sight of him made excitement flicker low in her belly.

Her husband.

As Father Gawen had wound the length of plaid around their joined hands and murmured the words that bound them in wedlock, the reality of the situation had finally sunk in.

She once dreamed of becoming Gavin MacNichol's wife. When she'd been young and foolish, she'd lain in her bed at night imagining the day of their wedding. There would be music—a harpist would play all day—and they would wed in spring when the first of the roses bloomed. She would weave meadow-flowers through her unbound hair and wear a wedding gown of shimmering emerald green with matching slippers upon her feet. Their wedding banquet would be a meal that folk would talk about for years to come, with a roasted and stuffed swan as the centerpiece. And that night she and Gavin would make love upon a bed strewn with scented rose petals.

All those dreams seemed to belong to a goose-witted lass now.

None of it mattered one bit.

She was sad that this was how it had turned out. Life wasn't like the songs the traveling minstrels sang. Gavin was a widower, and his late wife had been her sister. No minstrel would sing such a song.

"Aye," Ella replied. "But I would like to say farewell to the abbess first, if I may?"

Gavin nodded, stepping aside to let Mother Shona approach. "I will go and ready the horses."

He walked away, leaving the two women to speak in private.

Mother Shona's eyes gleamed as she moved close to Ella. Wordlessly, she reached out and took hold of Ella's hands, squeezing them tight.

"I'm sorry, lass," she whispered. "I know ye must think I am casting ye out without a thought." Her voice caught then. "But I can think of no other way to save ye. May the Lord watch over ye in the days to come."

"And may God keep ye and the Sisters of Kilbride safe, Mother Shona," Ella replied. "I know why ye must do this … and it is I who must beg forgiveness. I have brought MacKinnon's wrath to Kilbride. Maybe I should have killed him while I had the chance."

Mother Shona shook her head. "No … ye aren't a killer, Ella. Ye hurt him in self-defense, but if ye had taken a knife to his throat while he lay insensible upon the floor, that would make ye a murderer. The other clan-chiefs and chieftains of this isle would put a price upon yer head for such an act."

A shiver passed through Ella at the abbess's words. She was right. This way at least only MacKinnon was after her.

"I'll never be able to return to Kilbride, will I?" she asked softly.

"No, lass … not while MacKinnon still lives." The abbess released her hands and reached up to cup Ella's face. "But don't ye worry about that … it's time for ye to begin a new life, Lady Ella MacNichol. Seize it with both hands and don't look back."

25

Where is she?

MOTHER SHONA, ABBESS of Kilbride, arrived back at the abbey just in time for Vespers. She quickly saw to her pony and strode to the kirk, where the nuns were already gathering for the service.

Reaching the altar, the abbess smoothed sweaty palms upon her habit. She'd been dreading this moment. All the way back from Torrin, she'd gone over the words she would say to the sisters. None of them were adequate.

She couldn't speak the truth. The only way they would accept that Sister Ella had left them was to cast the woman in a dark light, to speak lies about her.

Of course, Sisters Leanna and Coira both knew the truth. Ella had told her that she'd confided in them both. However, she'd sworn them to secrecy.

Reaching up, the abbess's fingers clasped around the heavy iron crucifix that hung about her neck.

Forgive me Lord ... I do this for the greater good. I do this to protect these women.

When the last of the sisters had filed into the kirk and knelt ready to begin Vespers, Mother Shona cleared her throat.

"Before we begin the service, I have ill-tidings to share with ye." The abbess's voice echoed through the quiet kirk. "Sister Annella has left the order."

As expected, a gasp followed this news. Some of the sisters—the younger ones especially—merely gaped at her, while many of the older nuns—those who had been here before Ella's arrival and knew of her sad story—developed hard, pinched expressions.

A few of them, Sister Elspeth for one, had been vocal in their disapproval of Ella when it had been discovered that their new postulant was with child. The fact that the young woman remained tight-lipped as to the identity of the father of the bairn only made the older nuns suspect her further.

Ella had weathered their displeasure and eventually blossomed at Kilbride. Yet the abbess saw vindication flare in Sister Elspeth's eyes now.

"She has broken her vow of chastity," the abbess continued. It was a falsehood, and one that galled her to speak, yet it was a necessary one. "Not only that, but she does not repent ... she has wed MacNichol and is now his wife."

Even Sister Elspeth looked shocked. Mother Shona deliberately avoided looking at Sisters Leanna and Coira as she spoke. They alone knew the truth. She'd explained to them why it had to be this way, yet she didn't want to see the disappointment in their faces.

She hoped they understood why she had to do this.

But even if they didn't, it still had to be done. She'd bent many rules since becoming Abbess of Kilbride, had shaped the life here so that the sisters could live to their fullest potential while serving God. But she'd not risk the future unity of this order for one woman.

"It's forbidden to wed!" Sister Magda burst out. The old woman's dark eyes burned as she lurched to her feet, Vespers forgotten. "No priest will agree to it."

"No priest *knowingly* would, Sister Magda," the abbess replied, her voice deliberately calm. "But Sister Ella sinned again by not revealing who she was."

"But the union isn't valid!" Sister Elspeth exploded. She too rose to her feet, hands clenched by her sides. "The woman is a harlot, a fornicator, a—"

"Enough, Sister Elspeth!" Mother Shona's voice, harsh now, cut through the kirk, silencing the nun. This was exactly what she'd hoped to avoid. She'd not have the likes of Sister Elspeth stirring up ill-feeling inside the abbey. "Sister Ella has chosen her path, and I have made my decision. I have cast her from the order."

Silence settled after this proclamation.

It was unheard of, for the abbess to do such a thing. Usually, if a nun broke any of her vows, she was brought back into the fold and taught the error of her ways. Once a nun took her final vows, it was a lifetime's promise. It was a harsh choice indeed, for the abbess to cast her out.

Many of the nuns were watching her now with wary, frightened gazes. Would she do the same thing to them if they ever erred?

Something twisted deep within Mother Shona's chest. Again, she'd hoped to avoid this. All she could believe was that she had committed the lesser of two evils.

"There is something else ye should all know," she said, breaking the heavy silence. "Sister Annella has managed to fall foul of Duncan MacKinnon. I don't know the details, but he tried to force himself upon her ... and she fought back and stabbed him. He will come here, looking for her. None of ye are to speak a word about Sister Annella to him."

A beat of shocked silence passed.

"If MacKinnon asks whether ye have seen her, or if ye know where she is, ye are to answer 'nay'." The abbess's voice hardened now. "Is that clear?"

"Aye, Mother Shona." A chorus of cowed female voices answered her.

Guilt had tightened into a hard knot in the base of Mother Shona's belly when she emerged from the kirk. God would punish her for the sins she'd committed today, she was sure of it. Earlier in the day, she'd been so firm in her decision, so sure she was doing the right thing. Yet, seeing the alarm, fear, and wariness on the faces of the women she'd sworn to protect, she realized she'd failed.

Had she done the right thing throwing Ella into Gavin MacNichol's arms?

They'd been lovers once, and judging from the way they still looked at each other, that sentiment hadn't disappeared. Gavin gazed upon Ella in a way that made sadness quicken in the abbess's breast.

Many years earlier, in another life, a man had once looked at her like that.

The moment she'd seen Ella and Gavin together in the chapter house when he'd come to take her back to her dying mother, all the missing pieces in the puzzle that was Sister Ella had fallen into place.

She'd known then that MacNichol was the father of Ella's child.

The sadness that had cloaked Ella during her first months at Kilbride had been painful to see. Each morning the young woman appeared with a face swollen from weeping, while she moved through the day, through prayers and chores, as if she were sleep-walking. And when she'd discovered she was with bairn, she'd been inconsolable.

Mother Shona had asked Ella to tell her the name of the child's father—perhaps he could have helped. But Ella had been vehement in her refusal. The abbess had known then that the young woman bore a secret she would never share with her or the other sisters.

I've given her another chance, the abbess told herself as she stepped outside into the soft evening light. *But a price had to be paid in order to do so.*

The nuns went to wash up for supper, while Mother Shona took a walk in the gardens. She needed to be alone with her thoughts for a short while, to form a plan for the days that lay ahead. It would be a trying time for them all.

Deep in her own cares, the abbess circuited the neatly tended rows of kale and onions. It was only when a voice hailed her that she emerged from the fog of her thoughts.

Sister Firtha was hurrying toward her. The tall, lanky young woman, who was still a novice at the abbey, wore a strained expression, her eyes huge on a lean face.

The abbess stopped walking, turning to meet her.

"Abbess!" Sister Firtha called out once more. "We have visitors ... MacKinnon has just entered the abbey and is demanding to see ye."

Mother Shona walked toward the chapter house, where the visitors had been ushered in. Dread writhed in her belly at the thought of facing Duncan MacKinnon. The few encounters she'd had with the man over the years had troubled her for days afterward.

The clan-chief had a way about him that made all her instincts scream danger.

She'd had trouble with MacKinnon for the last few years. He disliked the influence the abbey wielded over the western edge of his lands. He especially hated how well-loved the Sisters of Kilbride were by the local folk.

It was a love he'd never been able to garner from his own people.

Dragging in a deep breath, and telling herself that a man such as MacKinnon didn't deserve her anxiety, Mother Shona pushed open the chapter door and entered the lofty space.

The clan-chief stood in the center of the flagstone floor, the stained-glass windows behind him. MacKinnon didn't look pleased. His gaze was bloodshot, his expression mutinous, and he held himself gingerly. No doubt, under that mail shirt he wore, the clan-chief's wounded ribs were bound. Two men flanked the clan-chief: one tall and raven haired with piercing blue eyes, the other heavily muscled with short blond hair and a forbidding expression. Ross Campbell and Carr Broderick—MacKinnon never went anywhere without his two henchmen.

"Where is she?" MacKinnon barked out as she entered. He didn't bother with greetings or preliminaries.

Having expected this, the abbess kept her expression neutral. "Please lower yer tone, MacKinnon ... this is a place of worship."

"Don't obstruct me, woman," MacKinnon growled. "Sister Annella. Bring her to me."

"Sister Ella ... what do ye want with her?"

"I ask the questions here, Mother Shona. Tell me where the nun is."

The abbess held his gaze, her own never wavering. "Ye have made a wasted trip here, I'm afraid. Sister Ella is currently at Scorrybreac Castle, visiting her ill mother. We have been praying for a miracle and that Lady Fraser might live."

"No, she isn't," MacKinnon barked, his dark brows knitting together. He was staring at the abbess with an intensity that made misgiving slither down her spine. "She accompanied MacNichol to Dunan and tried to kill me last night. She then fled ... west."

Mother Shona widened her gaze as she feigned surprise. "Well, she never arrived here," she replied, deliberately keeping her voice low and respectful. "Perhaps, she changed course during her journey?"

A muscle bunched in MacKinnon's lantern jaw. He was a handsome man; the abbess had noted that from the first time she'd met him. However, all one needed was a few moments in his company to realize that an attractive exterior hid much that was dark and unsavory. MacKinnon had a shadowed soul, and the abbess wondered if he had been born that way or if life had shaped his unpleasant nature.

"She traveled west," he growled. "To Kilbride."

The abbess inclined her head, as if his assertion confused her. "And I can assure ye that she never came here." She paused, her gaze narrowing. "In fact, we have been awaiting her return ... MacNichol promised to return her to Kilbride before now."

MacKinnon stared at her, and danger crackled in the air. His men, Campbell and Broderick, exchanged glances, their expressions veiled. They, like the abbess, were probably wondering what the clan-chief would do next.

When MacKinnon finally spoke, his voice was low and hard. "Ye lie, Mother Shona."

The abbess drew herself up. "How dare ye. I am a servant of God. I do not tell falsehoods."

MacKinnon took a threatening step forward. "Ye forget ... this abbey sits upon my land. I rule here, not ye." He paused there, letting his words sink in, before he shifted his attention to Ross Campbell. "Search the abbey," he barked. "Find that wee bitch."

26

In Name Only

THEY RODE HARD, cutting north into Fraser lands rather than risk the more direct, faster route home through MacKinnon territory. The day was waning, long shadows stretching across bare hills, when the party reached the tiny hamlet of Frithe nestled in the foothills of the Black Cuillins.

But as small as Frithe was, the village hosted an inn: a low-slung, white-washed building with a thatched roof and a weather-beaten sign revealing a dancing woman with flowing gold hair.

"The Fairy Maid." Perched behind Gavin, Ella squinted in the gloaming so that she could read the inn's name on the sign.

"Aye, the Lochans of the Fair Folk are just a short ride from here," Gavin replied, pulling up his mare, Saorsa.

Ella craned her neck then, looking north-west at where the great shadowy peaks of the Black Cuillins rose above them. She'd visited the Fairy Pools a few times, as a child, for they lay in Fraser land and the clan often celebrated weddings at the sacred spot. She remembered rushing water, the serene atmosphere, and a large turquoise pool that she'd bathed in.

If the situation had been different, if she hadn't been running from MacKinnon, fleeing her old identity, she'd have liked to see them again.

'The Fairy Maid' proved to be welcoming lodgings. The elderly couple who kept it directed Gavin and his men to the stables wedged between the two wings that stretched behind the main structure. There, they rubbed down their horses before retiring to the common room and a supper of roast mutton, mashed turnips with butter, and oaten bread.

There were no other travelers in the inn this eve, just two local men playing a game of Ard-ri upon a low table at the far end of the common room. Immersed in their game, the men barely looked up at the newcomers. Ella glanced over to see one of them grin as he moved a white counter close to a small stone figurine, while his opponent scowled. Ard-ri—or High King—was an old game that simulated a Viking raid. The grinning man was about to bring down the Scottish king.

Seated next to Gavin at the long table he shared with her and his men, Ella lowered her chin and whispered a prayer. It was a habit after all her years at Kilbride, one that she wouldn't lightly cast aside. Once she had given thanks for the food set before them, Ella ate with relish. After everything that had befallen them over the past day, she realized she hadn't eaten anything since leaving Dunan. Likewise, Gavin and his men ate as if they'd been starved for a week, washing down the meal with tankards of ale.

The food was delicious, and Ella focused upon it, happy to let the murmured conversation move around her rather than contribute. She was still reeling after the events of the day.

Ella helped herself to another slice of mutton, and as she did so, her hand brushed Gavin's. Her gaze snapped up, fusing with her husband's. Watching her, Gavin's mouth curved into a smile. Ella stared back, noting that dimple in his cheek that still gave him a boyish look.

"Is the meal to yer liking, Ella?" he asked softly.

"Aye," she replied, smiling back. "I imagine ye had forgotten how I can eat like a horse?"

His smile widened, although those warm blue eyes never wavered from hers. "I've forgotten nothing," he murmured. "Not one detail."

His words made a hot flush creep over her chest.

Not one detail.

Many years may had passed since they'd been lovers, yet they lived a lifetime in that one sultry summer. The memories of it all had tormented Ella when she initially left Scorrybreac. Eventually, with Mother Shona's help, she'd archived all those painful recollections, pushed them so far back into the recesses of her mind that she could barely reach them.

And yet, they were still there—they always would be.

The hours they'd spent in that clearing, laughing, talking, making plans, and exploring each other's bodies under the warmth of the sun.

Ella had told herself that Gavin had forgotten it all, that he'd laid the past to rest when he'd wed Innis.

Yet gazing into Gavin's eyes now, Ella understood that wasn't the case.

The meal concluded with another round of ale, and one by one, the members of the MacNichol party mumbled their excuses and went to find their beds.

Eventually, only Gavin and Ella were left at the table. It wasn't so comfortable there, so they took their ales over to the fireside, settling down into high-backed wooden chairs. The men playing Ard-ri had long since departed for the eve.

"The inn-keep has given us his best room," Gavin informed her, his mouth quirking. "He tells me it looks across his wife's rose garden ... I remember how well ye loved roses."

"I still do," Ella replied.

Gavin took a sip from his tankard, his gaze shifting to the glowing lump of peat in the hearth. "I have asked the inn-keep's wife to make ye up a separate room," he said. His voice was measured, as if he was carefully choosing his words. "Worry not, ye don't have to share my bed-chamber."

His words took Ella by surprise.

Of course—tonight was their wedding night. They had not yet consummated their vows. Unless they did so, they would not be officially wed.

The reminder made nervousness flutter up within Ella, like a cage of loosed butterflies. She'd done her best not to think of what the end of the day would bring; truthfully, she'd thought they'd be making camp under the stars rather than finding comfortable lodgings.

"We should share the same room, Gavin," she replied, her fingers tightening around the handle of her tankard. Such bold words made her heart race, yet she forced herself on. "And the same bed."

Gavin went still, his gaze widening.

"We are wed." She rushed out the words before her courage failed her. "And I'd rather it wasn't just in name only."

His blue eyes darkened. "Ye wish to lie with me again ... despite everything that has happened?"

The pair of them stared at each other for a long moment. Suddenly, it felt airless in the warm, smoky common room.

When Ella replied, her voice was barely above a whisper. "Aye."

Ella stepped inside the room the inn-keep's wife had prepared for them, and her heart started to race like a hunted deer's.

Indeed, she'd given them a lovely chamber. The rose garden was hidden from view, for the shutters had been bolted closed. Yet a vase of fresh pale pink roses sat on a table in the center of the space, their scent drifting through the warm room. Heavy beams stretched overhead, barely high enough for a tall man like Gavin to stand at full height, yet the white-washed walls gave the chamber a spacious feel. A screen covered one corner of the room, hiding the privy and wash-stand.

However, the sight of a large bed in the far corner, covered with a woad-blue blanket, made dizziness sweep over Ella.

An intoxicating blend of nerves and excitement.

She couldn't believe this was happening. After all these years—she and Gavin were going to lie together again.

The thought terrified her.

Gavin closed the door behind them, lowering the wooden bar so that they were secure inside the chamber.

Ella turned to him. Her heart was pounding so fiercely now that she was starting to feel ill.

It's Gavin, she counselled herself. *Ye know him ... why are ye so scared?*

And yet she was. So many years had passed. They'd both changed so much.

As if reading her thoughts, Gavin's expression, which had been serious just moments earlier, softened into a warm smile. "Do ye want to wash up first, or shall I?" He paused then before pulling a face. "I fear I stink like a goat."

"Ye go," Ella replied with an answering smile. She was grateful he was focusing on practical things, not the fact that the pair of them were now wed and standing alone together in their bed-chamber on their wedding night.

With a nod, Gavin threw his cloak over the back of the chair and heeled his boots off. He then loosed his hair from where it had been tied at the nape of his neck. The dark-gold waves fell over his shoulders. Ella watched, mesmerized. She'd always loved Gavin's hair.

Turning from her, Gavin disappeared behind the screen. Moments later Ella heard splashes as he poured water into a bowl for bathing.

She moved over to the fireplace, where the inn-keep's wife had left two earthen cups and a jug of wine. Pouring out both cups, Ella took a large gulp of wine. It was bramble—her favorite. The heat of it pooling in her belly calmed her nerves a little.

Presently, Gavin reappeared. Barefoot and naked from the waist up, the sight of him made Ella's breathing catch as it had that night in Dunan.

The soft firelight bathed his broad chest and the crisp blond curls that covered it. He had a couple of long, thin scars down his left side she hadn't noticed before.

Realizing that she was staring, Ella hastily put down her cup and picked up Gavin's before holding it out to him. "Here," she said. "It's good."

He took the wine with a smile, although his gaze smoldered in a way that told her he'd seen her frank appraisal of him.

Breathing fast, Ella hurried across the room and ducked behind the screen.

Hidden from view, she raised her hands to her cheeks to find them hot. Did Gavin have any idea what he did to her? Over the past two weeks, even a glance from him made her knees go weak.

She felt eighteen years old again, a maid who had never been touched by a man.

After years of wearing so many layers of clothing, disrobing was ridiculously easy tonight. Ella pulled off her snug leather boots and unlaced the kirtle, before she reached down and pulled the léine she wore underneath over her head.

Wearing only a thin sleeveless linen shift that reached mid-thigh, she moved over to the wash bowl. The water was still warm.

Ella washed deftly in an effort to keep her thoughts from the half-naked man who awaited her on the other side of the screen. It was futile. Her body felt sensitized, every nerve on alert as she dried herself with a cloth and adjusted the shift.

Glancing down at herself, she saw that the garment left little to the imagination. Her breasts, which had grown fuller since she'd carried a bairn, thrust out before her, her hard nipples clearly visible through the thin fabric.

Ella nervously licked her lips, smoothing down the flimsy shift against her thighs.

She felt as if she were standing on the edge of a cliff. Once she jumped there would be no turning back. Aye, she and Gavin were now wed, but it was only when they lay together that their union would be real.

Was she ready for this, for the upheaval taking this step would cause?

Not able to answer the question, for her thoughts were now lost in a churning sea of want, Ella stepped out from behind the screen.

27

Unforgotten

GAVIN WAS STANDING next to the fire, leaning up against the mantle-piece as he cradled his cup of wine. He looked up when Ella emerged, and their gazes locked. Then Gavin's gaze slid from her face, down the length of her body.

Ella watched his lips part, his gaze darken.

Slowly, deliberately, he put down the cup and walked toward her.

Reaching Ella, he lifted a hand and cupped her cheek. "Ye are lovely," he whispered. "Even more so than I remember."

Ella had to smile at that. At eighteen her body and been unblemished and lithe; she didn't think the same still held for her at thirty-six. Yet, his words made warmth flow through her. She was glad he found her attractive, for the mere sight of Gavin made her ache for him.

Ella reached up and cupped her hand over his, before she inclined her head so that her mouth slid over his palm. She kissed him there, gently, her eyes fluttering closed as she leaned into the strength of him.

His free hand touched her shoulder then, his fingertips sliding across her skin.

And then, with a groan deep in his throat, Gavin pulled Ella into his arms.

She sank into him, giving herself up to the moment as Gavin tangled his fingers in her hair, drew her head back, and kissed her.

The touch of his lips on hers, the feel of his tongue parting them, unraveled the last of Ella's doubts. Just like back in Scorrybreac, being in his arms, having his mouth on hers, felt right. She'd fought it then, struggled against an impulse that was as natural as breathing, but she didn't need to now.

She was no longer Sister Ella, but Lady Ella MacNichol.

She could give into this.

A soft cry escaped Ella, and she reached out, sliding her palms up his naked chest, before she linked her arms around his neck. Pressing herself up against him, she drank Gavin in, her tongue and lips exploring his mouth.

He groaned again, and the sound lit a fire deep within her core.

It was strange how memory erased many tiny details. There was much she remembered about what it was like to lie with Gavin, but that groan—both innately masculine and yet strangely vulnerable—was something she'd forgotten.

His kiss deepened, his hands splaying out across the back of her head.

Ella couldn't get enough of him. She pressed her body against the muscular length of his, and when she felt his shaft—hard and hot—against her belly, excitement rippled through her.

Panting, she drew back from him. Their gazes fused. Gavin's chest now rose and fell sharply. His lips were swollen from their kisses, his eyes hooded with desire. He wore a fierce, hungry expression that sucked the air from Ella's lungs.

How she wanted him. She'd never wanted anything more in her life.

Wordlessly, he reached down and caught the hem of her shift, drawing it upward. Ella helped him, wriggling out of the garment and tossing it aside. Gavin's stare devoured her nakedness. Then he undid his braies and pushed them down, before kicking them away.

Ella let her gaze travel down the length of him, taking in his swollen shaft that thrust up against his belly.

Her breathing caught. He hadn't been aroused that night at Dunan, and yet her gaze had still strayed to his manhood. But she couldn't stop staring at it now. She ached to touch it. She wanted to wrap her mouth and fingers around its strength, as she once had years earlier, and make his groans fill the room.

Before she could, Gavin took Ella by the hand and led her to the bed.

They sank down upon it, coming together with a hunger that took Ella by surprise. Gavin ravaged her mouth now, his big body sliding down the length of hers as his hands explored her. Ella arched up toward him, her own hands tangling in his thick blond hair.

Gavin tore his mouth from hers then, his lips leaving a trail of fire while he kissed his way down her neck to her breasts. As he suckled each one, Ella started to gasp and tremble, her fingers digging into his scalp, urging him on.

And then when he left her breasts and continued his exploration, Ella's gasps turned to groans. His lips, his tongue, his fingers. He knew exactly where to touch, where to stroke, where to lick. Gavin took his time, as if she were a banquet of delicacies he wished to savor.

It was only when Ella started to plead with him that he ceased his delicious torture. Lying spread-eagled on the bed, her body a pool of pulsing, aching need, Ella gazed at him as he rose up between her thighs.

His shaft thrust toward her, and Ella pushed herself up before reaching for it. Her fingers wrapped around the shaft, and she gasped at just how hot and hard it was, the tip swollen and slick with need.

"Ella," Gavin groaned. His voice was raw, a moan escaping when she slid her hand down his shaft's length. She watched Gavin's face, fascinated, while she pleasured him in long, gliding strokes. His eyes closed, a nerve flickering in his cheek. She loved seeing him like this, she loved knowing she was the one to transport him.

Moving closer, she bent over and took him in her mouth.

A low curse echoed through the room. Gavin made a strangled sound in the back of his throat, his body growing taut as she drew him deep into her mouth.

But after a few moments, he caught her by the shoulders, gently pushing her up. Reluctantly, Ella withdrew. She'd been enjoying herself; she'd wanted to bring him to the edge and then watch him topple over it.

She wanted to see Gavin MacNichol lose control.

"I have to be inside ye." He ground out the words, pushing Ella onto her back. "I can't wait any longer." With that he spread her thighs once more. He then took hold of one knee, lifting it high, and thrust into her.

The movement was swift and brutal—a shock after so many years of abstinence—and yet Ella welcomed it. She cried out, arching up against him. The aching, rippling pleasure of him deep inside her was almost unbearable in its intensity.

"Oh, Gavin," she whimpered. "I don't know ... I can't—"

Looming over Ella, he cut off her words with his mouth, kissing her hungrily, his lips bruising hers. And as he kissed her, Gavin started to move inside her—in slow, grinding thrusts.

Ella clutched at his shoulders as he rode her, digging her nails in with each movement. She kissed him back, frenzied now. She wanted to lose herself in this man, to forget the rest of the world existed.

The past ceased to matter, and the future was nothing more than a blank sheet of parchment waiting to be written upon.

The taste of him, the weight and strength of his body as he slammed into her with each thrust, pushed everything else from her mind. In the past, Gavin had been a gentle, sensitive lover, yet there was a tension to him tonight, a fire that consumed them both.

Tonight was a claiming.

He continued his steady rhythm, sweat sliding down his broad back. Gavin tore his mouth from Ella's then and stared into her eyes while he took her. He reached out, entwining their fingers, pushing her hands back against the pillows.

Ella gazed up at him, a deep, aching pleasure building in the cradle of her hips. It was almost too much, too intense to lock eyes with him while he slid in and out of her, driving a little deeper each time.

A wave of fierce tenderness crashed over her, making it hard to breathe. She'd lived apart from Gavin for years, yet the cord between them had never been broken. Giving him up had only made her realize how much she loved him, and bearing him a bairn had served to strengthen that bond. She'd known it was impossible, and that if she let it, her love for Gavin would destroy her. And so, she'd built herself a new life, with a new purpose.

But amongst it all, Gavin had always been there. In her heart he'd lived on, unforgotten.

Gavin sank down upon Ella, his body shaking as he found his release. Her skin against his was sweat-slicked, and he could feel her pulse pounding against the palm of his hand when he laid it upon her breast.

"Mo ghràdh," he murmured, leaning forward and kissing her once more. Ella's full lips were slightly swollen, her cheek bones were flushed, and her eyes gleamed in the lambent glow of the hearth that cast its light across the room.

Gavin wanted to say more, to pour out everything that lay within his heart, but their lovemaking had left him speechless. He could merely lie there, Ella curled in his arms, as they both recovered.

Rolling off Ella, Gavin drew her against his chest. She was a small woman, and he was afraid he might crush her under his weight if he fell asleep on top of her. Nestled against him, Ella lazily stroked the planes of his chest and belly, as if committing his body to memory.

A smile curved Gavin's lips, and he bent his head, inhaling the scent of rosewater in her hair. Never had anything felt more right than having her curled up in his arms. Their lovemaking had surprised him, for it had been very different to the past.

During that long, sultry summer, they had both been new to the pleasures of the flesh. They had explored each other's bodies eagerly, yet despite that he'd fallen in love with Ella then, there was always a part of him he kept back when they lay together. He never let go completely.

Tonight, Ella had stripped him bare.

He'd whispered words of love while he'd taken her, worshipped her body with his own. He'd given himself to her without keeping anything back.

As a young man, he hadn't had the courage to do so. That was why he'd been able to give her up all those years ago. That day in the clearing, he'd stepped into the role that had been expected of him: the clan-chief's dutiful first-born son. He'd deliberately shut Ella out.

It had hurt him to upset Ella, but he'd kept telling himself that he was doing the right thing—that his parents and clansmen would appreciate his sacrifice.

Strangely, none of them had seemed to care. Of course, few knew what he'd given up in order to wed his betrothed.

Gavin stroked Ella's thick hair, his vision misting. "I was a fool to let ye go, Ella," he whispered. "I will never do so again."

In response, she gave a gentle sigh, her small hand splaying over his heart. "I know ye won't," she murmured. "Sometimes life's lessons take us a while to learn ... but I think ye and I understand now."

Gavin's throat thickened. "Ye have always understood," he replied huskily. "It was me with a head as thick as an oak trunk."

Ella huffed a laugh against his chest, one slender leg curling over his hip as she drew him closer to her. "It matters not, love," she whispered. "The past can't be unwritten ... and maybe the Lord had this in store for us all along."

Gavin smiled. "So ye still have yer faith ... despite everything that's happened?"

Ella pulled away slightly, tipping her head back so that their gazes met. Like his, her eyes shone with tears. "I have it *because* of everything that's happened," she replied. "Ye and I were meant to be together, Gavin MacNichol ... and maybe God realizes that too."

28

Weathering the Storm

ELLA STEPPED OUT into the morning and raised her face to the gentle sun that was rising over the mountains to the east. Despite that she and Gavin had managed to sleep later in the night, fatigue pressed down upon her this morning. Her eyes were gritty, her limbs heavy—and yet she'd never felt better.

Last night had been the gateway to a better life, she could feel it in her bones.

"Tired?" Gavin stepped up next to Ella, placing an arm around her shoulders; it was a protective gesture that made warmth filter through her.

Leaning into him, Ella glanced up at her husband's face. "Aye ... but happy."

He smiled, and his eyes crinkled at the corners. "As am I."

They had shared a breakfast of fresh bannock, butter, and honey in the common room, before Gavin's men had gone out to ready the horses. It was now time to continue their journey.

"If we ride hard, we can make it to Scorrybreac by dusk, I reckon," Ceard announced. The older man approached, leading his bay and the clan-chief's grey.

Gavin nodded. "The inn-keep's wife has given us food for the journey ... so there shouldn't be any need to stop at Kiltaraglen on the way."

A tendril of nervousness wafted through Ella at hearing they would reach their destination by day's end. She'd hoped they'd spend the night at Kiltaraglen—a chance for her and Gavin to reacquaint themselves some more, as well as putting off the inevitable.

She didn't want to see the looks of shock, anger, and censure on his kin's faces—or suffer the condemnation that would swiftly follow.

As if sensing her shift in mood, Gavin's arm tightened around Ella's shoulders. "Ye worry about the reception we'll receive, don't ye?"

Ella swallowed before nodding. "Aye ... doesn't it concern ye?"

Not caring that his men now surrounded them and were looking on with interest, Gavin reached out and stroked Ella's face. "We'll weather it, Ella," he said softly. "Just remember, this is nothing compared to what ye have been through."

"But yer mother—"

"Will attempt to slay us with her tongue," he interrupted, his brow furrowing. "But they're just words ... surely ye aren't scared of Maggie MacNichol. Not after facing the likes of Duncan MacKinnon."

Ella snorted. "Lady MacNichol is terrifying, Gavin."

"*Ye* are Lady MacNichol now," he reminded her, a stubborn light gleaming in his eyes. "And my mother will have to accept that."

Ella pondered Gavin's words at dusk that evening as Scorrybreac's bulk hove into view. He was clan-chief, and set in his resolve, but she knew what folk could be like. His marriage would scandalize everyone at

Scorrybreac—from the high to the low. News of their union would ripple out from the castle, reaching all corners of Skye within days.

Sooner or later, MacKinnon would hear of it too.

Ella drew in a deep breath, squeezing Gavin's hand. She sat, perched before him, while he held the reins with his right hand, the other arm wrapped around her waist. "Home," she said softly.

"Aye," he replied, his breath feathering against her ear. "Remember what I said ... we'll weather this."

Outlined against a pale pink sky, the castle looked magnificent, as if it would endure forever. Not a breath of wind stirred the MacNichol pennant that hung from one of the keep's towers.

The road leading through Scorrybreac village was empty, for folk had all retired to their cottages for the evening. Smoke rose from the sod roofs, and the smell of overcooked vegetable stew—most likely pottage—wafted across the highway.

Up ahead the men upon the watch towers had spied them, and the heavy oaken and iron gates opened to receive the clan-chief and his men. They clattered into the outer bailey, which was empty at this hour, and continued on to the inner bailey.

Blair came out to meet them.

As Ella had expected, Gavin's younger brother's eyes widened at the sight of Ella riding with Gavin, dressed in a kirtle and léine instead of a nun's habit. As she was a wedded woman now, Ella had not left her hair unbound. Instead, she'd tamed her pale copper tresses into a long braid and wrapped it around the crown of her head.

"Gavin?" Blair finally spoke. "What's this?"

Turning from helping Ella from the saddle, Gavin met his brother's eye. "I'll save my explanations for when we're all gathered," he replied. His face was enigmatic, his tone even. Yet Ella detected the note of steel beneath; he was already preparing himself for the tempest. "Can ye tell everyone to meet us in the Great Hall?"

A heavy hush settled over the hall when Gavin finished his explanation.

He'd kept the details to a minimum, although Ella had been surprised about his candor relating to MacKinnon. He'd spoken frankly about the clan-chief's behavior, and detailed their escape to Kilbride, before explaining how he and Ella had come to be wed.

He did not speak of their still-born child. There were some details that were too private to be shared.

When no one broke the silence, Gavin spoke once more.

"Few of ye realize this, but I was in love with Ella years ago ... and wished to break my betrothal to Innis for her," he said, his gaze sweeping over the long table where his kin sat. Many of them stared at him as if he'd just sprouted two heads. Stewart Fraser was in attendance. Ella's father wore a stunned look, as if he was having difficulty grasping the clan-chief's explanation. "She fled to Kilbride and took her vows because I broke her heart," Gavin continued. "We now have the chance to start again."

A harsh laugh followed these words. Maggie MacNichol had drawn herself up, her features sharp, her grey eyes flint-hard. "Do ye think yer sordid wee affair was a secret?" Her voice lashed across the table, causing some present to flinch. "We all knew ... that was why yer father insisted ye honor the betrothal. It had nothing to do with his ill health and everything to do with saving yer honor."

Gavin's face went taut. He then shifted his attention to Blair, his gaze questioning.

"It's true," his brother murmured. "We all knew." Across the table Gordana dropped her gaze to her lap. Watching her, Ella realized that she too had known the full extent of Ella's relationship with Gavin—and yet she'd pretended otherwise.

Ella exhaled slowly. She stood at Gavin's side, yet her legs felt wobbly under her. She wished they were seated. Suddenly, it felt as if the walls were closing in on her. Had they all conspired to keep her and Gavin apart?

"Ye were a headstrong, foolish young man," Maggie MacNichol continued. "Ye had to be reined in. I wouldn't let ye humiliate us and risk our relationship with the Frasers of Skye."

Stewart Fraser's face grew taut at these words, while tension coiled within Ella, tightening with each passing moment. As she'd always known, Maggie MacNichol had dominated her husband's decision-making. She'd never let on, but she'd been set upon keeping the lovers apart.

She was a clever woman too—she understood that if she'd directly opposed Gavin and Ella, they'd have fought her. Instead, she'd used the clan-chief's ill-health and Gavin's sense of duty as her weapons of choice to manipulate him into doing her bidding.

Watching the gleam in the woman's eye, heat kindled in Ella's belly—a slow, pulsing anger. She glanced across at Gavin to see that his expression had turned hard. His eyes were cold as he watched his mother.

"Ye had yer victory, Ma," he said, his tone wintry. "And I congratulate ye for it ... but fortunately, fate has taken a turn. Ella and I are together now, and there's nothing ye can do about it."

"We'll see about that," Maggie MacNichol snarled, drawing herself up further. "It's a crime ye have both committed ... against the church, against decency."

"The abbess cast me from the order." Ella spoke up now. Her voice was low although it trembled with the anger she was now struggling to keep in check. "Gavin and I have committed no crime in wedding."

Gavin's mother glared back at her, not backing down an inch. This woman's viciousness was like standing under a lashing hailstorm. Maggie MacNichol still wielded a lot of influence and power at Scorrybreac. Ella could see from the surrounding faces that many seated upon the dais silently agreed with her. They had to act quickly if they wanted to stem the tide that now rose against them.

"A nun can't cast aside her vows as lightly as that." Her mother-in-law spat out the words. "I'll wager

MacKinnon would have something to say about her decision ... as would the Holy See."

Shocked murmuring rippled across the table at these words.

Ella's father's expression had turned thunderous now, although Ella wasn't sure if his anger was aimed at her or Maggie MacNichol. Across from Stewart Fraser, Gordana's face had gone the color of milk, her blue eyes wide as her gaze flicked from her mother to her brother.

Gavin stepped forward then. Leaning down, he placed his palms flat upon the table and fixed his mother with a penetrating stare.

"Mother Shona's decision was good enough for me." His voice was low, with a threatening edge. "I haven't gathered my kin here this eve to gain yer blessing ... but to do ye the courtesy of informing ye that I have taken a new wife. Whether or not ye agree with it means nothing to me ... do ye understand? *Nothing*."

His inflection on the final word made Maggie MacNichol's gaze narrow. However, the woman didn't flinch, didn't back down. Despite that she must have known that her son's temper was hanging by a thread, she held his gaze fearlessly.

"Annella Fraser always held an unhealthy influence upon ye, Gavin," she replied, her own voice brittle with anger. "I fear she has bewitched ye once again." Maggie's gaze shifted to Ella then, her face twisting. "Perhaps the abbess cast her out for she knew that Satan had taken up residence within ye." Her attention flicked to Gavin once more. "Ye have wed the devil's consort, son ... and yer very soul is now in peril."

Shocked gasps followed this pronouncement, although Gavin didn't move. His gaze didn't waver from his mother.

"Hatred and spite are Satan's work." His voice rang across the table, cutting through the whispers and mutters that had followed his mother's words. "There is nothing but goodness within Ella. Ye, on the other hand ..." He paused here as another hush settled over the table. "Ye spread ill-content like the pestilence that is bringing England and the continent beyond to its knees. If there is anyone doing the devil's work at Scorrybreac, mother ... it is ye."

29

Vengeance

"SHE'S A VIPER, Gavin," Ella whispered. She leaned into her husband's chest, pressing her hot cheek against his thudding heart. "Yer mother could turn the entire castle against us."

Gavin huffed a soft laugh, although there was little humor in it. She could feel the tension in his body; his pulse was rapid, and he hadn't spoken a word as they'd left the Great Hall and made their way to his solar.

"Do ye remember I told ye that Gordana has advised me to send mother away ... to our kin upon Raasay?" he said finally.

Ella drew back from him, nodding. Gavin's eyes were shadowed although his expression was still thunderous. "Are ye considering it now?"

An angry sigh gusted out of Gavin. He stepped away and dragged a hand through his hair. "Aye, although it pains me. I've always felt an obligation to my family ... Ma knows it ... and as ye have seen, she knows how to exploit it."

Ella frowned. "Aye ... she wields words like a claidheamh-mor."

"She is capable of causing great damage," Gavin admitted. He crossed the solar and poured two goblets of wine. The servants had been in here, and had closed the shutters and added another lump of peat to the fire. A warm golden glow bathed the chamber, highlighting the huge tapestry that hung on the rough stone wall behind them. It depicted a hunting scene in vivid detail. "As ye have just seen ... one under-estimates my mother at their peril. She is a scholar of manipulation. She knows how to read folk ... she always has."

He approached Ella and handed her a goblet. She received it gratefully and took a sip. "All these years and she never let on that she knew about us?"

Gavin shook his head. "She never needed to. She'd gotten what she'd wanted years ago. The knowledge she held was a secret weapon, to be kept in check just in case she needed it in the future." His face shadowed as he spoke these words, making it clear that he was worried.

They looked at each other once more. Ella saw how his gaze guttered and witnessed the tension upon his handsome face. Her ribcage tightened. She didn't want to bring Gavin grief and trouble.

Ella drew in a slow breath before taking another sip of wine. She needed something to soothe her nerves after that scene in the Great Hall. No one besides Maggie MacNichol had said much—although her outburst had been quite enough. Ella had looked around the table, noting that most folk—even Gordana—avoided her eye.

Only her father had met her gaze, his blue eyes gleaming, his face bereft.

"What if yer kin never accept me?" she whispered. Fear lanced through her as she said those words. "Many of them looked as if they agreed with yer mother. Blair had a face like thunder, and his wife looked as if she'd just swallowed a mouthful of vinegar."

"They'll accept ye." The fierceness in Gavin's voice took Ella aback.

"Not with Maggie MacNichol whispering in their ears. When she told them I was in league with the devil, some of the women looked as if they might faint."

Gavin's dark-blond brows knitted together. "My mother has a dangerous tongue, Ella ... I'm well-aware of that now. I also realize that her scheming goes far deeper than I thought." He stepped close to Ella and raised a hand, stroking her cheek with a tenderness that made her breathing catch. Nonetheless, she saw the concern in his eyes, and a glimmer of fear there as well that he tried to hide with his next words. "Worry not, my love. I'm keeping an eye on her from now on. And I will not tolerate my mother meddling in our lives any longer."

Alone, Lady Maggie MacNichol paced the length of her chamber. Heavy skirts hampered her stride, but she paid them no mind. Instead, her thoughts had turned inward.

Annella Fraser has bested me.

Maggie's hands fisted at her sides, squeezing so tightly that the rings encrusting them dug painfully into her palms.

That scheming wee whore always wanted to be Lady of Scorrybreac ... and now she has achieved her goal.

Maggie had never wanted a daughter-in-law, but Innis Fraser had been the ideal choice. Submissive and quiet, the woman had never spoken out of turn, had never challenged Maggie's authority.

Anger thrummed through Maggie, and she paced faster, circling the floor now. Gavin had proved to be a disappointment to her over the years, but she would never forgive him for this. Never.

After Iain had passed away, Maggie had assumed her son would be as easy to dominate as her husband had been.

But, despite that he had given up the woman he'd loved in order to please his family, Gavin had a core of iron she hadn't expected. Shortly after he became clan-chief, Maggie discovered that her son wouldn't let her guide him the way Iain had. He had his own ideas about how Scorrybreac should be ruled, and although he let his mother voice her opinions, he'd argued with her on every point she raised over the years. When he'd lowered the yearly tax for the cottars working his lands, she'd raged at him.

But her anger had washed off Gavin.

Years later, the MacNichol lands thrived. Maggie resented her son for that; she'd hoped he'd fail miserably so that she could sweep in and take control. Unfortunately, Gavin had proved himself highly competent over the past two decades. He'd also won the love and respect of his people—something his father had struggled with over the years.

And he'd developed a thick hide too. Her criticisms, scathing comments, and biting rebukes merely bounced off him these days.

But she'd managed to hit a raw nerve this evening.

When she'd accused his wife of being Satan's minion, Maggie had seen anger flare in his eyes. Finally, she'd discovered her son's weakness. Finally, she had a way to wield power over him.

Maggie stopped pacing as an idea took shape in her head. Her hands slowly unclenched, and she drew in a long, deep breath.

They won't beat me, she vowed, determination filtering over her. She crossed to the table that sat under her shuttered window. *I won't let Annella Fraser remain here as Lady of Scorrybreac. Something has to be done.*

Lowering herself upon her chair, Maggie took a sheet of parchment and smoothed it out before her. Then she reached for her quill and ink pot.

There was only one person upon Skye who would hate Annella Fraser with the passion she did. Only one person who would want to see her fall to the same degree.

Duncan MacKinnon.

The man was a brute. Maggie paused as she dipped her quill into the ink pot. She'd heard that his wife had died in childbirth and had felt a rare pang of sympathy for the dead woman. Men like Duncan MacKinnon made the worst husbands. They had no time for women, besides swiving them or having them wait upon their every need. Maggie had been fortunate in wedding Iain MacNichol, for if she'd been betrothed to a man like Duncan MacKinnon or his boorish father before him, he'd surely have beaten her to death for her sharp tongue and willful character.

Melancholy settled over Maggie MacNichol then, as memories of her dead husband surfaced.

She thought of Iain rarely these days, but sometimes she realized that there was an empty sensation in her breast, a dull ache that revealed she missed him. The early years of their marriage had been good. He'd once been handsome and strong, and she'd been happy to bear him three healthy bairns. But with the years, Iain had taken to eating and drinking to excess. He became slothful and lost interest in Scorrybreac. To compensate, Maggie's tongue grew sharper, her temper shorter, and her will stronger.

With each year after that, the passion she'd once had for her husband gradually burned out.

Even so, there were times, like now, when she missed his booming laugh and gentle gaze. He'd always tempered her sharper edges.

Pushing back the memories that wouldn't serve her now, Maggie lifted the quill from the ink pot, tapped off the excess ink, and began to write.

Scorrybreac's chapel was as cool and peaceful as ever when Ella stepped inside it. The hour grew late, yet a bank of tallow candles still burned against one wall. She was relieved to see that no one else was here. After everything that had happened since their arrival, she needed a few moments to put herself back together.

Crossing to the shrine of the Virgin Mary, Ella let her gaze settle upon the woman's serene face. She then slowly lowered herself to her knees, clasping her hands before her.

"Much has happened since I was last here, Mother Mary," she whispered. "And I beg yer forgiveness if I have done anything to offend the Lord." She broke off here, wondering if it was best to remain in silence rather than pour out her soul. However, the Virgin had always provided her solace in the past. Whenever she visited this shrine, she felt peace settle over her, a sense that everything would work out for the best.

Right now, she welcomed that sensation.

Closing her eyes, Ella bent her head and began to pray.

It was a while later when she finally rose to her feet and dusted off her skirts. It had been wise to visit the chapel, for she felt lighter, not so burdened with worries about what the future held.

Emerging into the cool evening, she was surprised to find her father awaiting her.

In the light of the torch that burned on the wall behind him, Stewart Fraser's face appeared austere, his gaze hooded.

"Good eve, Da," Ella greeted him cautiously. Since her arrival at Scorrybreac, they hadn't had a moment alone together. "How long have ye been waiting out here?"

"A while," he rumbled. "Ye take yer prayers seriously, daughter."

"Ye should have joined me," she replied with a smile. "I'd have welcomed yer company."

Her father shook his head with a grimace. "Yer mother was the pious one ... I've never felt at ease in a kirk."

Their gazes fused then and held, silence falling between them.

"Are ye angry with me, Da?" Ella asked finally.

"No, lass," he replied, weariness creeping into his voice. "Just confused ... I had no idea that ye loved Gavin MacKinnon. I feel a fool for not realizing that was the reason for yer decision to take the veil."

Ella sighed. "Well then, it seems that ye were the only one in this keep who didn't know ... if ye are to believe Maggie MacNichol."

A shadow moved across Stewart Fraser's eyes. "That woman has a poison tongue," he growled. "The things she said to ye today were unacceptable." A muscle bunched in his jaw. "If she continues her slander, I won't be held accountable."

Ella moved close to her father and took his hand, squeezing gently. "Neither will Gavin ... he was still angry when I left him earlier. I fear the time is coming when things with his mother will come to a head."

Her father nodded. "Aye ... it's been brewing for a while now. MacNichol is a good man ... but he's too soft-hearted with those who don't deserve it." His gaze gentled then as he looked upon her, and he covered Ella's hand with his own. "I am glad to see ye both happy together," he murmured. "I saw the way he looks at ye ... the man loves ye."

A soft smile curved Ella's mouth. "Aye, he does."

Duncan MacKinnon hurled the parchment away with a snarled curse.

At the opposite end of the table, Drew lifted her attention from where she was delicately spreading honey over a small wedge of bannock. "Ill-tidings, I take it?" she asked.

Duncan ignored her. "Whore!"

"MacKinnon?" Carr Broderick's rumbled question behind him was edged with censure. Through his haze of rage, Duncan realized that the warrior thought he was hurling insults at his sister. Carr could be ridiculously gallant at times. But, across the table, Drew's sanguine expression didn't change. She knew he wasn't speaking about her.

"That nun who stabbed me." Duncan whirled around, his gaze fixing upon the broad-shouldered man with short pale blond hair who stood by the door to the solar. "She's now Gavin MacNichol's bride."

Duncan heard his sister's sharply indrawn breath across the table, while Carr stared back at him, eyes widening. A few feet away, Ross Campbell, who also flanked the door, muttered an oath.

"That's impossible." Drew's voice was sharp with shock. "She's a nun."

Duncan whipped around, picked up the parchment that had just arrived by pigeon, and shoved it at his sister. "Here!" he barked. "Read it for yerself."

Drew did just that. Her eyes narrowed as she scanned the missive. "This is from Lady MacNichol?"

"Aye," Duncan growled, anger thrumming through him. He watched his sister's face go rigid.

"It says here that the abbess at Kilbride cast Sister Annella out."

"That scheming bitch." Duncan's hands fisted, for he remembered the challenge in the abbess's eyes when she'd given him permission to have his men search the abbey. They had, but had found no sign of Sister Annella. A visit to the nearby village had yielded nothing either. The priest there had denied ever seeing them. "She knew where the nun was … she helped them run off together."

Drew lowered the parchment. "Lady MacNichol says that the abbess doesn't have permission to cast out a nun who has taken her vows of perpetuity from the order."

"That's right." Duncan leaned back in his chair, the bannock he'd just consumed churning in his belly. "She should have applied to the Holy See … only the Pope himself can grant such permission."

Drew inclined her head, her gaze shuttering. "So what will ye do?"

Duncan glared back at her, outrage pulsing in his breast. "That woman tried to kill me," he ground out the words. "And I will have my vengeance upon her."

30

Always

"HAVE YE BEEN avoiding me, Gordana?"

Gavin's sister glanced up from her embroidery, guilt filtering across her face. Observing her, Ella's mouth curved. Gordana MacNichol had a gentle heart and an open nature. It wasn't in her character to be cruel to others. All the same, her mother had done an excellent job in making Ella an outcast in Scorrybreac.

In the two weeks since Ella's arrival, barely anyone save Gavin and her father had spoken to her. Even the servants avoided meeting her eye.

It was a drizzly grey morning, hence Gordana was not in her garden. Usually, if she sat in the women's solar, her mother would join her, but Maggie had retired to her bed-chamber after breaking her fast earlier that morning, complaining of a head-ache.

Ella wanted to make the most of their time alone together to speak frankly.

"I've been occupied of late," Gordana murmured, her gaze dropping to the coverlet she was embroidering with tiny pink roses. "The garden needs a lot of work at the end of the summer."

"I see the folk of Scorrybreac have been preparing for Lughnasadh."

"Aye," Gordana replied, her gaze still downcast. "Let us hope for fine weather tomorrow."

The festival, which marked the start of the harvest season, was one that Ella had always enjoyed when she'd previously lived in Scorrybreac. It had pagan origins, but now nuns and monks all over Scotland would make a pilgrimage to the top of nearby hills on the day of Lughnasadh.

In old times, folk had sacrificed animals and offered up gifts of the first cuttings of grain to the gods. These days though, there was eating, drinking, dancing, music, games, and matchmaking. As a lass, Ella had also enjoyed watching the athletic and sporting contests such as weight-throwing, hurling, and horse racing.

Silence fell while Ella took a seat opposite Gordana. To keep her hands busy, she picked up a spindle and a basket of wool and began to wind wool onto the spindle, teasing out the sticky strands with her fingers.

"Ye always used to make seed cakes for Lughnasadh," Ella said casually, eventually breaking the silence. "Will ye do so this year?"

Gordana shrugged. "I let the younger women do the baking these days."

"Gordana," Ella said gently. "Please look at me."

An uncomfortable pause followed, before Gordana complied. Her expression was guarded, her eyes colder than Ella had ever seen them.

"Do ye really believe I have manipulated yer brother?" Ella asked. She decided it was best to get straight to the point. She hadn't been deaf to the rumors that had been circulating the keep of late—no doubt thanks to Maggie. Folk whispered that she was a witch who kept Gavin captive with a vile spell.

It was dangerous talk, for Ella knew what people did to women they suspected of witchcraft. Only her position in Scorrybreac prevented them from stoning her, or worse. Two servant girls had spat on the ground after she passed them outdoors in the inner bailey that morning.

Not for the first time, oily fear pooled in the pit of her belly at the thought that everyone here might turn against her. Gavin was her only ally—and even he couldn't protect her if Maggie MacNichol incited mass hatred.

The rumors were gathering in intensity. Fear gripped Ella by the throat then as she remembered an elderly woman in Talasgair who'd been stoned to death after the locals had accused her of witchcraft. The rumors had to be stamped out.

"I don't know what to think," Gordana replied coolly. "I find it hard to believe that a woman who has dedicated her life to God can just change direction at a moment's notice."

"It wasn't like that," Ella replied quietly. "When I visited Scorrybreac during Ma's illness ... Kilbride was my life ... I couldn't see any other."

"What happened to change things then?"

Ella drew in a steadying breath. She didn't want to talk of the past, of the grief and pain that had nearly torn her to pieces, but if Gordana was ever to be her friend and ally again, she would need to.

"I loved yer brother," she said, her voice barely above a whisper, "and despite that I took my vows and dedicated my life to the Cluniac order, that feeling never went away. Love isn't something ye can just abandon ... although there have been times when I wish I could have."

Ella paused there. She could see she now had Gordana's full attention. The woman had stopped embroidering and was watching Ella steadily. There was no hostility in her gaze, but no warmth either.

"Shortly after I arrived at Kilbride, I realized I was with bairn," Ella continued. "The nuns let me stay on, allowing me to give birth within the abbey, but our son was born dead."

The words sounded barren, spoken so simply. Just a few sentences to encapsulate such pain, such loss. There were no words that would ever explain the grief that had consumed Ella after losing her son. She couldn't even begin to describe it now.

Gordana's gaze widened, the coldness disappearing as her eyes filled with tears. "No, Ella," she whispered. "Why did ye not send word?"

"Ye know why," Ella replied. "Foolishly, I thought our affair had been secret ... Gavin had a new life with Innis, and I didn't want to interfere. Telling him wouldn't change anything."

"Does he know now?"

"Aye ... I have told him everything."

The two women stared at each other for a long moment, before Gordana put aside her embroidery. Ella noted that her hands shook. She then moved to the stool next to Ella and placed her arms around her. "I'm so sorry," she whispered. "Ye must have felt so alone."

Ella swallowed. She didn't want to dwell on those dark days. "I did," she admitted, "but ye must believe me when I tell ye that none of this was planned. I hated leaving Kilbride and given the choice would have stayed there."

Gordana pulled back, her cheeks wet with tears. "Ye didn't want to wed Gavin then?"

Ella snorted. "It's not that ... yer mother talks as if I threw off my habit and ran naked into the sunset with yer brother without a second thought, but the situation was more complicated than that. Gavin agreed to wed me to save me from MacKinnon, and I agreed in order to save the abbess and the other nuns at Kilbride from MacKinnon's wrath." She paused there as she felt her own eyelids start to prickle.

Being with Gavin again, being able to touch him and kiss him, to drift off to sleep in his arms and awake cradled against his chest, made her so happy that she sometimes felt as if her heart would burst. She wasn't sure if she could describe such a feeling without weeping. "What I'm trying to say, is that both Gavin and I wed for other reasons ... but that doesn't alter the fact that we are meant for each other ... I feel as if I'm my best self when I'm at his side."

Gordana offered her a watery smile. "Despite all the tension since ye have returned, I've never seen him look happier. I'm sorry I've been so cold ... Ma has been filling my ears with awful stories about the two of ye over the past days. It's been wearing me down."

Ella smiled back. "So, are we friends again?"

Gordana covered Ella's hand with hers, squeezing hard. "Always."

Gavin went looking for his wife in the afternoon to find her resting in their bed-chamber.

Closing the door gently behind him, he moved across to the bed and sat down next to where Ella lay. She slept upon her side, still fully dressed in the cream-colored léine and dark-blue kirtle she'd donned that morning. However, she'd kicked off her slippers and unbound her hair. The long coppery tresses fell over the pillow in soft waves.

An ache rose in Gavin's chest at the sight of her.

Sleep had erased all the tension from her face; she looked young as a maid again, her full lips parted, her long lashes dark auburn against her smooth cheeks.

The past two weeks had been more difficult than he'd anticipated. His mother had launched a campaign against him and Ella, and had successfully turned most of the keep against them.

None of them were rude to his face, but he saw their expressions, the look in their eyes. He'd also heard the ridiculous yet damaging rumors his mother had spread about Ella being a witch. He'd have laughed them off, if he didn't know just how determined his mother could be when thwarted. He'd never seen her so bitter.

The time was coming when he'd have to make a decision about Maggie MacNichol. If she remained at Scorrybreac, she risked causing even greater trouble.

Ella stirred then, her eyelashes fluttering against her cheeks. "Have I slept long?" she murmured, her sea-blue eyes fixing upon him.

"I don't think so," he replied with a smile.

"What have ye been up to?" she asked, covering her mouth as she gave a small yawn. She then propped herself up onto an elbow. This kirtle was low-cut, revealing a deep, creamy cleavage.

"I've spent the afternoon dealing out justice to two men caught stealing cattle," Gavin replied. He reached out, brushing the upper swell of her breast with the back of his hand.

"What happened?"

"Some folk want them hung for the crime." Gavin began to unlace the bodice of her kirtle. "But I've ordered a flogging instead."

"Really?" Ella looked up at him, her gaze veiled, her breathing coming faster now. "Why is that?"

Gavin's mouth curved. "Cattle-rustling is a crime to be sure," he replied. "But I'd rather save hangings for outlaws and cutthroats."

Her gaze shadowed at his words. "It must be difficult to make such decisions."

"It's the lot of a clan-chief, mo ghràdh."

"And I'm sure ye do an admirable job."

He stopped unlacing her kirtle, his hand straying to her cheek. His chest constricted then as a tendril of fear spiraled up within him. He'd done his best to mend the damage his mother had wrought, yet he had seen the baleful looks some within the keep gave his wife when they thought he wasn't looking. "I wish the folk here were more accepting of ye, love. It's been a trying time for ye, and I'm sorry for it."

Ella caught his hand and pressed a soft, sensual kiss to his palm. "Like ye said, we shall weather it," she murmured. "Gordana and I have spoken today … we are friends again."

A little of the tension that had followed Gavin around these days like a heavy mantle eased, as did his fear. "I'm glad," he replied. "Although I always thought my sister too clever to allow my mother to influence her."

"Yer mother is a forceful woman, as ye well know."

"She won't win this … I promise ye," he replied, his voice hardening.

Ella's mouth curved. "I know."

Gavin pulled her into his arms then, covering her mouth with his. Ella's softness, the perfume of her hair and skin, enveloped his senses, and made the rest of the world—and all its cares—fade. Suddenly, nothing else existed but the two of them upon this rainy late-summer afternoon.

He kissed her hungrily, his lips and tongue exploring her mouth, before his hands returned to the laced bodice of her kirtle.

He continued his work, removing the garment, before his hands slid down the length of her and caught the hem of her léine.

Ella helped him remove it, wriggling out of the léine and the thin tunic she wore underneath so that she sat naked upon the bed.

Gavin's breathing hitched at the sight of her. He'd looked upon Ella's nakedness many times since their wedding night, and yet it was never enough. His gaze drew it all in: her smooth, shapely limbs; the lush swell of her breasts; the gentle curve of her belly; and the womanly dip of her waist.

Never taking his gaze from her, Gavin rose from the bed and started to undress.

And all the while, Ella watched him. He loved how boldly she did so, her lips parting when he cast aside his léine and began to unlace his braies. A soft sigh escaped her as he stood before her naked—her breathing hitching when her attention traveled down his torso and rested upon his groin.

Lord, how he loved her lustiness, the fact that her passion for him equaled what he felt for her.

They came together with a hunger that made a growl rise in Gavin's throat. Ella wound her arms around his neck, clinging to him as they collapsed upon the bed, mouths devouring, bodies entwining.

Gavin's hands slid down her back, cupping her buttocks. He pulled her hard against him, grinding their hips together. Ella gasped and bit his lower lip, her fingernails raking down his back. She wriggled under him, spreading her legs and arching her pelvis up.

"Please, Gavin," she gasped. "Now ... I want ye, now."

He'd planned to pleasure her for a while, to feast upon her body while she gasped and sighed his name. But Ella's urgency set Gavin's blood aflame, filled him with the ache to possess her.

He kneed her thighs apart and drove into her, groaning as her heat consumed him, as she drew him in.

Ella wrapped her legs around his hips, arching high with each thrust, while Gavin held himself up above her, watching her face transform.

She lost herself in their lovemaking: her cheeks flushed, her lips parted, and her eyes turned dark with passion. Her hair was now in disarray, spread out around her like a cloud. She grasped his biceps, nails digging in with each thrust.

Gavin could feel her core tightening around his shaft, and felt the ripples of her pleasure when she cried out, her body arching back against the bed.

It was too much. He'd wanted to take his time this afternoon, but this coupling was to be wild, fierce. It didn't matter if everyone upon this isle turned against them; they still had each other.

With each thrust, Gavin claimed her. With each thrust, he reminded them both that the promises they'd made to each other would not be broken this time.

Ella was his. She would always be his, and nothing besides death itself would part them.

"Ella!" Gavin gasped and closed his eyes and let go— let everything go. Shuddering, he spilled within her.

31

Bull's Eye

THE SUN CAME out for Lughnasadh. Ella was grateful it
did, and pleased for the folk of Scorrybreac too, who had
waited all summer for the chance to eat, drink, and enjoy
the games.

The festivities took place upon a grassy area behind
the village, a space that had not been used for growing
food. An old oak grew in one corner, its boughs
stretching out like embracing arms. Children played
under it, their laughter mingling with the trilling sound
of a bone whistle—a merry jig that a few young couples
now danced to.

Ella moved through the crowd, her arm looped
around Gavin's.

It felt good to be outdoors, away from the whispers
and pointed looks inside the keep. The villagers were a
merrier lot, too full of high-spirits and excitement to
bother with staring at the clan-chief and his new wife.

The savory aroma of food wafted across the pasture.
A number of village women were dishing out breads and
pies. Soon the games would begin in earnest, but before
they did, the folk of Scorrybreac wished to fill their
bellies.

Ella didn't blame them. The rich smell of venison was making her mouth water.

"Do ye want a pie, love?" Gavin asked, casting Ella a smile.

"Aye, please," she answered quickly. They had eaten simply but well at Kilbride, yet meat pie was not something the nuns got to enjoy, even on feast days.

Gavin's smile widened, and he left her to go and fetch the food.

On her own, Ella tensed a little. She preferred to be at Gavin's side these days, for the hissing and muttered comments ceased when he was about. She'd not told him about the servants spitting at her, for she knew the women would be punished if she did. Even so, the incident had made her wary of folk here. She had kept most of her fears to herself, as she knew Gavin worried for her—all the same, she was happier when her husband was present.

A few yards away, she spotted her father. Stewart Fraser held an untouched mutton pie and was deep in conversation with Gordana MacNichol. Seeing the two of them talking together, the warmth in her father's eyes as he spoke, Ella grew still.

Of course, little more than a decade separated the pair of them in age. Gordana's cheeks were slightly flushed, her gaze bright. Stewart and Gordana had lived under the same roof for years now, but with Cait Fraser's death, something had changed between them—Ella could sense it.

She was considering this change when she spied Maggie MacNichol making her way through the crowd. The sight of her mother-in-law made Ella grow tenser still. Unfortunately, she had to endure the woman at each mealtime in the Great Hall, but she did manage to avoid her at other times.

Yet not today.

Lady MacNichol wore an austere expression. She was dressed in a fine sky-blue kirtle that brought out the golden tones of her hair. Ella could see that Maggie had been a beauty in her youth, and would have still been a handsome woman, if she hadn't allowed bitterness in. The harsh lines, creased brow, and compressed lips aged her.

Seeing Ella, Maggie straightened her already stiff posture further. She barked out a command to Gordana, breaking off her conversation with Stewart Fraser. With a murmured apology, Gordana dipped her head and moved to her mother's side. Maggie muttered something to her daughter, her expression severe. She then hauled Gordana right, so that they would avoid walking past her daughter-in-law.

Relief washed over Ella. She didn't mind being avoided. It was infinitely preferable to insults and barbed comments.

Gavin returned then with their pies. His boyish smile made Ella's chest constrict. Sometimes she loved Gavin MacNichol with such fierceness that the emotion scared her. Yet it occurred to her that she was shy when it came to voicing her feelings toward him. She wasn't sure why.

"Thank ye," she murmured, taking the pie he handed her.

"Be careful," he warned. "It's hot."

Moving through the crowd, side-by-side, and gingerly beginning their pies, they took in the surrounding merriment. To one side of where the food and drink was being served, men were setting up a ring for the strength contests, as well as targets for archery and knife-throwing.

Ella finished her pie and brushed crumbs off her fingers, her gaze settling upon the targets.

"Fancy yer chances in the knife-throwing contest?" Gavin asked. There was a teasing note to his voice, for he'd seen the direction of her gaze.

Ella inclined her head. "Ye don't think I'd compete?"

His gaze widened. "Ye would?"

Ella considered it. Doing so would shock everyone, village folk and retainers alike—but what did it matter? She was already unpopular here; why not give folk something real to gossip over? A slow smile spread over her face then. "I would."

Ella drew in a deep breath, her gaze fixing upon the bull's eye target in the distance. She'd made it through the first four rounds, and with each round the targets had been moved back—starting at seven feet and now at sixteen feet.

Only three contestants had reached the final round: Ella, Ceard, and a wiry young warrior named Iver.

A huge crowd had gathered around them now, heads straining forward, while bairns peeked out from between their father's legs and mother's skirts.

By now, all had heard that Lady Ella was competing at knife throwing.

Initially, Ella had weathered some jeering. A few of the warriors had laughed, before Gavin stopped them with a glare.

And then, when she made it through the first round, the grins and smothered mirth stopped.

Ella was aware that Maggie MacNichol had pushed her way up to the front of the crowd and was now looking on. Next to her stood Gordana, her cheeks flushed and gaze gleaming. She'd cheered Ella on at the end of each round, only to earn vicious looks from her mother. Ella was pleased to see that Gordana had ignored her mother's glares; their conversation the day before had mended things between them, and it appeared that Gordana had thought on the matter further since then.

Blair and his wife were watching too. Both of them wore bemused expressions.

Catching Gavin's eye, they shared a smile. Then, her husband winked.

Ella turned back to the target, deliberately shutting everyone out as she focused. Around her waist Ella wore a belt with her throwing knives. She had thrown five during each round: twelve-inch blades with slender wooden handles.

Readying herself to throw, Ella positioned herself with one leg before the other, her weight resting on the leg opposite her throwing arm. She then raised the knife, gripping it by the handle, presenting it at the target. She sighted the target and brought the blade back behind her shoulder.

Around her the crowd hushed. Ella kept her eye on the target, swung the knife in an arcing motion, and released it at the arc's zenith. The knife flew easily from her hand, completing two full spins before it thudded into the target.

A grin spread across Ella's face.

Bull's eye.

It had taken her years to master blade throwing. Every afternoon, before Vespers, Mother Shona had taken her through endless drills.

Let the knife slip easily from yer hand. Do not whip yer wrist. Follow through. Transfer yer weight from the front to the back foot during the throw.

Mother Shona's instructions came back to her as she readied to throw her second blade. She'd been clumsy at first when she'd started with the knives, but the abbess assured her that she had a steady hand and a keen eye.

Forget the other weapons, the abbess had told her. *Make blades yer specialty.*

And she had. When Ella had finally gotten to the point where she knew where her knife would find its mark, a feeling quite unlike any other had filtered through her. She'd never been as good at anything as she was at this. She knew that if she was ever called upon to defend herself, or the other sisters, she wouldn't let them down.

Four more blades hit the target, each within the bull's eye.

Ceard was good, but one of his knives strayed outside the bull's eye line, making Ella the winner.

A roar went up amongst the crowd; men and women cheered while Gavin walked across to Ella, gathered her up in his arms, and kissed her for all to see. The cheering grew louder till it became nothing but a roar in Ella's ears.

Her cheeks were warm when Gavin set her down. His arm curled protectively around her waist as he did so, before he turned to the crowd and raised a hand, signaling that he wished to speak.

The applause died away. "For those of ye who have not yet been acquainted with my wife, I present Lady Ella of Scorrybreac to ye all," he called out, his voice ringing over the hillside. "A woman who stole my heart many years ago, but who has now returned to me … returned to us all." Gavin paused there, his gaze sweeping over the now silent crowd of onlookers. "I wish ye to all welcome her into yer hearts, for she is a kind and talented woman who will rule MacNichol lands at my side."

Smiles and applause followed these words, and for the first time her return to the castle, Ella felt welcome. It warmed her to see friendly gazes upon her. It was a good day to stand before the folk of Scorrybreac. The sun was shining, they had the day off work, and their bellies were full of food and drink. It was easy to accept a newcomer into their midst on a day such as this one; it was easier to like a woman who'd arrived under a cloud of scandal when they could spend the day doing as they pleased.

"What kind of woman throws knives?" A harsh female voice cut through the applause, causing it to die away. All gazes shifted from the clan-chief and his wife, to the tall, statuesque figure of Maggie MacNichol, who still stood at the edge of the crowd. Unlike Gordana and Blair, who'd been smiling along with the rest of the onlookers, Ella's mother-in-law's face was pale and taut. Her eyes blazed with fury. "An unnatural woman. Didn't I tell ye all that my husband has wed a consort of the devil?"

A shocked hush followed these words, and Ella felt the cloak of contentment that had briefly settled over her shoulders slough away. Maggie MacNichol would give her no peace, not even today. She was determined to bring her low, and she would use whatever means.

"Mother," Gavin growled. "I warn ye now … cease talking or ye shall regret it."

Maggie ignored her son. Instead, her gaze was riveted upon Ella. She raised up a finger, pointing it at her.

"Look upon her ... can ye all not see how she has ensnared my son? She has blinded him with her wiles, but no lady knows how to wield a blade like that. She is unnatural, I tell ye. She is a witch!"

"A bold assertion, my Lady." A loud voice boomed through the crowd before Gavin had the chance to answer. "We shall see if there is any truth in it."

A heartbeat later a portly figure swathed in black, astride a finely bedecked mule, rode into their midst. An iron crucifix gleamed upon the man's breast, and a row of tonsured monks in black habits shuffled on foot after him.

Ella stared, her lips parting as shock rippled through her.

Abbot Camron.

She hadn't seen him in nearly a decade. The abbot had only made one trip to Kilbride in her time there; he and his monks had stayed nearly three months, and all the nuns—including Ella—had been relieved to see him go.

One look at Abbot Camron's high-colored, pugnacious face, and the last shreds of Ella's buoyant mood disintegrated.

There was only one reason why the Abbot of Crossraguel, a Cluniac monastic located in Carrick, south-west Scotland, would be visiting Scorrybreac.

He had been called here.

32

All Lies

"I'M THE MACNICHOL clan-chief." Gavin stepped forward, his brow furrowing. "What brings ye to Scorrybreac ... abbot?"

"Good day, MacNichol." The newcomer inclined his head, acknowledging Gavin. Then with the help of two monks, he dismounted from his mule. The beast, bedecked with bells, silver ornaments, and tassels snorted, as if relieved to be free of its burden. "I am Abbot Camron of Crossraguel Abbey." The newcomer's attention shifted to where Ella stood behind her husband. "Unfortunately, I have been hailed here to deal with an errant nun."

Gavin's frown deepened. "On whose summons?"

"MacKinnon," the abbot replied, his tone haughty. "He advised us that something of great concern to the order had occurred at Kilbride."

"And have ye been to the abbey?"

Abbot Camron's full lips thinned. He didn't enjoy being questioned by the MacNichol clan-chief. Having spent time with the man, Ella knew how the abbot preferred to be in control of any given situation. During his visit to Kilbride, the sisters had ceased their arms training. However, Abbot Camron and Mother Shona had butted heads on a number of occasions; he had disapproved of what he called her 'lenient ways'.

"Not yet," he replied, his tone clipped. "MacKinnon's missive concerned me so much that I was compelled to travel directly here." He paused, his dark eyes now boring into Ella. "And I see that I was right to do so."

His gaze raked down Ella, taking in her knife belt and the target full of blades a few feet away. "What devilry has taken place here?"

Ella folded her arms across her chest and held the abbot's gaze. How fortunate she had been in Mother Shona over the years; the monks who followed Abbot Camron were a cowed lot. They stood now, clustered together, heads bent as if the abbot's very presence made them nervous.

"There hasn't been any devilry," Ella replied. She was surprised how calm, how dispassionate, her voice was. Underneath she could feel her temper starting to simmer, yet she wouldn't let the abbot see it, for he'd only wield it as a weapon against her. "It's simply the day of Lughnasadh, and we are playing games."

"Ye are throwing knives?" the abbot countered, his tone sharpening. "The Lady speaks true." He acknowledged Maggie MacNichol then with an approving nod. "It is unnatural. How is it ye know such a skill?"

Ella stared back at him. She wouldn't tell him of Mother Shona, and of all the skills she'd taught the Sisters of Kilbride over the years. The abbot would suffer a fit of apoplexy if he ever found out—and the abbess would be punished, perhaps even cast from the order.

Ella would never put Mother Shona at risk.

"It is a pastime I have always enjoyed," she answered. "When I was a lass, I used to practice in secret, although the opportunity to do so at Kilbride was obviously limited. I preferred instead to devote my attention to Christ."

"Devote yerself to Christ? The truth is that ye are a wicked woman, Annella Fraser." The abbot's voice became chill. "MacKinnon told me that ye tried to stab him to death, and that ye then fled, fornicated with MacNichol, and forced him to wed ye. Worse still, ye didn't repent yer sins. The Abbess of Kilbride had no choice but to cast yer corrupting influence from the abbey."

"MacKinnon lies." Gavin's voice lashed through the humid afternoon air. "He attacked Ella ... he would have raped her if she hadn't defended herself."

Ella stepped forward and placed a hand on Gavin's arm. She appreciated him defending her and shared his outrage. Yet this was a battle she had to fight herself. Their gazes locked and held for a long moment. Ella saw his struggle, noted how his jaw bunched, but he eventually gave a curt nod and held his tongue, allowing Ella to face the abbot on her own.

"MacKinnon entered my bed-chamber at Dunan," she said, her voice low and strong. Nonetheless, it galled her to have spell this all out. "He threatened me and tried to force himself upon me. I did what I had to in order to get away from him. As for the rest of the tale ... my husband speaks true. They are all lies. I never broke my vows. After Mother Shona cast me from the order, Gavin MacNichol offered me protection, and I accepted him."

Abbot Camron stared back at her, before his lip curled. "Ye were lovers?"

Ella nodded. "Once ... many years ago ... before I joined the order. But then MacNichol wed my sister, and I took my vows. I did *not* break them."

Her words faded, and the crowd that had grown larger still since the arrival of Abbot Camron and his monks shifted. Many of the faces of those watching the scene unfold looked uncomfortable. Both Gordana and Blair were frowning at the abbot, while Ella's father glared openly at him.

Stewart Fraser's meaty hands were clenched at his side. He looked as if he wished to launch himself at Abbot Camron and pummel his face into a bloody pulp. Anxiety pumped through Ella at the thought. She couldn't let him.

The abbot was enraged. His fury rippled out from him as he drew his bulky figure up, squaring his shoulders. His face had gone the color of a ripe damson, his eyes glittered with the force of his outrage.

"Annella Fraser," he ground out. Ella noted that once again he used her maiden name. He refused to acknowledge her union with Gavin. "Ye are indeed a consort of the devil. This brief interview is all I need to condemn ye as a witch. Such a woman is dangerous and cannot be allowed to live." The abbot broke off there. "Who here has the courage to do the Lord's work? She must be stripped naked and burned at the stake, only then will her wickedness be purged from the earth."

Shocked gasps followed this outburst.

A wave of dizziness washed over Ella, and the world tilted. For a moment she thought she might faint.

Reaching for Gavin's arm, she clung to him.

The abbot took a menacing step toward her, one hand clasping the crucifix about his neck, while the other pointed at her. "Ye will burn ... only then will yer soul be cleansed."

"Enough!" Gavin stepped in front of Ella, shielding her from the abbot's wrath. "One more poisonous word, and I'll shove yer teeth down yer throat."

"Satan lives within this woman," Abbot Camron continued, ranting now. "She has sinned grievously and will not repent. She must die. She must—"

Gavin didn't utter another warning. Instead, he lunged forward and slugged the abbot in the mouth with his fist.

Abbot Camron staggered back, eyes bulging. His hands went to his mouth, and he stumbled once more, sinking onto his haunches. When he removed his fingers, Ella saw blood leaking from between his lips. It trickled down his chin.

Gavin loomed over him, his right fist still clenched. "As I told ye, abbot, ye are grossly misinformed." The words were spoken in a low, threatening voice. "MacKinnon has filled yer head with lies ... and like the bigot ye are, ye believed every one of them." Gavin paused, letting his words sink in. "But now, it is I who should inform ye that ye are trespassing on my land. And if ye and this murder of crows that follow ye do not depart this instant, I shall have ye stripped and stoned as ye flee … is that clear?"

The abbot merely stared up at Gavin, his eyes glittering with hate.

"Is … that … clear?" Gavin repeated.

Ella watched her husband, shocked by his brutality. She hadn't realized Gavin was capable of such violence. Yet she wasn't sorry he had lashed out. The abbot had spewed ugly words, accusations that could incite an angry mob if not quashed. Gavin knew that, hence his harshness.

He'd told Ella he wouldn't let any harm befall her, and he was now showing her that he'd meant his promise. The abbot and his monks would indeed be stripped and stoned if they didn't obey him.

Slowly, Abbot Camron nodded. Moments passed, and then the abbot heaved himself to his feet. He was trembling, both in fear and rage, while behind him one of his monks started to whimper.

No one said a word as the abbot, with the assistance of three monks, clambered back on his mule. Then he and his flock turned and departed in the direction they'd come, the crowd closing behind them.

A heavy silence settled over the field once they'd gone.

Tearing her gaze from the direction that the abbot had disappeared in, Ella saw that Gavin's expression hadn't softened. Instead, he was glaring at his mother.

Maggie MacNichol's face appeared carven from stone. Her grey eyes were flint-hard as she stared back at her son.

"Ye contacted MacKinnon, Ma," Gavin said, splintering the tension. "Didn't ye?"

His mother's lip curled. "Someone had to."

"And why's that?"

"This business ... ye wedding yer sister-in-law ... a nun ... it's unseemly. Ye have brought our family low, Gavin. Ye have tarnished us all."

Gavin held her gaze. Ella felt the arm she gripped tense. "This ends here, Ma," he said roughly. "Long have I put up with yer venom, but now it risks poisoning us all. Ye would destroy Scorrybreac in yer quest to control it ... to control me."

"Has she fed ye this nonsense?" Maggie countered, casting Ella a look of pure hatred. "This *whore*."

"Ye have insulted Ella for the last time," Gavin cut in. He twisted then, catching Ceard's gaze. The warrior stood on the edge of the crowd with a group of Gavin's most trusted men. "Escort my mother to the Isle of Raasay," he instructed coldly. "Tell my uncle that she is to remain there. I never want to see her at Scorrybreac ever again."

Shock rippled across the crowd. Even Ceard, who was usually unflappable, gaped at the clan-chief.

Ella stared at Gavin, as if she was seeing him for the first time. She couldn't believe it. He was sending his mother into exile.

Love for Gavin MacNichol surged through her—the emotion so strong that Ella's breathing hitched. She realized then why she'd held back in expressing how she felt for him. There had been a kernel of fear within her that for all his promises, Gavin might let her down again.

But now he'd proved to her that he never would.

"Ye can't send me away, Gavin." Maggie MacNichol's voice, harsh now, slashed through the shocked chatter, dousing it. "I won't go."

Gavin inclined his head, fixing his mother with a long look. In response, the woman's throat bobbed, her cheeks flushing. It was the first time Ella had ever seen Maggie look unsure of herself. Suddenly, she realized—too late—that she'd pushed her son beyond his limits.

"Let me put it this way," he replied gently. "Ye can either depart from Scorrybreac upon yer palfrey with yer dignity intact ... or I'll have ye hog-tied and thrown over

the back of a mule for yer departure. Either way, ye are
leaving at first light tomorrow."

33

Fear Not

MOTHER SHONA'S HEART sank when she spied Abbot Camron. The noon meal had just concluded, and the nuns were filing out of the kirk, heading toward their sleeping quarters, where they would rest a while before beginning their afternoon chores.

The sight of the heavy-set figure riding toward her upon a mule, his monks shuffling in his wake, made a heavy sigh rise up within the abbess.

It had taken many days for the atmosphere in the abbey to calm after MacKinnon's disruption. Now, the abbot risked upsetting the sisters again. His visit a decade earlier had been three of the most unpleasant months she'd ever passed. Yet she instinctively knew that his appearance at Kilbride now had nothing to do with paying the abbey a visit.

The abbess halted, watching as the abbot struggled off his long-suffering steed, and turned to her.

"Peace be upon ye, Father," she greeted him with a tight smile. "How unexpected ... we did not receive prior word of yer arrival."

"Peace be upon ye, Mother," the abbot mumbled through swollen lips. "That's because I did not send it."

Close up, the abbess saw that Abbot Camron had received a harsh blow to the mouth. His lips were swollen and encrusted with scabs.

"Our Holy Father," she murmured. "Were ye set upon by outlaws?"

"No," the abbot snarled before wincing. Reaching up, he dabbed a handkerchief to his mouth. It came away bloody, for one of the scabs had just split open once more. "Gavin MacNichol, curse him to hell, is responsible."

Shocked murmurs followed these words as the monks, who had halted behind the abbot, started to whisper amongst themselves.

"Silence, ye chattering fools," the abbot growled, dabbing his mouth again. He then shifted his attention fully upon the abbess.

Mother Shona felt herself stiffen under his scrutiny. Abbot Camron had small, dark eyes that reminded her of a bird of prey. They gleamed now as he observed her. "I've just come from Scorrybreac."

"MacKinnon contacted ye?" Heaviness settled over the abbess. She should have realized that the clan-chief would do so; he'd certainly been angry enough when he'd left Kilbride. Surprisingly, no one in Torrin had betrayed them, not even the priest. Nonetheless, the abbess knew he'd learn that Gavin and Ella had wed sooner or later. Skye wasn't large enough for such events to go unnoticed.

"Of course he did!" The abbot spat out the words, his ruddy cheeks deepening in color even further. "As ye should have, Mother Shona."

"I saw no need. I dealt with Sister Annella as I saw fit."

The abbot drew himself up. "Ye take too much upon yerself, abbess. The nun had taken her vows of perpetuity. Ye could not cast her from the order without requesting permission from the Holy See."

The abbess frowned, her irritation rising. "There was no time for that. We live far from Rome, abbot … I had to make a decision, for the welfare of this abbey."

"The Pope will hear of this," the abbot ground out the words, his portly frame vibrating with fury now. "I will write to him ... I will inform him of yer arrogance ... yer *incompetence*."

Mother Shona let out a long, measured breath. She'd been ready to invite the abbot and his monks in. They all looked hungry and travel-weary. Yet Abbot Camron's threat made her temper flare. After her election, she'd worked hard to strengthen Kilbride over the years; the previous abbess had left it weak and impoverished.

She knew she was unorthodox in her views—and if the abbot knew the full extent of her activities, he'd have written to the Holy See years earlier to demand her removal—but she had always served God faithfully.

"Well, if ye intend to do so, I won't keep ye," she replied crisply. "Good day, abbot ... if ye travel hard, ye should make Dunan by nightfall."

Abbot Camron's face stiffened. "We are remaining here overnight."

The abbess made a clicking noise with her tongue before shaking her head. "I'm afraid not. Since ye find me arrogant and incompetent, I feel it wouldn't be right to invite ye into the abbey overnight. Ye should continue on yer journey and find lodgings somewhere that is less offensive to ye. May peace be upon ye."

The abbot's cheeks deepened to puce. Glaring at the abbess, he drew his robes around him, turned, and attempted to mount his mule. The beast side-stepped, the ornaments and bells that adorned it jingling, before it let out an ear-splitting whinny; it wasn't like the sound of a horse, but rather a strangled noise that sounded like someone was sawing wood with a blunt iron saw.

"Help me, ye fools!" The abbot wheezed. An instant later two monks were at his side, helping him into the saddle.

Watching him go, Mother Shona felt a pang of misgiving.

I shouldn't have done that.

Sometimes she forgot she possessed a fiery temper. Life in the order had softened her, as had the passing years, yet the sin of pride occasionally raised its head.

Abbot Camron wasn't a man to make an enemy of. He was haughty and petty. She'd just humiliated him, and he wouldn't forget it easily.

Once the abbot and his monks had disappeared, the abbess heaved a sigh and turned away from the gates.

For years she'd managed to keep the peace here at Kilbride, but a sense of foreboding settled over her now. The incident with Ella had set things in motion that couldn't be stopped. The abbey had two enemies now: MacKinnon and Abbot Camron. She would need to be wary of giving either of those men further offense.

A chill wind whipped through the abbey then, tugging at the abbess's habit and veil. The sky had darkened, and the scent of rain was in the air.

Despite herself, Mother Shona allowed a grim smile to curve her mouth. It looked as if Abbot Camron was about to get a soaking on his way to Dunan.

What a shame.

"Mother Shona." A voice hailed her, and she turned to see a small figure hurry across to her.

"Sister Leanna," Mother Shona greeted the young woman with a frown, waiting while the nun knelt before her, before she made the sign of the cross to bless her. "Ye shouldn't be outdoors at this hour."

"I know, Mother Shona." Leanna rose to her feet, her gaze pleading. "But I had to speak to ye ... when the other sisters weren't present."

The abbess inclined her head. "What is it, Sister?"

"Sister Ella ... Ella ... brought back a message for me from Dunan," Sister Leanna replied hastily. "She wanted me to warn ye and my father, when I was ready."

The abbess tensed at these words, but didn't reply. After a brief pause the novice continued. Her voice was unusually high-pitched, betraying her nervousness. "As ye know, MacKinnon wished to wed me ... but my father was against the match and sent me here so that I would be free of him."

Mother Shona nodded. Niall MacDonald of Sleat had been wise to protect his daughter from MacKinnon. Apart from Sisters Ella and Coira—whom the novice had confided in—they'd decided to keep this news from the other nuns. Sister Leanna was leaving her past behind her, after all.

Sister Leanna's gaze grew haunted. "Ella told me that MacKinnon intends to come for me ... he gave her a message. He says that the walls of Kilbride will not protect me. Sooner or later I will be his wife." The nun paused, dropping her gaze. "When his men searched the abbey for Ella, I hid in the pig sty."

The abbess grew still. Alarm filtered through her. The news shouldn't have surprised her, yet it did. Of course, MacKinnon had wed Siusan Campbell after being thwarted by Niall MacDonald. Unfortunately, he was now free to wed again—and he had not forgotten Lady Leanna.

Troubled, Mother Shona resisted the urge to mutter an ungodly curse. Life had become increasingly difficult of late. She didn't like that MacKinnon had yet another reason to disturb their peace.

"He cannot touch ye here, child," she said finally, hoping that her voice didn't betray the unease that simmered in her breast. "Next year ye shall take yer perpetual vows."

Did she imagine it or did Sister Leanna's hazel eyes shadow at that? Mother Shona knew that coming to live at Kilbride had not been the lass's choice, yet she had adapted well to life here. The abbess had thought she was content in her decision, but maybe she wasn't.

"Yer father would never permit the union," Mother Shona continued. She reached out and placed a comforting hand upon Sister Leanna's arm. "Fear not."

Sister Leanna's chin firmed, and she managed a wan smile. "Thank ye, Mother Shona. I apologize for burdening ye."

"And I'm glad ye shared this news with me," the abbess replied. "Go now and get some rest. We have archery practice this afternoon."

Sister Leanna nodded before turning and hurrying away.

Mother Shona watched her go, misgiving settling upon her.

This was ill-news indeed. She hadn't realized that MacKinnon still wanted the lass. He was a strangely obsessive man; once his mind fixed upon something, he would never give it up. It made her fear him a little.

I need to increase our training sessions, she counselled herself as she turned on her heel and set off across the yard. *The sisters must be ready to defend themselves if the need should arise.*

The abbess entered her hall, a narrow annex that abutted the refectory. Stepping inside the dimly lit space, she felt her shoulders lower, a little of the day's tension draining from her. This was her sanctuary, a quiet space where she could let herself relax. In this place she wasn't 'Mother Shona', but just merely 'Shona of Lismore'.

Her hall was sparsely furnished, with a desk and chair at one end and a narrow sleeping pallet at the other, shielded from view by a heavy curtain. A large hearth, unlit at this hour, sat alongside one wall, flanked by two high-backed wooden chairs. Mother Shona lowered herself onto one.

A sense of disquiet settled over her, causing her belly to tense and her breathing to quicken. Kilbride had been her life's work. She had poured her passion, her soul, into making it strong, into making the women who lived within its walls independent and learned.

But now, a shadow had fallen over them. Dunan was half a day's ride away, yet it now felt as if MacKinnon lived far too close. There had been times over the years when she'd almost forgotten that the abbey sat on MacKinnon lands—but of late she'd received a sharp reminder.

Difficult times lay ahead, she sensed it in her bones.

Epilogue

Remember But Look Ahead

ELLA SWUNG UP onto the courser's back, a smile spreading across her face. It felt good to sit astride a horse. She knew it wasn't 'ladylike', but she preferred this style. She'd never enjoyed riding sidesaddle.

"Ready?"

Ella turned to see Gavin smiling at her. He'd already mounted Saorsa and was awaiting her. Gavin had gifted her the leggy bay gelding. She'd named the horse Fàd—Peat—for his coat was so dark brown it almost appeared black in certain lights.

Nodding, Ella gathered up the reins. "Let's go."

They clip-clopped out of the inner bailey, through the high stone arch, and into the rectangular-shaped outer bailey beyond. It was a windy morning and gusts blew straw around the wide space as lads mucked out stables and a servant girl threw grain for the geese and fowl that roamed the outer bailey.

Folk waved as they passed, and both Gavin and Ella acknowledged them. Spying the warmth on the faces of Scorrybreac's retainers, their ready smiles, a sense of belonging settled over Ella.

Maggie MacNichol had departed two days earlier, and the moment she had, it was as if a shadow lifted from

Scorrybreac. The woman hadn't gone quietly. Her shrill voice had echoed across the castle and beyond while Ceard and the other warriors escorted her out.

And with Lady MacNichol's departure, the cruel whispers and cold glances ceased. Those women who'd been influenced by Gavin's mother lost their leader. Overnight, their manner toward Ella softened. No longer did the ladies rise from their sewing and embroidery, mutter excuses, and hurry off when Ella approached. No longer did servants sneer and turn their backs upon her.

Of course, everyone had witnessed the ugly scene with Abbot Camron, and the one that followed with Lady MacNichol afterward. They'd seen Ella throw knives during the games and defend herself verbally against the abbot—and they'd seen Gavin's harshness toward those who crossed him, toward those who threatened his wife.

It wasn't a lesson any of them were likely to forget soon.

Ella's attention shifted ahead to where Gavin urged Saorsa on. He'd tied his thick blond hair back at his nape this morning, and a cloak hung from his broad shoulders. The warmth of summer was indeed fading, and as such both she and Gavin had donned plaid cloaks for their ride. The mantle emphasized the strength and breadth of Gavin's shoulders, his straight yet relaxed posture in the saddle.

Excitement fluttered in the base of Ella's belly at the sight of him. Gavin had always been handsome and charismatic, but ever since Lughnasadh, she'd found him irresistible. It shocked her a little that she'd liked seeing the ruthless edge to his character. He was a fair, kind-hearted man, but he wasn't to be crossed. Her chest constricted then.

Lord, how she adored him.

Up ahead Gavin waved to his brother. Blair was in the midst of shoeing an ill-tempered horse. The beast nipped and kicked at him as he struggled with it. Sweat trickled down Blair's red face when he glanced up and grunted a greeting.

Gavin led the way out of the castle, under the portcullis, and down the causeway to the village. Ella followed close at his heels. Although the wind was cold, she enjoyed the feel of it on her face. They had been riding a few times since their return to Scorrybreac, but this outing was special; this time they were alone. Not even Ceard accompanied them.

As soon as they left Scorrybreac behind, Gavin urged his mare into a swift canter. Ella did the same, and moments later they were racing south-west, over undulating hills toward the thick woodland that filled a shallow inland vale.

The excitement continued to tighten within Ella's belly as she rode. They hadn't spoken of today's destination, yet she knew where Gavin was headed.

They were going to a place where she hadn't set foot in eighteen years—a place where their story had begun.

The clearing in the heart of the copse of birches looked exactly the same. The burn still trickled across mossy rocks. It was as if time had stood still there.

Glancing around her, Ella drew Fàd up. It was sheltered in the glade, the gusting wind hardly seemed to touch them.

Wordlessly, both she and Gavin dismounted, tying their horses up to a coppicing tree.

Picking up her skirts, Ella walked into the center of the clearing, her boots sinking into the carpet of soft moss that grew upon the banks of the burn. And as she stood there, all the memories she'd kept locked up for so many years flooded back.

Her breathing hitched, and when Gavin stepped up beside her, she turned to him, burying her face in his broad chest. In response, Gavin's arms encircled Ella's back, and he drew her close.

"I used to come back to this place sometimes," he murmured into her hair. "When life at Scorrybreac grew wearisome, I'd escape and lose myself in my memories. It made life easier to bear ... the knowledge that ye had once been part of my life."

"I tried not to think of this place," Ella admitted softly. "It was too painful."

"Ye are strong, Ella," he whispered, his fingers wreathing through her hair. "I always knew it."

"And stubborn," she reminded him with a wry smile he couldn't see. "Don't forget that."

His hands still entangled in her hair, Gavin gently pulled Ella's head back so that their gazes met. "I never thought this day would come," he whispered, his eyes gleaming, "that ye and I would stand together in this place again."

"And yet it did." Ella raised a hand and placed it over his heart. She could feel the strong, steady thud of his pulse against her palm. "I want to come back here often, Gavin. I don't want to ever forget the past, or about the fires we had to walk through to reach this point."

"I'll always have regrets," Gavin replied, a shadow passing over his face. "I don't think they will ever leave me."

"Some things we just have to live with," she murmured. "What's important is we learn."

His mouth curved. "*Meminisse sed providere: remember but look ahead.*"

"Aye," she replied softly. "The past is part of us ... as is Finn."

Gavin's gaze guttered at the mention of their son. Although they didn't speak often of the bairn, Ella knew that the loss weighed upon Gavin. She'd seen the devastation on his face when they'd stood in the graveyard together at Kilbride. She'd never planned on revealing her secret to him, but fate had forced her to. And now, although it hurt him to learn of Finn, she was glad she had.

There would be no secrets between them now.

"I love ye, Gavin MacNichol," she whispered, her voice trembling with the force of her feelings. "Every morning I awake and thank the Lord for being so blessed. I couldn't wish for a better man than ye."

His lips parted at this, and his gaze shone. "I've longed to hear ye say that ye love me," he replied softly.

"But I feared … after everything I put ye through … that I didn't deserve to hear the words."

"I've always loved ye," she said. Her eyes prickled with tears as she spoke. "I never once stopped."

Silence fell between them then, and when Gavin spoke, his voice was husky. "I want us to have a family. I don't know if it's possible … but I wish for it nonetheless."

Ella smiled, although the expression was tinged with sadness. The same thought had also been on her mind of late. However, Ella wasn't sure if at thirty-six, she was too old now. Maybe that chance was lost forever. "I don't know if my womb will ever quicken again," she replied, her fingertips sliding down his chest to the hard planes of his belly. "Time will tell …" Her smile turned wicked then. "But perhaps if we try hard enough, it may come to pass."

Gavin's lips curved, his gaze hooding in that sensual way that never failed to make desire kindle in the cradle of her hips. "If we *try* hard enough?"

Ella's pulse accelerated, and she leaned into him, her mouth grazing the column of his neck. "Let's start today," she murmured. "Right now."

Gavin didn't reply. Instead, with a grin, he scooped Ella up into his arms and carried her under the spreading boughs of an old birch.

The End

From the author

Wow, that was quite a start to the series! Gavin and Ella's story had me in tears more than once during the writing of this novel … and I hope you enjoyed reading it as much as I loved writing it. I enjoyed exploring the idea that love can blossom from tragedy, and that it's never too late. Gavin and Ella needed their happy ending, and I wanted to give it to them.

Second chance romance is one of my favorite themes, but when you combine it with forbidden love, you get conflict at every turn and a bit of hand-wringing angst!

I've read a few romances that start in a convent or abbey over the years, and many of them portray the heroine trying to escape the confines of a religious life. I didn't want that to be Ella's story. I wanted her to have a strong faith that carries through the whole novel, and I wanted her experience at Kilbride to be a positive one; hence why I created the abbess, Mother Shona (she has her own story, which will be revealed as the series progresses) and her unorthodox ways.

I liked giving the Sisters of Kilbride different fighting skills. Why couldn't nuns learn to defend themselves? They lived in dangerous times, and I wanted to make Kilbride a place where women could flourish.

This story ended up having a lot of 'big' themes, making it far more emotional and heart-wrenching than I'd ever intended. It's also what makes this story so epic and sweeping. It doesn't matter what time period we're born into—people are people, and we all want love and to be loved in return. We all make mistakes, and sometimes we get a chance to put things right.

For those of you who have read my BRIDES OF SKYE series you will remember that Gavin appeared in Book #3, THE ROGUE'S BRIDE. This story picks up one year after the conclusion of that series, and as such, much of the same historical context applies. Scotland had recently lost a major battle against the English, and as a result times were tough. Near the start of UNFORGOTTEN, I also mention that the Black Death arrived in Scotland around this time ... more on this in later books in the series!

Kilbride Abbey never existed on the Isle of Skye, so to make it authentic I researched contemporary Cluniac abbeys of the time. Likewise, Dunan (although an actual location on Skye) is entirely a figment of my imagination. I needed a suitable stronghold for the MacKinnons and like to think something similar to Dunan might have existed.

Scorrybreac, however, did exist. It was the MacNichol stronghold although the castle was likely to have been a bit smaller than the one I describe. These days nothing but scattered ruins remain of it.

Of course, anyone who knows about medieval marriage law will realize that I've taken liberties with this novel. The law of 'affinity' existed in medieval times—which prevented widowed men and women from marrying their brother or sister-in-law. Unlike today, once you married into a family, they officially became your 'blood' relatives. The only way around this was to obtain Papal dispensation (a lengthy and costly procedure). Gavin and Ella already break taboos in this story—so I thought they might as well do it in style! Hence, I have allowed them their happy ending, which the church would have otherwise forbidden.

All the clans that I mention in this book (except the Frasers) were actual clans of the time upon the Isle of Skye in the 14th Century. Malcolm MacLeod was a real clan-chief, although all the other chieftains and clan-chiefs (including our hero, Gavin and the nasty Duncan MacKinnon) are fictitious.

Get ready for Leanna and Ross's story up next—it's going to be exciting!

Jayne x

Acknowledgements

Many people deserve thanks for this one. First of all my husband Tim, who edits all my books. We make a great team!

Thanks to Deb, for her help with getting the religious facts right (any errors remaining are entirely mine!).

I'm also immensely grateful to RWNZ (Romance Writers of New Zealand) and especially the Otago/Southland chapter. This organization and its wonderful members have been a constant source of inspiration and encouragement. I attended the RWNZ 2016 conference, and it lit a fire under me. I decided then and there that I would make becoming a full-time author my goal—one that I've now achieved. I don't think I could have done it if I hadn't seen others achieving the same thing!

About the Author

Jayne Castel writes Historical Romance set in Dark Ages Britain and Scotland, and Epic Fantasy Romance. Her vibrant characters, richly researched historical settings, extensive world-building and action-packed adventure romance transport readers back to forgotten times and imaginary worlds.

Jayne is the author of the Amazon bestselling BRIDES OF SKYE series—a Medieval Scottish Romance trilogy about three strong-willed sisters and the men who love them. In love with all things Scottish, she also writes romances set in 4th Century Isle of Skye ... sexy Pict warriors anyone?

When she's not writing, Jayne is reading (and re-reading) her favorite authors, learning French, cooking Italian, and taking her dog, Juno, for walks. She lives in New Zealand's beautiful South Island.

Jayne won the 2017 RWNZ Koru Award (Short, Sexy Category) for her novel, ITALIAN UNDERCOVER AFFAIR.

Connect with Jayne online:
www.jaynecastel.com
www.facebook.com/JayneCastelRomance/
Twitter: @JayneCastel
Email: contact@jaynecastel.com